A SNAKE IN THE GRASS

A JESSE JAMES DAWSON NOVEL

K.A. STEWART

Jesse James #4

Dedicated to Dedication

Acknowledgements

So many aspects of my life would be impossible without my family, and I'm lucky enough to have more than one. So, for the family I was born to: Grammy, Butch, David, Gary, Eric, Laura, Jimmy, Lora, Jackie, Jason, Chase, Rylee and Cashlee. For the family I chose: Scott, Gita, Paul, Jayson, Dawna, Melissa, Caron, Faith, Josh, Jenn, Erin, Andy, Ethan, Rachel and Will. And for the writing family that chose me: Anne, Ginger, Alice, Caleb and Janet.

Thank you.

Also, a special shout out to Paul Henri Alanís Noyola for his diligent efforts in correcting my gawdawful Spanish. *Gracias*.

1

Forever ago…

It's no secret that I was a hell-raiser as a kid. Well, more teen than kid, but you know what I mean. If there was trouble, I found it. If there was petty crime, I committed it. If there was a drug, I did it. A lot. Seriously, I did my fair share of drugs. Hell, I did my share, and your share, and a couple other people's shares. If I hadn't been arrested at fifteen, I'd most likely have been dead before eighteen.

In contrast, my little brother had known he wanted to be a cop from the time he was three years old. While I embraced the reputation of my outlaw namesake, Jesse James, my brother Cole Younger Dawson was destined to be the exact opposite of his. Straight A student, honor society, volunteer work, you name it, he was there. He was the kind of guy that you just knew was going to rip open his shirt to reveal a Superman emblem underneath. Still is, to this day.

You'd think that such a disparity in personalities would cause friction, and yeah, we did our damnedest to kill each other on several occasions, but in the end, it always boiled down to blood. He was my blood, and there was no power on earth that could help the person who laid hands on my little brother. We were close, even when we absolutely didn't understand each other. That's what brothers do.

So like I said, I tore up the town with some buddies one night, and I got arrested while my so-called friends high-tailed it over the chain-link fence out back. Can't even remember what I was running on that night, but I tried like hell to take a chunk out of the cops that put me down. I failed, of course. I seriously weighed maybe a hundred pounds soaking wet. Bet it was like getting attacked by a broom straw. Those guys probably still laugh about it, and I deserved it.

Judge Carter, known for his unusual sentences especially in juvenile cases, opted to suspend any time in Juvie for me, so long as I attended a court-selected martial arts class twice a week. Everyone around me, including me, expected it to be a spectacular failure. Turns out, it wasn't.

If Judge Carter saved my life, then Carl Bledsoe set my path from that moment on. Sensei, disciplinarian, smacker-of-hard-heads and later, friend. He taught me everything I would need to know to become the man that I am today. He drove the tenets of *bushido* into my head until I could recite them in my sleep (and have). He taught me to value honor and integrity. He taught me that there are things greater than just one man, and that sometimes, doing the right thing may suck, but it's always worth it.

And of course, he taught me to kick a lot of ass. That's one of those things I'm not supposed to say, but hey, it's come in handy in the years since. Sometimes, when I have nothing to do but think back on what my life has become, I have to wonder what would have happened to all the people that I've helped if I'd never learned the skills that I have. If I'd have dropped the classes, or if I'd climbed over that fence after my friends, or if I'd just stayed in that night and smoked another bowl. If I wasn't who I am, where would my baby brother be now?

He was young when he came to me for help, but we were both old enough to be fathers. My Annabelle and his Nicky were less than six months apart in age, just at the age where they should be toddling. Well, Anna was toddling. Nicky, so frail and weak, had spent the best part of his first year in and out of hospitals with so many ailments that I think the doctors despaired of ever discovering them all.

Nicky was five months old the first time they called the priest to perform last rites. He pulled through that time, somehow, but the next time was barely a month later, and even Mira was convinced to bless the tiny little life that was surely passing on to the next world right before our eyes. Mira held Stephanie, Cole's wife, as she sobbed silently, and I couldn't do a thing but stand next to my brother, watching the grayness of sick certainty settle over his face. Parents aren't supposed to outlive their children, and we all knew it, even as young as we all were.

Finally, he ducked out of the room, unable to stand and listen for the inevitable long tone in his tiny son's heart monitor. I wanted to go after him, wanted to take some of that horrible, inexorable burden off his shoulders, but I didn't. For probably the first time in my life, I couldn't think of the right words to say, or even the wrong ones. All I could think was how I would feel if that was my Annabelle in that bed, and the sick dread of it threatened to choke me to death. So I let him go to face whatever he had to face all alone.

I hate myself every day for that. I probably always will.

That night, the night that should have been the end of the world as we knew it, Nicky's vital signs suddenly got stronger. His oxygen came up, his heart rate stabilized. He opened his eyes, and when they landed on his mother, he smiled around the tubes that were taped to his face.

They were able to take him home two days later, and everyone thanked whatever god or goddess they believed in for the miracle. We didn't know, back then. We had no idea what had actually happened.

Cole withdrew. I saw it, and I chalked it up to stress over bills, over Nicky's health, over a lot of things. He found excuses not to hang out with me, to skip family gatherings. He took extra shifts under the pretense that they could use the money. On the few occasions I saw him, the hollows in his cheeks seemed deeper, the shadows under his eyes darker. Other than our hair color – his chestnut brown to my blond – and the fact that he packed on about thirty pounds more muscle than I had, we were supposed to look alike. In those days, I thought we still did, though he looked fifteen years older than me instead of three years younger.

Nicky had been out of the hospital for five months, growing stronger all the time, though he still had a lot of ground to make up. Through rampant bullying, I managed to get Cole to my parents' house for a shindig, convinced that some good old-fashioned family shenanigans were just what he needed to lighten his spirits.

We stood off to the side and nursed beers as the kids played, Anna taking charge of Nicky with a watchful eye that said she understood even then that he wasn't capable of the same things she was. Mira and Steph calmly navigated the sea of Dawson family lunacy, setting out the giant barbecue dinner we were going to have if my parents could ever quit arguing over the proper settings for the grill. There was no venom behind my folks' grumbling. We'd been hearing the same old snarks for decades at that point. It was just…normal. This was how life was supposed to be.

Up until the moment that Cole cleared his throat to get my attention. "Jesse?"

That made me look at him sharply. We never used our names. It was always little brother and big brother. Sometimes Beavis and Butthead. Occasionally asshole and dipshit. But never, never ever Jesse and Cole.

There was something strange in his blue-gray eyes, something I had never seen there before. A flatness, maybe, or just… Something not right. Something was missing. "What's up, little brother?"

"Can you…can I talk to you for a minute? Inside?" With a raised brow, I followed him into the house, stopping in the living room where he rolled up his long shirt sleeve. "I think… I think I've done something really bad."

He revealed what looked to be a black tribal tattoo on the inside of his left forearm, stretching from wrist to elbow, and I swear, I busted out laughing. "Oh shit, little brother. The nineties called, they want their tattoo back." He gave me a pained look, but I was on a roll, there was no way I was letting that one go. "Seriously, how drunk were you? Did you actually pay money for that piece of crap?"

"*Jesse*!" He grabbed my arm and gave me a good jerk, one that went beyond just playful. When I stopped to give him a "what the fuck" glare, he thrust his arm before my eyes again. "Look closer. Really look."

And I did. I looked. *Really* looked, and the black marks on his arm swam before my eyes. They writhed and stayed still all at the same time, they intersected at impossible angles and dipped in and out of view in a way that was simply not possible. I stared at it until my eyes watered, until I felt like someone had driven an icepick up into my eye socket. It was *wrong* in a way I had no words for at that time (and have failed to find words for in the time since). "What the ever-loving fuck, Cole?"

Only then did he drop his arm and release his grip on me, a shudder passing through his body. "You see it. Thank God, you see it too."

"Well yeah, you let someone tattoo…what the hell is that? It's kinda hard to miss."

"Steph can't see it."

I snorted. "I think it's going to be a bit hard to hide it from her, little brother. It's not exactly subtle."

He shook his head, obviously frustrated at my lack of understanding. "No… She isn't *able* to see it. It's just…not there for her. The…wiggling, the movement. I wasn't sure… I wasn't sure if you would be able to."

"I think maybe you better sit down and explain yourself, little brother."

We found ourselves staring at each other over my parents' coffee table as Cole laid it all out for me.

"The night in the hospital…The night Nicky almost…" I nodded quickly. Yeah, I knew which night he meant. He didn't need to say it. "When I left his room, I was going to go to the hospital chapel. But when I got close, I just… I couldn't go in there. I was too angry with God to go asking him for favors at that moment, y'know? I mean, why would he help us when he'd allowed Nicky to suffer so much already? So I just kept walking."

I could understand it. I wasn't a confirmed believer in God-with-a-big-G myself, but we'd been raised with the church in our lives and Cole was more comfortable with his faith than I was. I totally understood being angry with God in that moment. I would have been too.

"So, like, I went out to that big courtyard they have, y'know where the smokers all go. And I sat down on this bench and I just put my head in my hands, and I tried to cry, 'cause it seemed like the thing to do. But there weren't any tears anymore. I was all dried up, all numb. All I could see ahead of me was this long, black, cold tunnel, y'know? No light anymore. The world was never going to be the same again."

I just sat and let him talk, knowing this had all been coming a long time.

"So I was sitting there, and suddenly, there was this guy in hospital scrubs sitting next to me. I didn't see him come out the doors, or walk up, but he was just…there. And I looked up at him, 'cause I figured he was the one who had come out to tell me Nicky was gone." He shuddered again, and I reached across the table to rest my hand on his shoulder. "But that wasn't what he wanted. He looked at me, and he smiled, and he said 'what if I told you that you could save him?'"

My brother's face was pasty in an unhealthy way as he recounted the conversation. "He wasn't...he wasn't human, Jess. I know you're thinking I'm nuts, but if you could have heard his voice... It wasn't like anything you've ever heard. It wasn't something you could ever doubt, if you'd have heard it. He offered...if I would give him my soul, he would make Nicky healthy again. And I believed him, totally and completely. There was no way this guy, this thing, was lying to me. And I thought... I thought, if Nicky dies, I don't want my soul anyway. I don't want to live in that world where I go on and my son can't."

"Jesus, Cole..." Ignoring the soul-selling part, just to know that my brother had hit that level of despair was...sobering on a level I can't describe.

"So I told him yes. He asked me if I was really sure, and I said yes again. Then he grabbed my arm, and it started burning. I mean, I could smell my own flesh smoking, and this black mark crawled its way up my arm like it was alive." He rubbed at the tattoo, then snatched his hand away like he could still feel it wriggling under his skin. "About half an hour later, Mom came to find me, to tell me that Nicky was stabilizing. That's when I came back in, because I knew it had worked."

I sat back on the couch with a sigh, running a hand through my long hair. Cole sat with his elbows on his knees, his eyes on the carpet, shoulders tense like he was braced for...something. Finally, I just shook my head. "I don't know what to even say to that, little brother. That's the weirdest story I've ever heard in my life."

"I know." He nodded quickly. "Trust me, I know. I hear myself saying these words, and I want to go lock myself up in a loony bin. But then I look down, and the mark is still there. And you can see it move, too."

"So… So it worked, right? I mean…aside from the whole not having a soul thing – and we're not even going to address how much I don't believe that at all – you saved Nicky. That's good, right?"

"Yeah, that part is good. Except now he can't stand for me to touch him. He screams, Jess, if I come anywhere near him. Screams and screams and screams like I was dunking him in boiling water. He'll only quiet down if I give him back to Steph." He dropped his head, wrapping his arms over it like that was going to muffle the faint sob. "He *knows*, Jesse. He's just a baby, but he knows what I did, and he knows I'm a terrible person now."

"You don't have the ability to be a terrible person." He refused to look up at me, and I poked him in the arm. "Hey. Hey! Look up at me, asshole." He did, finally, his eyes ringed in red and as empty as a bottomless pit. "There has to be a way to fix this. Right? If it can be done, it can be undone."

"I don't want it to be undone. Nicky is healthier now than he's been since he was born. I just want him to not be afraid of me."

I pursed my lips as I thought, going over the details of what Cole had told me. "So this thing that talked to you, the not-a-man thing. It was…the devil?"

He snorted a small laugh, and shook his head. "No, nothing so grand. Just a demon. I guess I didn't rate the Big Guy himself coming up to bargain."

"And do you know how to get ahold of this thing again?"

He nodded. "He gave me his name." When I opened my mouth again, he held up his hand quickly. "I'm not going to tell you what it is. It's… It lives in my head now. It crawls around and it feels…terrible. I don't want that in your head."

"Okay. I assume, if books and movies haven't lied to us all these years, that if you call his name, he'll come a-runnin', and he'll be willing to make another deal."

"What do I offer him? I kinda only had the one soul, and that's gone now."

"I have one. Little dark around the edges, but perfectly usable." I raised a brow at him and let that sink in for a moment.

"No. Absolutely not." He shook his head until I thought his brains might rattle out his ears. "I can't let you do that, big brother, not after what I just told you about how Nicky reacts to me. Do you want Annabelle to shriek every time you get near her?"

"Well I'm not just going to walk up and hand it over to the thing."

"What, then?"

I gave him a slow grin. "I have a plan."

As plans go, I've had better ones. Had worse ones, too.

A few nights later, I met my brother in the back acreage of some local park land. It was as far away from prying eyes as we could manage on short notice, and one of the few places that I felt I could safely pull out three feet of sharpened steel without getting arrested.

The sword was one that my blacksmith buddy Marty had made me a couple of years prior, as a Christmas present. It was supposed to just be something to hang over my mantel, if I ever had one, and look wickedly pretty. That didn't mean, though, that it wasn't a perfectly functional weapon, or that I didn't know how to use it.

I gave Cole a small smirk. "And you said that a thousands-of-years-old martial art wasn't going to be applicable to my everyday life." He probably would have laughed at me if he hadn't been busy looking like he was going to puke.

After swallowing a couple of times, he said "Are you ready?" and when I nodded, he opened his mouth and the nastiest thing I have ever heard in my life came spewing out of it. Seriously, the thing had no vowels, or consonants, it was just poison wrapped in hate, and smothered in a nice layer of bloody thorns and acid. My body had an instant and violent reaction, and I hit the ground with a sharp pain in both knees as I heaved up my guts into the grass. Cole was faring no better, by the sound of it, coughing and gagging just out of my sight.

My throat and nose burning with my own stomach bile, I finally managed to force myself to my feet. Meeting a demon on my knees seemed like a shitty first impression, especially given the deal I intended to offer him.

The first thing I noticed, aside from the fact that Cole was still crouched down, trying to regain control of himself, was that the night had gone absolutely still. The birds that had been serenading us just moments ago had fallen silent, and the insects that were feasting on us had found somewhere else to be. Even the breeze had stopped, and the late spring air felt heavy with the night's dew still settling onto the foliage around us.

If it hadn't been so still, I'm not sure I'd have noticed the faint movement across the clearing, and I murmured "Incoming" to Cole as something stepped from the trees. It looked like a man, at first, dressed in nondescript green hospital scrubs. But as the thing drew closer, the scrubs melted away, first into a suit and tie combo, and then into faded jeans and a black T-shirt, and I realized that it was trying to look like me. Trying to set me at ease. 'Cause yeah, magical melting morphing clothes was *normal*.

The thing stopped a good ten yards away, giving me a slow smile for a moment before turning his eyes on my brother. "Cole Younger Dawson. I have come to your call."

Ew. Ew ew ew! Cole was right, there was something in the voice, something that tasted like rancid lard at the back of my throat and felt like an oil slick over my skin. No human sounded like that. I wanted to spit until that taste was erased from my mouth, but I didn't have time for such nonsense.

Cole, on his feet again, visibly flinched when the thing said his name, his shoulders up like he was sheltering from an incoming blow. I couldn't have that. I couldn't let this thing beat him down without even raising a finger.

"Hey, tall-dark-and-devilish. Over here." I snapped my fingers to get the thing to look at me, which it did with a raised brow. "You're here to talk to me, not him."

"I am listening."

"Oh I just bet you are. Well listen up good, Sparky, 'cause it's time to play 'Let's Make a Deal'."

The thing grinned at me, showing pretty much more teeth than a human head holds. "I will hear you."

"You have his soul, yes?" I nodded toward Cole. "You possess the soul of one Cole Younger Dawson." The thing had said Cole's full name. That seemed important.

"Yes. I am in possession of such."

"I want it back."

The demon – I was still having trouble thinking of it like that – chuckled, and its eyes flashed a bright red, lighting up the night for a moment. Okaaaay. That was…weird. "And what do you offer in exchange?"

"I will fight you for it." I brought my other hand out from behind my back, displaying my sheathed sword. "If I win, you will return his soul to him."

"And if you lose? What is my prize?"

He knew the answer already, he just wanted – maybe needed – me to say it. "You can have my soul, if I lose the fight."

It hissed in displeasure, the human-ish face wrinkling up in a way that no real human could. "Your name! You must give your name, fool!" Oh. Oops. "Jesse. Jesse James Dawson."

"Jesse James Dawson…" My name from that thing's lips just made me want to cringe like a kicked puppy. There were things inside me trying to crawl out and away to safety at the sound of that voice caressing the syllables of my name. No wonder Cole had cowered away from it. "This is your wager, then. A soul against a soul, on a challenge of combat."

"Yeah, I can't play the fiddle for shit." It gave me a slightly puzzled look, and I sighed. Nobody gets my jokes.

"Accepted." The thing's eyes flashed red again, and I felt something hot slice down the back of my right hand, a sharp line between the first two knuckles.

With a startled cry, I looked down to find a scorched black mark there, the edges glowing faintly like embers in the darkness. The smell of smoke reached my nostrils, my own skin cooking as the glow died out. Oh, that was just nasty.

"Name your next term, champion."

Terms? Oh hell, we got to set terms? This could either be really good, or really bad. "I'm guessing that every time we agree on a term, I'm gonna get another line branded into my skin?"

"This is how the contract is sealed, yes."

"Great."

"Unless you wish to withdraw. I am willing cease this now and depart, if you have…doubts."

This was gonna hurt like a mother fucker. I could tell that already. I glanced once toward Cole, his eyes large and glassy even in the darkness. He looked back at me, and the emptiness behind his eyes was like a kick in the gut. No. There was no withdrawing.

"Okay, my first term. You don't get to use any magic. No spells, no hocus pocus, no blipping in and out of existence. Just stand there and have a physical fight."

The thing paused, like it was thinking it over, then nodded. "I require the same of you. No spells of protection or enhancement, no blessings upon your person or your weapon."

Shit, I didn't have any of that stuff anyway. Joke was on him. "Done." Another black line burned its way across my hand, this one ending in a cute little curlicue. My breath hissed between my teeth, but I bit back the cry that wanted to escape.

Every time it hurt, every time I wanted to gag on the smell of my own scorched flesh, I would look at Cole, and I kept going.

This is what you do for family.

2

Now…

The sound of glass crashing at around five o'dark in the morning was followed by several other distinct sounds. The first was a woman's voice snarling in Ukrainian from the living room, the second was the slide on a semi-automatic racking, and the third was the gallop of large, guilty puppy feet.

"Do *not* shoot the dog, Sveta!" My feet hit the floor a second after that, and I didn't even bother to pull on my pajama pants. Everyone in the house had seen my boxers by now.

Chunk, our canine midnight vandal, was disappearing into my daughter's room as I padded down the hallway, and the door slammed shut behind him. I heard the scraping sound of Anna's toybox being shoved against the door, and nodded to myself. We'd practiced, for just this occasion.

At the end of the hallway, I paused, pressed against the wall for safety's sake. "Sveta? Can I come around?"

There was a long moment of silence before a woman's heavily accented voice answered. "Slowly."

With both hands raised, I stepped into the kitchen, turning to face the living room door with supreme caution. "It was just the dog. You can stand down."

The barrel end of a gun, no matter what kind of gun it is, looks goddamn big when you're staring down it. Add to that the pre-dawn darkness and the fact that I was the next best thing to buck-ass naked and "vulnerable" didn't even begin to describe my situation. But I was sure she wouldn't actually shoot me. Pretty sure. Eighty-five percent sure. Maybe.

There was no wavering of the weapon as I looked past the dangerous end to the woman holding it. Her dark hair was back in a loose ponytail for sleep, and she was dressed only in a light tank top and panties, but there was no hint of sleepiness in her pale blue eyes. She focused on me, calm, cool, and entirely capable of blowing my brains out if she thought it necessary. "You are certain? Only the dog?" Her lilting Ukrainian accent even managed to sound menacing.

"You can sweep the house if you want, but stay out of my bedroom, and give me the gun. Deal?" I held my hand out expectantly, but kept my voice level. We'd done this dance before in the few months since Sveta had come to live with us. Nothing like having a paranoid, trigger-happy demon slayer sleeping on your couch.

After a moment, she flicked the safety back on the gun and spun it in her hand, handing it to me grip first. The knots in my shoulders relaxed. "I will get my sword." Turning on her heel, she disappeared back into the living room to retrieve one of her other weapons.

"Oh damn…" Mira's voice behind me was sad, and I turned to see her crouch down near the stove, looking at the shards of purple glass all over the linoleum. "That was my mother's vase." She picked up a few of the bigger pieces, cradling them gently in her palm. With her head down, her dark curls hung all around her face, and I think she thought it would hide the tears.

"Sorry, baby." Stepping gingerly through the remnants of the beautiful vase – Mira had thought to put shoes on, I hadn't. – I bent down to wrap my arms around her. "I'll clean it up for you, why don't you go back to bed?"

She almost succeeded in hiding the sniffle. "No. No, I'm up now. I'll get it. Here, help me up so I can get the broom."

As requested, I laid Sveta's gun on the counter and gave my wife an arm to lean on so she could heave herself back to her feet. Only six-ish months pregnant, but she was carrying differently with this one than she had with Anna, and her hips were hurting her already. Watching my wife go through everything that pregnancy requires always makes me marvel that our species has survived. If it were up to men, we'd be extinct by now.

Like a ghost, Sveta padded through the kitchen behind us and down the hallway, her shaska blade bared like most of the rest of her. I knew she wouldn't be happy until she'd done a sweep and clear of the house, the yard, and possibly the entire neighborhood block. I just hoped she'd put clothes on before going outside this time. We'd had to call Cole to get her out of jail, last go around. Having a cop in the family comes in handy from time to time.

"Jess?" I glanced back to Mira. "You're glowing." She nodded toward my bared back.

Dammit. I wasn't actually glowing, not to normal eyes, but the unexpected noise in the night had brought me up battle-ready too, and now that Sveta was under control, I could feel the souls just under my skin writhing in agitation. Two hundred and seventy-five of them, ready to spring to my defense if needed. I knew they were willing, though I couldn't have told you how. We'd gotten to know each other fairly well since January, and they were as attuned to my moods as I was to theirs. It was a very odd, very unwelcome symbiotic relationship.

It should have been a dream come true for someone like me. Almost unlimited power to destroy pretty much anything I wanted. For a champion who had never had magic before, you'd think I'd be doing a jig on a daily basis and slaughtering demons left and right. But I knew that if I cast one spell, even one tiny bit of conjuring, one of those souls would cease to exist. Poof, burned up, ashes, gone. And the person connected to that soul would drop dead on the spot. The souls were willing to make that sacrifice. I wasn't.

While my wife flipped the light on and went about cleaning up the broken glass, I stood in the kitchen and did a few deep breathing exercises. Slowly, my adrenaline faded and the riot of movement under my skin died down. "There we go…"

"Five bloody o'clock in the morning, and everyone's up traipsing around in their skivvies." A large grumpy form shuffled out of the hallway, already reeking of gin and pipe tobacco. With gray hair sticking out at wild angles, a scruffy coat of more-salt-than-pepper whiskers, and a heavily patched bathrobe over possibly moldy house slippers, it looked like something out of that movie with the puppets and the glam rocker in the tight pants. You know the one I mean. "Can't get a solid night's sleep for all this bloody noise!"

"Want me to put the kettle on, Terrence?" Mira was nicer than I was at this hour of the morning.

"Yes, missus, if you would please." The

curmudgeon shuffled his way over to my kitchen
 table and plopped down, producing a hip flask from
somewhere in his moth-eaten robe and taking a swig.
"The crazy bint clearing the house?"

"Yeah, Sveta's taking a look around, but it
was just Chunk being a pest."

Terrence snorted. "And the one time you
think it's 'just', it'll be something worse. You let her
do her job." He eyed me up and down from under his
bushy gray eyebrows. "And go put some pants on,
for the love a God and wee fishes."

"Yessir." With a sigh, I retreated toward the
back of the house, brushing past Sveta in the hallway
as she returned. "You, too. Pants." She only grunted
at me.

I pounded my fist on one of the closed doors
as I passed. I knew if Terrence was up, he'd roused
the kid too. They made such lovely roommates.
"Up! Work!" If I was going to see the sunrise, then
Estéban could see it with me. The kid had been
slacking on his workouts lately anyway. We all had.
Hazard of this new, totally bizarre, living
arrangement.

I understood, on a theoretical level, why Ivan
believed I needed bodyguards. One person had
already died over the souls I was now carrying under
my skin, and there was no lack of evil creatures and
nefarious doers who would be happy to make me
casualty number two. But I would forever question
the old man's choice in who he had assigned me.

Sveta I understood, in a "I'm actually kind of
scared of her" way. She was good with every weapon
I'd ever seen her pick up, alert bordering on paranoid,
and practical in the cold way that mercenaries grow to
be. She was the only female fighter I knew of in an

occupation that typically chewed up the men and spit them out if they stepped wrong by an inch. I'd seen her fight once, years ago, and even then, I knew that I'd never hold my own against her. It was just a good thing she was on my side.

Terrence, however. Terrence Smythe was what Great Britain inflicted on us in retribution for that little revolution we had a few centuries ago. The information on him in our champion database, Grapevine, was spotty at best, despite my newly expanded access. I assumed the lack of info was because he was mostly active before computers were invented. Maybe before the invention of the abacus.

From what I understood, he had been a champion in his younger years. He'd survived to become a retired champion, which told me that at some point, he'd been a badass in his own right. Now, though, he was pickled on gin more often than not, and hobbled around with a cane when he thought it might earn him some sympathy. For him, people fell into two categories: those with names, and those without. For example, Sveta had been "that crazy bint" since day one, but Mira was either "Missus" or "Miss Mira." Me, I was "you." Estéban was "boy." Guess it could have been worse.

His only redeeming feature, that I could see, was that as far as magic went, he had it practically oozing out his pores. I mean, I'd seen strong magic users before. My wife, when she wasn't pregnant, was one of the strongest, most precise spell-casters I knew. I'd met a Maori native who, while completely untrained, literally had more power in one hair than I did in my entire body. But Terrence managed to combine the two, and he tossed spells around like they were water with very few ill effects. (Though I will say it's hard to tell the difference between passed out drunk and passed out spell-sick.)

I retrieved my sweats from the foot of my bed and paused to examine my back in the mirror. In the dim light from the bedside lamp, the pale white tattoos were almost impossible to see, and yet I could have traced each one precisely. In the right lighting, they would shine like the iridescent scales of a butterfly's wing, and they stretched from the tops of my shoulders down to the waistband of my pants. Elaborate whorls and spirals, things that connected at impossible angles and twisted through each other like vines... I caught myself touching one of the ones at the top and made myself lower my hand. They were mesmerizing, at times, and it was best not to get caught in it.

I kicked Estéban's door again as I passed, and made my way out into the early morning while Terrence and my wife chatted over tea at the kitchen table. The grass on my lawn made my bare feet tingle when I stepped off my back patio, and I rolled my head on my shoulders, letting the goosebumps crawl across my skin then fade into nothing. Where once that would have been a sign of danger looming, now it just meant that the souls in my skin were reacting to the latent magic around me. The tiniest glimmer of a spell would set them clamoring, friendly magic or not. Nothing like having your advance warning system completely short-circuited. The one thing I had always relied on was now completely useless to me.

Terrence had placed formidable magical wards around the borders of my yard, something I had long threatened to do, but never done. That he'd done it with liberal application of blessed alcohol from his flask (holy gin, kid you not), was something of a sore point where Mira was concerned, but for the safety of our unborn child, there was nothing she could do about it. She was on spell-casting time out at least until the baby was born. We still had about two and a half months to go.

The sliding glass door opened and closed, and I felt more than saw Estéban step up beside me in the grass. He stood out in my mind now, a tall, slender outline, the glimmer of magic inside him speaking to the barely contained ocean inside of me. It was eerie, to me, but I'd started to understand that this was what it was always like for them. Estéban, Mira, Sveta, Terrence, all the others. They knew each other instinctively, drawn by like talents. It explained a lot about how Ivan had started rounding up all the champions, so many years ago. Easier, when you can just pick a guy out of a crowd and go "Ah yeah, that's the one."

"C'mon, kid."

He followed me out into the yard without questioning, silently gliding through the kata forms at my side like my darker twin. He'd come a long way in the last year or so. The angry kid that had come to me was calmer now, more thoughtful. I was pretty sure I couldn't take credit for that, but I was really glad to see it. It gave me a little more hope that the kid would survive whatever life was going to throw at him.

We went through every form I'd taught him, and I was pleased to see that his movements were almost perfect. He had a good head for this stuff. I was proud of the kid, but part of me felt like I had to test him one more time. Just in case it was the last time.

"What are the seven virtues of bushido?" Part of his test was to see if he could carry on a conversation and keep up with the kata at the same time. He knew this one. I knew he knew it.

"Righteousness, courage, benevolence, respect, honesty, honor, and loyalty." Not one movement faltered, each one punctuated by a correct answer.

"Are you packed?" I abruptly changed subjects, to see if I could throw him off.

"Yes."

"Did you get your posters?"

"They're rolled. Miss Mira is going to mail them to me later."

"You get emails and phone numbers for all your friends?"

"They're all in my notebook."

"You got your phone charger?"

"Yes."

He was leaving, you see. Tomorrow, we were getting on a plane to Mexico, and I was taking Estéban back to his mother and the rest of his demon-slaying family. There was a ton more I could teach him, sure, but now, with things like they were… I had a target on my back in the most literal sense, and the kid was just collateral damage waiting to happen. It was time for him to go home, back where it was safe.

I should have taken him home earlier, but some pleading on his part (and Mira's) had convinced me that the kid should at least be allowed to finish out his senior year of high school in peace. *"Give him a few months to be normal, Jess. Please. Once he goes home, you know that's gone for him."* What could I say? When she was right, she was right. So here we were, end of May, and we were packing the kid up to go home for the first time in over a year.

Between you and me? I was gonna miss him.

The secondary part of the mission, of course, was to see if Estéban's mother, a powerful *bruja*, could figure out how to rid me of these extra souls without harming me, or them. Someone, somewhere, had to know how, and while Carlotta had never heard of such a thing before, she was willing to see if she could figure it out. I was hoping between she and Terrence, they could solve this little problem of mine and I could get back to *my* normal life. For some loose definition of the word "normal."

"Jesse?" Estéban stopped in the middle of his kata, but I finished the last move before I turned to look at him. "Do you think I'm ready? Tell the truth."

A year ago, he'd believed with the absolute certainty of bull-headed youth that he was ready. A year ago, he'd arrived in Kansas City in pursuit of the demon who had murdered his older brother. He was guided by fury and bravado, and together, we'd taken the thing down. Now... Now he asked if he was ready. I was so damn proud of this kid it hurt.

"I think... I think that it is my strongest wish that you *never* have to fight another demon battle in your life, kid." I watched him wilt on the inside, and kept going. "But I also know that you will, and I am ninety percent sure that you'll live through it. I can't make you any more ready than you are, k-...Estéban. Whatever's left to do has to come from you."

A ghost of a smile flickered across his face, and I snaked an arm out to yank him into a quick noogie. "Just remember I'm older, and faster, and meaner. 'Kay?"

"'Kay." He shrugged me off with a small

chuckle. "Whose turn is it to come with you to It today?"

"Sveta." We both made a face. Taking Sveta out in public was like walking around with a rabid honey badger on a dental floss leash. But taking Terrence into the mall where I worked was little more appetizing. The last time I'd worked, I'd caught him out in front of the store where I worked, berating a group of kids with fluorescent hair and skinny jeans, informing them just why they were what's wrong with the world. Considering that those kids were my store's target demographic, you can see how this wasn't helpful.

I think the only reason Mira wasn't protesting this Mexico trip more was that she was relieved I was taking my two "bodyguards" with me. To say things had been unsettled in the Dawson household was putting it mildly.

And it wasn't just Mira. I was reminded of that as Estéban and I came back inside to find my six-year-old daughter facing down with the potential Ukrainian psychopath.

"You leave my doggy alone! He doesn't like you, and I don't like you either!" My angelic little redhead hid a fiery temper, and her sense of self-preservation hadn't kicked in yet. This much was obvious. She was standing almost nose to nose with Sveta, who had obligingly crouched down to be more on the child's level. Thankfully, neither my child nor her adversary had any weaponry in evidence.

I looked at Mira and Terrence, who were still contentedly drinking tea. "Was no one going to put an end to this?"

"I think Anna has it under control, actually." Mira gave me a small smirk, telling me I was on my own.

Sveta, ignoring the presence of all the adults in the room, nodded solemnly to my daughter. "It is not necessary to like everyone all of the time. But sometimes, we must live with them anyway. Understand?"

Anna's nose wrinkled up a little as she pondered that. "Yeah…" It was clear she was mentally looking for the trap.

"So, I will make a bargain with you. You know what a bargain is?"

Again, the wary "Yeah."

"I will not harm your doggy. In return, you will do your best to keep him from startling me in my sleep. To keep him safe, you must teach him. It is part of being a responsible pet owner. Understand?"

Annabelle thought it over for long serious moments, then spit in her own palm and stuck out her hand for a shake. "Deal." I glanced at Mira, who gave me a shrug and a shake of her head. No idea where our child had learned that.

Sveta spit in return and shook the offered hand without a trace of amusement or condescension, then stood up. "And now, we should eat breakfast, I think. After we wash our hands."

The war abruptly over, Anna obediently followed the dangerous woman over to the kitchen sink so they could both wash their hands together. Within moments, my daughter forgot her ire, and was chatting away with Sveta about doggies and kitties and whatever else popped into her curly red head. It boggled the mind.

"You're all crazy. I'm gonna go take a shower." I left a chorus of chuckles behind me, though I failed to see the humor.

In our newly expanded, overly chaotic household, the shower was one of the few places I could get some time to myself, and that was only because I'd put my foot down early on and insisted that Sveta was *not* allowed to follow me in there. Seriously, if a demon was gonna come at me in the shower, it was just gonna have to happen. A man has limits.

As the hot water sluiced down over my shoulders, I rested my head against the cool tile wall. I was so done with all this. This whole demon-slaying, soul-selling, war-in-Hell circus, you could have it. I was supposed to be *retired*, dammit. Of course, I'd seen enough cop buddy movies to know what happens when you say you're going to retire. Might as well have painted the cross-hairs on my forehead myself.

With my eyes closed, there was nothing to stop the images from coming back. The most vivid one was a beautiful blond woman, toppling backwards in slow motion, my fingertips just barely brushing hers as she fell. It was night, and the lights of a distant city twinkled behind her as she plummeted down and down and down. Over and over again, that graceful pirouette into oblivion.

It hadn't happened that way. I knew that. The night Gretchen Keene leapt to her death from the roof of her hotel, I hadn't been anywhere near close enough to stop her. And even if I had, she wouldn't have been reaching for me. She'd gone willingly in a last ditch effort to protect her loved ones from the chaos I was now facing. But regardless of how it had actually gone down, it haunted me. Somehow, some way, I should have been able to stop her.

Until recently, my visions of past failures had

been limited to my dreams. Anymore, though, they crept up on me when I least expected it. I knew the flashbacks were a sign of PTSD. The nightmares, too. And there was that really nasty hypervigilance episode a few weeks ago where Sveta and I prowled the house for hours, looking for the threat I just *knew* was there.

When it was happening, it was terrifying, both for me and for everyone around me. After, I was mostly pissed off at myself and embarrassed. At worst, I was becoming a danger to my family. At the very least, it was inconvenient.

And we weren't even going to mention what I'd come to think of as "the tunnel dream." Not a night went by that I didn't find myself stepping out of some mysterious tunnel, facing down a long, empty, dirt field. I was never alone in those dreams, but I could never quite see the dark, slender figure that waited for me at the other end, and I was never able to turn around to see who was taking shelter in the tunnel behind me.

I stood under the shower until the water started to get cool, then went to get ready for work.

3

My real job, when I actually get to spend time there anymore, involves selling snarky tees, band shirts, and various clothing items with artfully placed holes in them. I get to listen to really loud, abrasive music, and give advice on tattoo and body piercing care to kids who are probably too young to actually have either. I love my job, and I wear my OLD DUDE name badge proudly.

Funny how a tiny little chain retail store can come to feel like home. From the blacklight painted walls, to the endless bass thumping through the overhead speakers, to the rows and rows of goth-clothed mannequins hanging up near the ceiling. I'd touched pretty much everything in this store at some point or another in my way-too-long tenure. Walking in felt comfortable. Normal.

My boss, Kristyn, her hair an obnoxious shade of fuchsia this week, threw her keys at me as I came in the door. "I gotta run to the Oak Park store. You're in charge, Abe will be in at noon, and Lex will be in at two. I'll be back before five." Poof, she was gone, leaving me alone to open the store. Technically against the rules, but after so many years working together, we fudged now and then. And it was only for a couple of hours.

Being alone in the store for a bit meant that I was free to give the place a good once over. Y'know, mop the bathroom floor, straighten the cash wrap, scope for demonic fleas…

The mirror on my keychain looked like any

trinket you could get out of the dollar bin at any discount store. In fact, I think that may be where we got it. It was the runes scratched into the back of it that made it something special.

I examined the entire store with that mirror, checking out the high shadowy corners, crawling under the clothing racks, even opening the new boxes of shipment, just in case.

I was looking for something I called a Scrap demon. They looked like greasy black mop heads with four insectile legs poking out, though most of their body was taking up by a gargantuan, shark-toothed mouth. They were the parasites of the demon world, unintelligent but crafty when it came to their own survival. They usually operated at the behest of a stronger demon. Attached to a person, they could suck energy, will, even the very life out of their prey, leaving their host a husk of their former self. And that's *if* the host survived.

There'd been one in the store once, and I'd dispatched it posthaste. There was still a gouge in the tile floor where I'd skewered the thing with a novelty letter opener. Now, with so much more on the line, I couldn't afford for one to sneak up on me again.

Once I was satisfied that the place was clear of creepy crawlies, I went to open up. Standing at the door, I caught the eye of the woman across the street and gave her the all-clear nod.

My punk co-workers didn't know about demons, or slaying, or trapped souls or anything like that. And quite frankly, Sveta wasn't going to fit in as a customer or an employee, so while I puttered around inside It, she took up camp on a bench across the courtyard where she could see the door. She could cross that distance in three seconds. I know, because she had me time her the first few times, just for practice.

Every time I passed near the front window, I checked on her, but as near as I could tell, she never moved. She could have been any woman, anywhere, dressed in blue jeans, heavy work boots, and a thin gray T-shirt. Her brown hair was pulled back into a utilitarian ponytail, and she wore no makeup at all. At first glance, she appeared perfectly normal. Young and athletic, pretty even.

But if you watched long enough, you'd realize that no one else tried to sit on her bench, ever. Parents pushed their strollers in a wide arc around her, small children made it a point to scamper in the opposite direction, and teenagers found other places to loiter. It was like she exuded the aura of a predator, and normal people steered clear on pure instinct.

It could also be the scars. Being a champion demon slayer wasn't exactly a safety-conscious occupation, and like any of us, Sveta's arms were peppered with scars varying from tiny blemishes to one that wrapped completely her left biceps and told the story of how she'd nearly lost the arm. There were more, concealed by her clothing. Down her legs, across her ribs. Reminders of battles won. We'd had one very PG-13 game of "compare the scar" when she came to live with us. While Terrence won by default – no one wanted him taking off his clothes, I mean really – I think Sveta probably topped even my spectacular marks.

She never wore long sleeves, though, never tried to hide them. Most likely, she never even thought about them anymore. I know I didn't think about my own, until I caught the sidelong glances, the whispered conversations as some stranger caught a glimpse. I think it was worse for Sveta. People don't like to see scars on pretty women. It violates the natural order of the world or something.

Both her elbows hung over the back of the bench, her hands dangling near her sides where I was certain some type of weapon was hidden just out of reach. Her pale blue eyes moved constantly, scanning the crowd. I wasn't exactly sure what would happen if she thought she saw a potential threat, but so far, we hadn't had any incidents.

Of course, I had one frequent visitor to the store that would have tripped every alarm bell she had, if she'd ever recognized him. I'd been forced to tell Ivan about Axel, my personal demon, and I was certain that he'd informed Sveta and Terrence. Luckily, neither of them knew what Axel looked like, and so he continued to slip under their radar. (Quite frankly, if they failed to recognize the most powerful demon I'd ever been around, I wasn't sure this gave me a lot of confidence in their ability to protect my body. Just sayin'.)

And speaking of the devil, Axel showed up a few hours into my shift, as expected. His visits to my home had been curtailed by Terrence's over-zealous wards, and with my two guardians providing constant watch, having conversations had become difficult. We'd had to resort to more clandestine methods.

I spotted him across the courtyard, his blond mohawk and excessive facial piercings kinda standing out in a crowd. Nonchalantly, he sauntered right past Sveta's bench, dragging his fingers across the back within inches of her shoulder, smirking to himself when she didn't even look twice. I shouldn't have been surprised at his audacity. He was a demon after all, he just couldn't help pushing the envelope.

The minute he cleared the door, I made a beeline to get ahead of my coworkers. "Welcome to It! What can I help you find today? Our band tees are all buy one, get one half off."

The man-demon gave me a small smirk as I ushered him over to the tween girl section. "You do this on purpose."

"Every time." Once I was sure our words would be drowned out by the thumping bass overhead, I gave up the pretense. "So, what's the word?"

Axel sighed at me. "Always right to business with you. No 'how was your day?' or 'my, did you lose weight?'" He clicked his tongue piercing against his teeth in disapproval.

"How's about I whistle real loud and introduce you to a lovely single Ukrainian I know?" Not that I would. As much as I hated to admit it, I needed Axel too much right now to sic Sveta on him. And truth be told, I was pretty sure she wouldn't win.

Axel swiveled around to glance out the plate glass window. "Little Svetlana... My, how she's grown." For a heartbeat, his eyes flared red, until I elbowed him in the ribs. "Ow."

"Dude, either talk or buy something." I grabbed a shirt and shoved it into his hands, belatedly realizing it was pink. That made me grin.

The demon rolled his eyes, thankfully returned to their normal color, and tossed the shirt on the floor. "It's pretty much the same. They know the souls are in the wind, but no one can seem to track where they went." He smirked. "You're welcome."

A few months ago, shortly after my return from L.A., it had become very clear that keeping my little extra-souls problem a secret was going to be next to impossible when I glowed like a fifty-thousand watt bulb to anyone who could see magic. That included any demon who came within fifty yards of me.

So Axel, in all his magnanimous (read: self-serving) glory, had performed some of that voodoo that he do so well, and cloaked me from demonic prying eyes. Now, so long as the souls were calm, and I didn't have a demon sitting right on my head, I was relatively safe, for some loose definition of the word.

I could still feel Axel's spell if I thought about it, though I tried very hard not to. It slid across my skin like a faint sheen of baby oil, and it smelled like rancid butter. I didn't like it, and the souls under my skin had put me through excruciating pain at first, trying to burn it off. I'd struggled for days before I'd managed to wrestle them under control.

So far, though, it seemed to be working.

"So you're still the only one that knows I have them?" Every time we talked, I lived with the dread that the secret was out. Because I knew what would happen then. Then, all bets were off, and they'd come for me, and everyone I'd ever cared about. It's what they did.

"I, and I alone." He idly thumbed through the rack of shirts. "Though everyone's pretty sure you know where they are."

I kept yanking shirts out of his hands before he could litter the floor with them. "Well, you do whatever it is you do, but let them know that I won't be home for a while. I don't want anyone coming to the house while the girls are alone."

"I still can't talk you out of that, I guess?" Axel sniffed in distaste. "Nothing good in Mexico, you know. Cacti and big lizards. The occasional chupacabra. Dead Mayans."

"I thought they were Aztecs."

"Whatever. You all look alike."

"Still not coming with, hm?" For reasons known only to him, Axel had adamantly refused to shadow me on my trip south. The one time I'd mentioned it, he'd acted like I'd tried to say the Lord's prayer over him or something. *"You're going to have a sleepover with a family that has been banishing demons since before the Europeans set foot on this soil. Do I look crazy?"* If I didn't know better, I'd say Axel was scared, which amused me greatly.

"I have other things to do. You'll be fine."

I snorted softly. "If you really thought they could get these things out of me, you'd be down there damn quick." He didn't want to lose two hundred and seventy-five souls, and keeping them in my skin was as good as a bank vault as far as he was concerned. If he truly believed that Estéban's mother could release them, he'd be stuck to my side like glue.

Axel just smirked at me. "It's my week to wash my hair."

I rolled my eyes. "God forbid I interrupt your beauty regimen." The mention of the G-word got a wince and a glare from him. "You better go. Kristyn's eyeing you like she just knows you need a pair of pirate footie pjs."

"I've worn worse. If something changes, I'll be in touch." He waggled his fingers at my boss as he made his way out of the store, and when he was gone, she raised a brow at me. I just shook my head and went about straightening up the racks he'd wrecked.

Axel was…Axel. He was an unrepentant

demon – though in all fairness, I'd never seen a repentant one – and never did anything unless it directly benefitted himself in some way. It galled me that I was dependent on him for information and protection. It seemed that no matter how I played things, my life just got more and more tangled up with stuff I wanted to leave behind.

Later that night, I lay in bed with my arms around my pregnant wife, and I tried not to think about what was going to happen if Carlotta and Terrence *couldn't* get these souls out of me.

"If you think any louder, you're going to wake the house," Mira murmured quietly, proving that she wasn't any more asleep than I was. She shifted a little, snuggling closer into me, and I buried my face against her neck, just breathing in her scent.

"Sorry. My brain is all buzzy."

"I know." Her hand found mine and drew it down to her belly, pressing it flat so that I could feel the roll of motion within. He was a kicker, our little one. Or she. Mira refused to find out ahead of time, and when her doctor was her best friend, there was no sneaking around behind her back. I just kept thinking "he" like that would make it so.

Don't get me wrong, my daughter is the absolute center of my universe. She's a tough kid and plays with swords and trucks just as much as she does Barbies and toy ponies. I'd had an equal number of tea parties and snowball fights, and there wasn't anything in the world I wouldn't do for that little girl.

But part of me wanted a son, too. A boy to carry on my name when I was gone. I guess it didn't help that "when I was gone" felt like it was going to be sooner rather than later.

My unborn child elbowed me square in the

palm at the same time that Mira said "Stop it."

"Stop what?"

"Stop brooding." She laced her fingers through mine. "We'll get this fixed. I've talked to Carlotta, I'm sure that she and Terrence can solve this."

"And if they can't?"

"They will."

I sighed and leaned up on my elbow so that I could look down at her. "But if they *can't*."

She rolled over onto her back so that she could look me square in the eyes, the green of her own impossible to see in the darkness. "Then we try something else. I refuse to believe that this is a permanent situation. And once the baby gets here, maybe I can…do something."

I knew it was killing her that she could do literally nothing to help me, at least in a magical sense. Mira was not the type of woman who waited around for someone else to do the rescuing. The fact that she'd been benched ate at her, even if it was for the best of reasons. "A few more months. Let's get him here safely, then we'll worry about…other things."

"Or her."

"Or her," I agreed, and lay back down, cuddling together as we felt our child move inside her. "While I'm gone, if you need anything, call the guys, okay?"

Mira sighed and rolled her eyes. "Cameron for magic, Cole for anything else. I know. We've talked about this about twenty times now."

"Sorry. Pre-travel jitters." The little alien in her belly rolled against my hand again, as if to assure me that everything would be all right. "You probably won't be able to get ahold of me, 'cause cell reception is crappy down there, but I'll call whenever we go down into town."

"Jesse Dawson, I swear to the goddess, if you go over all this crap again, I will punch you in the throat." She'd do it too. I believed that.

I sat up again, resting my elbows on my knees and running a hand through my hair. It was getting longer again, hanging past my shoulders now. I should have gotten it cut before we left. I'd learned the hard way that long hair was a liability in a fight. "Sorry, Mir. I just… I hate this. You know how frustrating it is to not be able to work magic to help out… Well I can't do *any*thing. I can't stay here, because sooner or later they're going to come for me, and I can't endanger you and Anna. And even when they *do* come after me, I can't risk fighting. I can't risk all these people's lives, and I feel so damn *helpless.*"

"I know. It's not in your nature to stand by and let others fight your battles for you." I heard a ghost of a smile in her voice, even if I wasn't looking at her. Her hand came to rest on my back, one of the rare times she'd touched me there since…since. The extra souls made her uncomfortable. In response to her touch, they flexed a little, stretching maybe, but didn't become agitated. I think they knew her, they knew she wasn't a threat.

"You'll be safe, down there. If I had to rely on someone else's magic to protect you, it would be Carlotta's. The very land they live on is blessed after so many centuries of magic being worked there."

Like Axel had said, the Perez clan had been challenging demons for longer than written memory. Sure, now they used an odd combination of native magic and Catholic prayer, but the power was the same. Only a suicidal demon would think of coming after me there. Suicidal, or one that had just been tempted beyond the limits of endurance. I guess it remained to be seen if two hundred and seventy-five souls qualified as such a temptation.

Sleep wasn't going to come easy, I could tell that already. Leaning down, I kissed Mira on the head. "Go to sleep. I'm gonna go watch TV or something. I don't want to keep you up."

"Hey." She grabbed my hand as I slid from the bed, halting my retreat. "I love you."

Words I never got tired of hearing, ever. "I love you, too." We squeezed hands, than I slipped into my sweat pants and out into the darkened house.

Ducking my head into my daughter's room, I was pleased to note that she was sound asleep, sprawled in some impossible position. Chunk, sleeping on the floor beside the bed, raised his head curiously, tilting it so that one ear flopped over. *Good dog.*

At just over nine months old, the English mastiff was still a puppy at heart, but he was already tipping the scales well over a hundred and twenty-five pounds. If he turned out like his dam and sire, he promised to grow into the size of a small buffalo before it was all said and done, which was just fine with me.

His sole purpose was to protect my daughter from the nasty things that I knew were out there, and the bigger he was, the better. I'd stood my ground against some of the worst the demon world had to offer, with one of Chunk's relatives at my side, and there was no better guardian I could ask for. He'd watch after my Annabelle when I no longer could.

As I padded down the hallway, I heard him slip from Anna's room, his nails clicking against the hardwood floor. By the time I got to the kitchen, I had a big square head shoved up under my hand, those liquid doggy eyes begging me for the treats he knew we kept in the cabinet.

"You giant mooch," I whispered, but slipped him a biscuit anyway. What can I say, I'm a softie.

Chunk took his treasure and disappeared with it back into the depths of the house.

Night had settled over the back yard, and I stood at the sliding door and looked out over my patio, resting my forehead against the cool glass. Things looked so peaceful out there, and at an earlier time in my life, I could have found peace out there, just meditating to the sounds of the fountain running into our little decorative pond.

Now, I knew the second I opened the door, Sveta would be on my heels – she had awakened the moment I left my room, and was currently lurking in the kitchen doorway while I pretended not to notice – and it was impossible to relax while an armed woman paced a track in the grass behind you. Not to mention that the sheer amount of magic wafting around through my yard was enough to set the souls in my skin jangling like a four alarm fire. My sanctuary had turned into my prison, it seemed.

I guess lack of sleep makes me a bit melodramatic.

"We have a long flight tomorrow. You should sleep." Hunh. Didn't expect her to break the silence first. I glanced over my shoulder to see her leaning against the door jamb, gun hanging loosely against her bare thigh.

"I can sleep on the flight." She made some

kind of vaguely agreeing noise. "You should crash while you can. I'll just hang out in here a while."

"All right. Call if you need me."

"Hey, Sveta?" She paused, only the tilt of her head telling me that she was listening. "Do you ever think of quitting? Of not...doing this anymore?"

There was no hesitation in her answer. "No."

"Why not?"

She turned just enough that she could look directly at me. "Because I do not know how to be anything but this."

I had to wonder if I did.

4

Morning came all too early, as those following sleepless nights are wont to do, and there wasn't enough coffee in the *world* to help me deal with the small whirlwind of chaos that settled over my household.

Surprisingly, the problem wasn't Sveta and Terrence, who set about loading everyone's gear into the rental van with quiet military efficiency. No, the herding of the cats was related directly to my family, and their desire to say a proper goodbye to Estéban.

His packing job had to be checked and rechecked. His room was searched at least twice to make sure he hadn't forgotten anything. Annabelle's hair had to be put up in pigtails, and only Estéban's skill would do. Chunk, sensing that something major was happening, anxiously kept getting underfoot, and the debate over what snacks Estéban was allowed to take on the plane in his carryon nearly started World War III.

"Take your coat." Mira pressed the heavy winter parka in to his arms, and he gave me a helpless look.

"It does not really get cold at my mother's, Miss Mira." He put the coat down.

She picked the coat up. "Take it anyway. Just in case." Back into his hands it went.

"I do not have room in my bags for it." The coat was down.

The coat was up. "But…"

"Mira!" Finally, I stood up, taking possession of the much-contested garment. "He can leave it here for now. If he needs it later, we can ship it to him. I promise, I will not let him freeze to death in Mexico in the middle of summer."

She gave me the same helpless look the kid had just shot me, and I sighed. "Baby, he'll be fine. I promise."

Tears glimmered in her eyes, and she ducked her head under the pretense of adjusting her ponytail. "All right, but when I get a phone call saying 'please send me my coat', don't say I didn't warn you."

I swear, my wife isn't normally crazy. But the pregnancy had her maternal instincts in overdrive, and whether we'd intended it or not, Estéban truly felt like one of our own kids. In the year or so that he'd lived with us, he'd become family, and he was the first child to leave the nest. Mira wasn't dealing well. I wasn't sure I was either.

And as far as Annabelle was concerned, we were taking away the big brother she'd always wanted. She fixed those devastating blue eyes on him and let the tears spill forth, clinging to the teenager's knees with all her might. "I don't want you to gooooo!"

"Oh, Bellita…" The kid got down on his knees and hugged her tightly. "I will miss you very much, too. But I promise I will write you letters, so you must practice your reading every day, all right?"

Anna sniffled, but nodded solemnly. "But you're still my big brother, right? For always? Pinky swear?"

"Pinky swear." He sealed the deal with a handshake of linked pinky fingers, then stood up with her in his arms. "And you can walk me out to the car, all right?" He gave me a significant look over Anna's head as he turned to head out front.

Right. A moment alone with Mira. She had taken the coat again, holding it in her arms like it was going to fly away without restraint. Her eyes were a little red, but she wasn't actively weeping, so I counted that as a good sign. "Hey. You gonna be okay?"

"Did I seriously just lose my mind and insist that he take a parka to a nearly tropical environment?"

"Yeah. A little." I opened my arms and she stepped into them, her belly interfering just a little with our usual snuggling position. "It's okay. He knows you love him."

She sighed, resting her forehead against my chest. "I know he needs to go home. I can't imagine not seeing Anna for over a year, I'm sure his mother is about to go crazy for missing him. But the house is going to seem pretty empty without him."

"I know." I rested my chin on top of her curly head, stroking her back soothingly. "But hey...we'll still have Sveta and Terrence. You can mother them. Maybe see if Sveta will let you paint her nails or something."

She snorted softly, but her shoulders shook with silent laughter. "I think I'll pass." Finally, she looked up at me, drawing my head down to kiss me gently. "Be careful. Come home to me."

"Always. You know that." I crouched down to rest my head against her stomach, but the occupant inside was quiet at the moment. "You take care of your mom, you hear?" Mira's fingers tangled in my hair, and we sat like that for a moment, just breathing together. Then, something crashed outside and broke the spell. "Time to go."

Somehow, we got everyone herded into the

car that was supposed to be there, and no one stashed away that wasn't supposed to be – though Anna tried – and with a last few tears and kisses-and dear god would *some*one just drive, we managed to get on the road.

Kansas City's airport is actually pretty easy to navigate, compared to some other places I've passed through, and we arrived with plenty of time to get our bags checked and get through security.

All four of us had demon slaying gear to pack – mailing things to Mexico wasn't an option – and since the government tends to frown on weapons like that on airplanes, we were forced to check the heavy duty crates. They were locked and tagged with all the proper paperwork to ensure that they'd remain that way, and for extra precaution, Terrence had placed some magical locks on them too.

As the sky-hops loaded them onto the cart to wheel them away, I could see the sigils flare into visibility from time to time. Only to me, though, and presumably the three champions with me. Ordinary people would never see the magic right under their noses, and if they did, it could usually be explained away as a trick of the light, or fatigue. Hopefully, the physical locks would keep out the airport thieves, and the mystical locks would keep out…worse things.

Checking our bags was the easy part. Getting through security, however… That was another issue.

I'd flown a lot in the last few years, I knew the drill. Anything that even looked like it contained liquid – like my mace canister – was in my suitcase. I wore my scuffed up sneakers instead of my combat boots, and I had my key chain collection of other anti-demon paraphernalia ready to dump into the bin to go through the scanners. No big deal.

Terrence, on the other hand, would try the patience of a saint on one of his *good* days. This was not such a day.

"Sir, you can't take that on board." The TSA agent patiently held his hand out for the silver flask that the old champion was clutching protectively to his chest.

"It's for medicinal purposes!"

"Sir, all liquids have to be in a three-point-four ounce bottle, in a Ziploc bag, and no one believes that your gin is medicinal." The security guy looked terminally bored, and I had to wonder how many times a day he had this argument.

"You can't have my flask! It's real silver, you know what this costs?"

"Then you'll have to dump it out, sir."

From the look on Terrence's face, that suggestion seemed tantamount to offering to kick the baby Jesus or something. "That's expensive gin!" Even his hair was offended, standing out from his head in irate disarray.

"I'm sorry, sir, regulations."

I could see actual security guards starting to mass off to the side, and knew we were about two more tirades away from seeing Terrence get strip searched. Leaning close, I muttered into his ear, "Just go dump it out before they send you into a little room with a big burly guy and some rubber gloves."

With a look of utter disgust at the TSA agent, Terrence hobbled off toward the restrooms to dump out his flask, slamming the point of his cane down loudly with every step just so that the entire world could know that he was pissed off. When he returned, the smell told me that more of the gin had gone down his throat than down the sink.

"Sir, we'll need to x-ray your cane, too."

"Oh for the love a Saint Peter. You'll deny an old man his cane, too? Is that what we've come to in this world now?"

Before his voice could rise any higher, I snatched the cane from him and threw it on the conveyor belt. "Get on the damn plane, Terrence."

With an insulted sniff, he marched through the metal detectors – showing no need for the cane, I might add – displaying his now-empty flask, and collected his cane on the far side. Behind me, Estéban muttered to himself in Spanish. He and Mira had been giving me a crash course in Spanish in preparation for the trip, and I knew none of the words were complimentary. I was inclined to agree with him. Sure, being old and crotchety meant that you pretty much got to do whatever you wanted and hang thoughts of etiquette and proper behavior, but if that was how this whole trip was going to go, I was seriously thinking about misplacing Terrence somewhere down in Mexico.

I watched carefully as Sveta passed through the checkpoint. She looked normal enough. A plain gray T-shirt (she must have a dozen of the same shirt), jeans, ponytail. And if her eyes swept the crowds around us with a bit more scrutiny than the average person, well, nobody seemed to notice. I knew perfectly well, though, that she had to have at least one weapon on her, if not more, and when she slipped through without comment, I had to wonder just where she'd stashed them and what they were made out of. When she caught me eyeing her, she gave me a raised brow and a faint smirk. On second thought, never mind where she'd hidden her weapons. I didn't need to know that badly.

The first leg of the flight passed without incident, and we changed planes in Houston with little to no drama. There would be one more stopover in Mexico City, and then we'd hit our final destination something like twelve hours after we started. I mean, what do you say about being in the air that long? The food sucks, and always looks like it's about one stray solar flare from becoming sentient. One airport looks very much like another when you get down to the nuts and bolts of it. The passengers sitting around you sometimes change, but they've all got that same 'dear god let it be over' look on their faces.

It wasn't my first long plane trip – wasn't even my longest – but there is just something about being forced to maintain a seated position for that long that is exhausting. My whole body ached, just thinking about it, and my usual plan for this sort of this was to just close my eyes and think of England. (No, not really. Closing my eyes, though, that was on my list.)

My seat was next to the kid's, and Sveta and Terrence had been spread out in the rest of the cabin. I made a solemn vow to myself that if I saw a sky marshal towing Terrence down the aisle, I was going to swear I didn't know him. I let Estéban sit at the window and settled in to reclaim some of the sleep I'd missed out on last night.

Somewhere near the halfway point, I opened my eyes to see the kid staring out the window, a pensive look on his face. "Kid? You okay?" "I'm fine." He sighed a little, giving me that all-purpose teenage shrug. "Just thinking."

"About?" Estéban was the typical adolescent male, he viewed 'talking' as one of the greatest

punishments that could be inflicted upon him.
Sometimes, though, just sometimes, he'd open up,
and when he did, I figured it was best for me to listen.

"Miguel."

That was to be expected. I'd been thinking
about him too.

Miguel was one of the kid's older brothers.
He was one of the first champions I'd ever met, and
while he'd been quite a bit younger than me, he'd
been fighting demons for much longer. He was quick
to laugh, always smiling, like the darkness we dealt
with on a daily basis had never touched him. We'd
struck up an instant friendship, and as he'd begun
courting the love of his life, Rosaline, we'd traded
demon slaying information for relationship advice.
I'd liked Miguel. A lot.

The last time I'd been to Mexico, it had been
for his wedding. I still had the picture sitting on my
desk at home, Mira and I on one side, Ivan on the
other, flanking a young couple who obviously had no
eyes for anyone but each other.

A year later, Miguel was dead, slain in a
rigged demon battle. I'd managed to free his soul,
with Estéban's help, but it wouldn't bring him back,
and it didn't make his loss any easier to those he'd
left behind.

I gave the kid a small nod, to let him know it
was okay. "I think about him a lot too. I think he'd
be very proud of you, y'know."

"Maybe." His gaze drifted out the window
again, watching the world pass by far below us. "I
just keep thinking... Why are we doing this? Papa is
gone, Joaquin and Miguel. Me, someday, and then
one of the little ones will have to step into my place.
And for what? All these years, all these centuries,

and they don't stop coming. There will never be an end. No one wins."

Pretty damn deep, for a kid, and he wasn't wrong. "I think… I think we do it because for that one person, that one single person at that one single moment, that we help, it matters a lot."

"And if that's not enough?"

"Then you walk away." He jerked his head back toward me like I'd scalded him, shock evident in those dark eyes. "You always have that option, kid. If your heart's not in it, you won't fight well, and your end will come sooner rather than later. Better to walk now than throw your life away."

"This is what we *do*, my family. I cannot just walk away from that." He shook his head and looked out the window again. "You do not understand."

I did, though. Better than he realized, but it wasn't an argument worth pursuing. I think all of us felt that way, to some extent. All of us who chose to put our lives and souls on the lines to help out complete strangers. Even with my retirement dancing within tantalizing reach, a part of me wondered if I'd truly go through with it. When it came down to the actual moment when I could say no, would I? I hadn't so far.

Maybe it was like Sveta said. Maybe I didn't know how to be anything else. Sleep wouldn't find me again, after that, but I sat with my eyes closed, trying to meditate my way out of the dark spiral of what-ifs and mighta-coulds.

Our wheels finally touched down in Culiacán, which is the capital of the state of Sinaloa. Before I'd met Miguel, I didn't have the foggiest idea what that meant, but I'd learned a lot in the time since. Things like it got just as freakin' hot down there as it did back at home, though I personally thought the humidity was better. Things like the mountains are really damn beautiful, and the trees and bushes didn't really look a lot different than Missouri. Things like tequila is a whole different beast on its native soil. Y'know, important stuff.

We all shuffled along like rigor mortis had set in on the flight, stretching and working the kinks out of annoyed muscles as we waited for our luggage and our crates. Only Sveta seemed unaffected by the flight, finding a place to stand with her back to a wall as she let her blue eyes sweep the crowds around us.

I'd only seen her a few times on the flight as she'd passed by us on the way to the restroom or whatever it was she did, but I didn't believe for a second that she had been unaware of anything that had happened on that plane. I was willing to bet she could tell me the full descriptions of every person who sat near me on the plane, as well as what they ordered for the meal, and maybe even their date of birth and favorite ice cream flavor.

Even standing to the side as she was now, I could see the gears spinning in her mind, how she catalogued every single person she saw, analyzing their threat potential. Most she dismissed, but I saw her gaze track a few men across the terminal until they disappeared from her sight. I couldn't say for sure what she was looking for, and I'm not sure I wanted to know what would have happened if one of those men had stopped and looked back at her.

Estéban was searching too, no doubt trying to find a glimpse of a familiar and long-missed face amongst the strangers. The longer he went without finding anyone, the more his brows drew together in concern. "Mamá said that someone would come pick us up. I hope that nothing has gone wrong. Maybe we should call…"

"Chill out, kid. We just got here, and we don't even have our stuff yet. Maybe there was traffic."

He made some kind of noise indicating that he heard me, but he never stopped scanning the crowd, tension growing in his lanky shoulders. I finally gave up on trying to talk sense into him and snatched his bags off the conveyor belt when they came trundling by, setting them next to mine.

Sveta finally left her post when our crates were wheeled up on a flat cart, and she and Terrence went about checking them over, making sure nothing had been tampered with. I saw the locking sigils flare into view as the old man's hands passed over them, the magic answering its maker, but none of them looked altered to me. Both he and Sveta made approving noises over the boxes, so I guess that meant our gear had made the journey unscathed.

"*Oye! Primo!*"

Estéban's head jerked around at the shout, and a huge smile split his face. "Paulito!" Before I could even spot the source of the call, the kid had bolted across the terminal and was engaged in a very rough back-slapping hug with a strange man. What followed was an exchange in Spanish so rapid that I with my very rudimentary language skills couldn't hope to keep up. I mean Mira and the kid had done a bang up job pounding the language in to my head, but my major accomplishment was knowing "*Dos cervezas, por favor.*" The kid looked happy, though, real happy.

Whoever Paulito was, the Perez family resemblance was stamped indelibly on his features.

An inch taller than my protégé, maybe a couple of
years older, but I could see hints of both Miguel and
Estéban in the shape of his jaw, the angle of his eyes.
They moved the same too, I realized, as I watched
them walk toward us. Something about the set of
their shoulders, or maybe the same slight bounce in
their stride.

And like Estéban, Paulito gleamed to my
newfound magical senses. There was magical talent
there, and given that he was undoubtedly a Perez, he
was probably well trained in its use.

"Paulito, this is Jesse Dawson, and Señor
Smythe. And this is Sveta. Everyone, this is *mi
primo* – my cousin – Paulito."

Terrence shook the young man's hand when
offered, as did I. Briefly, the almost invisible
symbols across my back crawled, no doubt in reaction
to the touch of the unfamiliar magic. They settled
though, the moment I broke contact.

Paulito tried to offer his hand to Sveta, but he
made the mistake of giving her an appraising once-
over first. By the time his gaze got up to her face, he
found only ice-cold blue eyes waiting for him, and he
dropped his hand after a few moments. His
apologetic shrug was ruined by the almost leering
grin on his face. Yup. Sveta was gonna throw him
through a wall before the week was out. I could tell
that already.

"I brought the truck, for the crates, but
someone will have to ride in the back with them.
There are only so many seats." His English was
accented, but easily understandable. In fact, most of
the Perez clan probably spoke English better than a
lot of American high schoolers I knew.

"Not a problem, bugs are pure protein."

Estéban smirked at my joke, but it was clear by the puzzled look on Paulito's face that he didn't get it.

The two young men took possession of our luggage cart, and we followed them out to the truck, left out of the conversation as they chattered back and forth in Spanish.

"Why can't they just speak the King's English?" Terrence grumbled, loud enough that I knew he meant to be overheard.

"Because we aren't in Kansas anymore, Toto."

"What the bloody hell is that supposed to mean?"

5

The thing that action movies and TV shows never show when following the intrepid hero about his adventures is how freakin' long they have to sit in the car to get where they're going. I mean, in TV-world, the drive from Alabama to North Dakota takes like ten minutes, but in reality, there are road tunes and pit stops, greasy gas station food, and more empty roadside whooshing by the windows that anyone cares to remember.

While we weren't exactly going quite that far, there was still a two-hour drive ahead of us, uncomfortably wedged between three weapons crates in the back of a seventies-era pickup truck. Paulito got the unfathomable privilege of riding with Terrence in the cab, and the rest of us got as comfy as we could in the bed, gritting our teeth as we jounced over potholes and dodged insects flying at warp speed.

Only Estéban seemed immune to the discomfort, leaning over the sides of the truck to point things out to Sveta as we barreled down the highway. Twice, we had to make a wild grab for his belt as his antics and his cousin's driving threatened to jounce him right out over the battered tailgate. Nothing would dim his enthusiasm, though, and I even saw a faint smile curve the corners of Sveta's lips in response, the kid's excitement downright infectious. Dorothy was right, I guess. There's no place like home.

We hung a left once we hit Cosalá, a small city that could have been taken right out of the pages of a fairy tale. The buildings were all the old traditional Spanish style, painted bright colors, and the streets were all cobblestone. It wasn't some backwoods nowhere, though, they were a thoroughly modern vacation destination. We were an hour and a half from Mazatlán, and spitting distance from the Gulf of California coast and the beaches. I knew from talking to Miguel and Estéban that tourism was booming in the area, people drawn to the authentic food and old world atmosphere. When we'd visited before, we'd seen one of their local festivals, and I remembered how Mira's green eyes had sparkled as we danced to the music under strings of colorful lights. She'd had this loose, patchwork skirt on, and her blouse hung off her shoulders...

I think I must have been wearing a dopey smile, lost in my thoughts, because Sveta kicked me in the ankle then rolled her eyes at me when I protested. "You're heartless, you know that?" She only snorted at me.

The sun was slowly sinking toward the ocean, just visible in the distance, when we pulled to a stop in front of a storefront, painted a charming coral color. Paulito hopped out, mumbling about picking something up for his aunt, and vanished inside, while the rest of us nearly fell out of the bed of the truck, rubbing feeling back into our lower extremities.

Estéban inhaled deeply, and let it out in a contented sigh. "Now it is beginning to smell like home."

Some locals were seated out in front of their shops, and Sveta let her gaze roam over them without hint of apology. They eyed her back in turn with as much – if less hostile – curiosity. "We are not yet at your home, yes?"

The kid shook his head. "No, another half an hour or so. Maybe less, the way Paulito drives." He pointed west, toward the darkness of the mountains. "Up there." Even with twilight barely trickling down the sides of the range, we could already see the twinkling lights of the houses up there, tiny outposts of homes on the mountainside. "The road will be rougher though." He grimaced a little.

Terrence, who had been blessedly confined to the cab of the pickup until this point, rolled the window down to snarl at us. "Any chance of getting a move on? Some of us aren't as young as we used to be, and this is hard on my old bones."

He thought *that* was hard? I had half a mind to make him take my place in the bed of the truck for the last leg, but somehow I knew that Mira would know, and she'd give me that disappointed look. I hated that look. "You could get out and stretch, you know."

The old curmudgeon just grumbled and rolled the window back up.

I was about to make some smart remark to Estéban – would have been supremely witty, I'm sure – when a hand closed around my forearm, and I turned startled eyes on Sveta. Despite her vice-like grip on my arm, her icy gaze wasn't on me. "Ten o'clock."

I followed her gaze to the corner of the building, and found a pair of dark eyes watching us in return. Half-hidden in the shadows of the alley, the young woman looked like a local girl, dressed in cut-off jean shorts and a tank top, showing off a lot of darkly tanned skin. Her black hair hung in loose waves around a heart-shaped face, and if she was wearing makeup, it was the kind that was meant to look like she wasn't. She glanced at Sveta and I briefly, not seeming to care that she'd been noticed, and then her eyes settled on Estéban with frank curiosity.

I grinned a little, and elbowed the kid. "Hey. You've got an admirer."

"Hunh?" Turning, he blushed faintly to find the very attractive girl staring at him. "Oh. Um...*hola*." She smiled a little at his clumsy greeting, but didn't answer him, only tilting her head so that her hair draped artfully across her bare shoulders. Estéban swallowed hard and seemed to have lost all words in every language he knew. Me, I settled back to see how long the two were going to stare at each other without talking, 'cause this was damn funny.

Unfortunately, Paulito chose that moment to return, and the spell was broken. Settling a few grocery bags into the back of the truck, he followed his cousin's entranced gaze to the alley, and broke into a broad grin himself. "Reina!"

The mystery girl dragged her gaze away from the kid, and she gave Paulito a teasing smile as he went to greet her. Despite my newness with the language, it was very clear that they knew each other. Very, *very* well, if you get my meaning. They murmured between themselves in Spanish for a bit, while Estéban shuffled his feet and did his best to look anywhere but. Finally, Paulito remembered his audience, and turned to make introductions.

"*Primo, señor* and *señorita*, this is *mi novia*, my girlfriend, Reina."

We all made noises of hello, though Estéban's mumbled "*Encantado*" was lost in the shuffling of his feet. For her part, the newly named Reina just inclined her head a little, that same small smile crossing her lips as her eyes swept over the kid, but she never said a word.

"I could die in here and no one would care!" Terrence had rolled the window down again, and we all jumped at his grumpy shout. He fixed us with a glare from under his bushy eyebrows, like he could kill us all with his brain.

"C'mon kid, let's go." I thumped Estéban in the shoulder, and we reluctantly piled back into the bed of the truck as Paulito made his farewells with his girlfriend. They disappeared into the alley for a moment, where I'm sure there was much kissy face going on, and then he returned alone, hopping behind the wheel again. The truck started up with a jolt that smacked my head against the back window, and I sighed, rubbing it ruefully. *Almost there. Almost there.*

The drive up into the hills was rough, but the promise of the journey's end made up for the kidneys we were surely damaging with all the bouncing. The trees closed around us as we climbed our way through the foothills, bringing dusk on early, and the lights from the small homesteads that we passed gleamed through the leaves like fireflies.

The Perez family home was actually more of a small compound, almost a village in and of itself. Many houses and outbuildings, several small barns for the variety of livestock, even their own small chapel. It was bigger than the last time I was here, I realized, marking a few structures that were missing from my memory. No doubt each building had been crafted by loving hands, probably a weekend event for the family as the need arose.

As we pulled up into the big circular drive,

Paulito beeped the horn a few times, and the place exploded as people flooded out of every doorway in sight. I felt Sveta tense up beside me, unprepared for the sheer human tsunami that was Estéban's family. Her hand slipped behind her back, where I knew she had a knife or a gun or something.

I wasn't stupid enough to touch her when she was like that, but I leaned close to quietly remind her, "Easy. There are children here." She blinked at me a few times, and I saw her forcibly relax the tension in her shoulders. After a moment, she nodded, and I felt safe getting out of the truck.

Dear god, there were so *many* of them, and all of them were trying to get close to Estéban, mussing his hair, giving him rough hugs, clinging to his knees when they were too small to reach higher. So many voices in both English and Spanish, shouting and calling greetings full of joy and welcome. I lost sight of the kid, but I could hear his laughter, somewhere in the middle of the throng.

I helped Terrence out of the truck and the three of us started unloading our things, staying safely out of the melee. We stacked the crates and piled our luggage up against it, and then there was nothing to do but lean against the truck and wait for someone to remember that we existed. It was likely going to be a while.

I let my gaze wander over the clearing again, noting how different things looked now since my…circumstances had changed. Even through the soles of my sneakers, I could feel the land almost pulsing under my feet, magic flowing through the dirt like an enormous heartbeat. Every wall, every window, every door was decorated with sigils and marks, some so new that they were almost painful to

look at, others so faint and worn that you just knew
their creators had long since forgotten them. Some of
them were precisely etched by an experienced hand,
some of them looked like the equivalent of a child's
crayon drawing. Even the youngest Perez children
were schooled in the use of magic, marking down
their first protection symbols alongside their ABCs.
Seeing layers upon layers of magic, each spell
worked immediately atop the one before it, was
almost like looking at a family tree, dating back more
generations than I could imagine.

I rolled my head back and forth a little, trying
to ignore the dance of goosebumps across my skin.
There was no danger here, obviously. How could
there be? It was the sheer quantity of magic, laid over
everything like a thick comfortable rug. The souls
rippled under my shirt, under Axel's spell, wanting to
explore their new surroundings. I closed my eyes for
a moment, silently willing them to calm. The last
thing I needed was for them to put on a show when
every person in sight would be able to see me going
up like a homing beacon.

"Jesse!" I had an instant of warning before
arms were around my neck and I was being hugged
whether I liked it or not. With a chuckle, I returned
it, then leaned back to look down at the young woman
in my arms.

"Rosaline. How have you been?" Miguel's
wife, widowed so very young. My heart hurt, just
thinking about it, but I carefully kept those thoughts
off my face. I hadn't talked to her much, since the
fight to retrieve Miguel's soul, mostly because I was
never quite sure what to say to her. Every time I
tried, all I could think of was how I'd feel if I lost
Mira, and then my throat got all thick and I couldn't

say anything intelligent. Best to not subject her to my inane babbling.

"I have been well." She grinned as she stepped back, tucking a strand of hair behind her ear. She looked just like she had on the day she wed, dark eyes aglow with an inner joy that had always been echoed in Miguel's smile. They had been so perfect together. "Mama Carlotta is teaching me to be a midwife."

"Oh! That's…interesting." I had no idea what to say to that, but a part of me was very glad to know that Rosaline had stayed with Miguel's family after his death. He would have liked that.

"It is very good to see you again." She took one of my hands in both of hers. "Everyone is so happy to have Estéban home again, and honored that all of you have come."

"Ah, speaking of everyone…" I turned to make our own small round of introductions. "Sveta, Terrence, this is Rosaline Perez. Midwife in training, apparently."

Sveta inclined her head, which was as good as a hallelujah chorus from her, and Terrence made a small bow as he kissed the back of her hand, proving that he could be a charmer when he was so inclined. "Missus."

"Mama Carlotta will be along in a moment, but she wanted me to tell you that we have rooms set up for everyone, and there is dinner waiting, because she knew you would all be hungry."

"Wouldn't say no to a small bite, and that's a fact," Terrence patted her hand with his gnarled fingers, and Sveta rolled her eyes behind his back. Funny how his mood changed the moment a pretty face was involved. "And might there be a chair for an old man to sit in?"

"Oh! Of course, this way." Linking her arm through his, Rosaline led Terrence toward the main house.

I looked to Sveta. "We just got stuck carrying the bags, didn't we?"

"Mhmm."

Before we could pick up our gear and follow, the crowd parted like the Red Sea, and the matriarch of the Perez clan appeared, immediately enveloping me in one of those hugs only moms have. "Jesse. It is so very good to see you."

Carlotta Perez was a short woman, her head barely coming up to my shoulder, somewhere in her late fifties or early sixties if I had to guess. Her dark hair, cut short but styled in neat curls, was a bit more salt than pepper since the last time I'd see her, but her round face still glowed when she smiled. She still had her apron on, with a fine dusting of flour decorating one cheek, and I wiped it off for her with a chuckle. "Baking?"

She nodded proudly. "There will be cake!" My stomach growled at that, and she laughed, delighted. *"Carlos! Pepito! Tomas! Cárguense las cosas!"* At her command, several adolescent boys darted out of the throng to take possession of our crates and luggage, and began the process of hauling everything into the house. Despite her short stature, there was something about Carlotta that made her seem eight feet tall, and even I had to suppress the urge to hop to when she barked.

"Carlotta, this is Sveta." It occurred to me, not for the first time, that I had no idea what Sveta's last name was. Maybe she didn't have one, like Madonna or Prince. I stepped back so the two women could make their greetings, and Carlotta tilted her head curiously as she looked the young woman over. Sveta just returned the look, and the silence dragged on long enough that I started to get uncomfortable. Had something gone wrong when I wasn't looking?

Finally, Carlotta sniffed. "You need feeding up. You're too skinny." And then she pulled Sveta into her arms for the same motherly embrace she'd given me. Sveta's blue eyes went wide, looking at me for help, but after a moment she relaxed and awkwardly returned the hug. Like I said, it was something about Carlotta. What could you do?

Estéban, suddenly appearing at my shoulder, gave me a shrug. His cheeks were marred with lipstick from half a dozen kiss marks, and he scrubbed at his face with the back of his hand self-consciously. "Everyone is very happy to see me."

"I can tell." The crowd was breaking up, hastened on in no small part by the shooing motions Carlotta was making in their general direction.

She nodded her satisfaction as the family slowly dispersed, then turned her gaze back on the three of us. "Come. You will have dinner, and then you will sleep. We have tomorrow for catching up."

"Yes ma'am."

"*Sí, Mamá*." The kid and I exchanged sheepish chuckles at our automatic responses, and Sveta just shook her head at us, falling into step behind Carlotta as she led us into the main house.

The Perez kitchen was enormous. It had to be, to feed so many people at a time. Four ovens, three stoves, a sprawling kitchen island with a butcher block top where they could roll out loaf after loaf of handmade bread or piles and piles of tortillas. Ropes of onions and dried peppers hung from the rafters of the high ceiling, and there was a large pot of something bubbling on the farthest stove.

The smells alone were enough to have me drooling on myself, and I was a bit envious of Terrence who was already seated at the large table with a bowl of something soup-like in front of him. Rosaline sat next to him, giggling at something he was telling her.

"Sit, sit. I will bring dinner." We found ourselves mom-bullied onto the bench seats at the table, and food appeared as if by magic, everything from soup to tortillas to something with a ton of seafood in it. "Simple food tonight, I am afraid, but for the *fiesta*, I will be making *chilorio*."

Oh God. I'd had her *chilorio* at Miguel and Rosaline's wedding, and I'd almost moved to Mexico after that. It was a local specialty, mostly resembling the barbecue pulled pork from back home, but then they fried up the meat in this chili sauce that was…I just…no words. "If I wasn't married, Carlotta…"

She laughed and patted me on the head. "Eat." And we did. I personally ate until I was hurting, and even then that last bite of homemade tortilla made me consider whether or not I was really done.

"That was spectacular, missus." Even Terrence seemed happily content, which I counted as a small miracle. "Much thanks." He spoiled the moment with a thick belch, but no one but me seemed to care.

"Now. Señor Smythe, you will be sleeping in the room at the very end of the hall. Estéban can show you the way. Jesse, I have put a cot in the boys' room for you. Señorita, there is an empty bed in the girls' room that you can use, but you should know that little Elena tends to have nightmares, so she may wake you."

Sveta frowned faintly at that thought. "It would be better if I slept elsewhere, then." I tended to agree with her. That was just going to end all kinds of bad. "Could I not also have a cot in the boys' room?"

Estéban choked on a shrimp, and I pounded him on the back until his face turned back to its normal color. "I…the boys' room is very small and crowded." And the last thing we needed was an armed woman sleeping in the midst of all the budding male hormones, dressed only in her panties.

"Do not worry for me, then. I will find somewhere." It was Carlotta's turn to frown at that, but Sveta pretended that she didn't see it. Easier that way, I'm sure.

The room at the end of the hall, where Terrence would sleep, turned out to be Carlotta's own room, though she would never have admitted it. Rosaline quietly confided to me that Carlotta would be sharing a room with her instead for the duration of our visit. I was pretty sure Terrence would be offended to know that he'd ousted our host from her own bed, but I said nothing. Wasn't my battle to fight.

The boys' room, as promised, was not small so much as it was occupied by six Perez males. Esteban's bunk – yes, there were bunk beds, lord help me – had been left empty for his return, and the other five beds were home to two of his younger brothers and three cousins of varying ages, all somewhere between ten and fifteen years old. It was eerie, watching five almost identical sets of dark eyes peering at me as I tried to get settled on my assigned cot.

Sveta herself prowled the room for a moment, examining the windows, peering at the scenery outside. Finally, she nodded. "It should be secure."

"Hey." I stopped her as she started to leave. "Where are you going to sleep?"

She smirked. "Do not worry. I am a big girl." She flipped the light switch as she disappeared out the door, dropping us into darkness.

Once my body was actually horizontal, the long hours of the day caught up to me, and I almost groaned as the aches and pains all materialized at once. Sleeping on a cot possibly left over since World War I was not going to be pleasant. "I'm too old for this," I muttered, but apparently not quietly enough, because I was answered by snickers from the bunk beds.

"Shh." That was Estéban. "*Silencio. Ya váyanse a dormir.*" My mental translation was laborious at best, but I got the general gist of "Shut up and go to sleep already." It had the exact opposite effect, as a chorus of indignant protests broke out, and one pillow flew through the darkness to pelt him in the head. "*Ay! Quieren que le vaya a decir a Mamá?*" Even I understood the threat to go tell mom, and the peanut gallery lapsed into silence.

The peace lasted approximately thirty seconds, before one brave voice carried out of the darkness. "Señor Dawson?" One of the younger boys, I thought.

"Hm?"

"The lady with you. She fights the demons too?"

"She does. She's very, very good."

Estéban snorted softly from atop his upper bunk. "And she sleeps with a gun, so do not try to surprise her. Ever."

The boys murmured amongst themselves at that, though the Spanish was muffled enough to be lost on me. I knew they'd come to some kind of consensus about what question to ask, though, when they switched back to English.

"You fought the demon that killed Miguel." That from Estéban's younger brother, I thought... Javier, maybe? There were so many of them, I mostly called them "Thing 1" and "Thing 2" in my head.

"I did. Estéban and I killed it together."

"He killed it. I just distracted it by letting it chew on my arm." The kid's arm had healed well, really, for as bad as the break had been. But he didn't give himself enough credit. I'd been injured already, gimping along, and without Estéban, that demon – a hellhound the size of a small horse – would have eaten me alive.

"You have killed many demons, yes?"

With a sigh, I leaned up on my elbows to find a host of dark eyes gleaming at me expectantly. "Boys, I will be happy to tell you stories all you want while I'm here, but right now, I'm jet-lagged and stuffed full of your mother's truly amazing food. Let me sleep tonight, and tomorrow night, we'll stay up 'til all hours and talk about whatever you want. Deal?"

There was a disappointed chorus of agreement, but they settled down, and I rested my head back down on the extraordinarily flat pillow. Estéban watched me from his high vantage point, and when I caught his eye, he smiled a little before rolling over to his own rest. He wasn't a champion to them yet, I realized. To them, he was still just big brother, or cousin. He was the same kid who had wrestled with all of them in the dirt, played pranks, went fishing or surfing or whatever they did for fun.

Carlotta had mentioned a *fiesta* before, and I knew that was a simple word for something that was going to be much more complex. A party, yes, for the returning Perez family member, but also a time to finally lay Miguel to rest, and to officially install Estéban as the family champion. Jesus, he was only eighteen. So young. So freakin' young.

Despite my overwhelming exhaustion, I lay awake for a long time, listening to the kids snore. It reminded me of Annabelle a little, and it made missing my girls a little easier to bear.

6

Morning in a household the size of this one is always inhumanly early, and never quiet. I awakened to the sounds of a herd of elephants stampeding down the hallway, and it took me a few minutes to realize it was actually just a group of teenage boys, trying to be the first to breakfast. Once the intoxicating aromas from the kitchen wafted far enough to hit my cot, I was up and right behind them.

The kids jostled and jabbed at each other, elbows flying and forks clashing over eggs and chilis, beans, tortillas. I admit it, I was right there in the midst of them. I had a brother, I knew the drill, and it was amusing to see the same antics with these kids that Cole and I had always engaged in. Some things are universal, and a teenage boy's appetite is one of them.

As we playfully bickered and stole tidbits off each other's plates, I noted that Estéban held himself apart, helping his mother bring more platters of food to the table rather than engage in the silliness. When he caught me looking, I raised a brow at him, and he just shrugged, finding something else to look at. I got it, though. He had to prove them that he wasn't just one of the kids anymore, and acting like a responsible adult was his first step. It didn't sit easily on his lanky shoulders, and I could see a hint of wistfulness in his eyes as he watched Thing 1 'accidentally' slosh a full glass of water into Thing 2's lap.

The brawl that could have ensued was quickly quashed by Carlotta's fierce glare, and in no time at all the boys had eaten and scattered, leaving the place looking like a horde of locusts had passed through.

Once my competition was gone, I helped myself to a second plate full, and ate at my leisure. The kid – Estéban, I really had to quit calling him 'kid' – sat across from me, and we were soon joined by Sveta who appeared from outside looking fresh as a morning daisy. "And where have you been?"

"Sleeping." She gave me a smirk and slid in beside Estéban, nodding to Carlotta as she was handed a plate. "Thank you."

We ate in companionable silence, several members of the family wandering in and out to take their breakfast to go, and by the time we were done, Terrence had shuffled in, fully dressed if not fully awake. Carlotta filled a mug with coffee for him without being asked, and he grumbled under his breath.

"What he means is thank you, Carlotta. He's British, his English is terrible." That earned me a baleful glare from the old man, and I grinned in return. "So, what's the plan for today?"

Carlotta slid in on the other side of her son, finally taking a moment for her own breakfast. "I thought it would be best if we began with…that…" She nodded toward me, but we all knew she was thinking of the scrawl of iridescent tattoos across my back. "Before I get too involved in preparations for the *fiesta*."

"And when will this fiesta be happening?"

"A few days, still. We are waiting for more relatives to arrive. Some of them must travel far." She slipped her arm around her son's shoulders. "All of them wish to come see Estéban." He blushed and ducked his head.

"And you, kid? You got plans?"

He wiped his mouth off and stood, gathering up his own plate, then reached for the others to begin cleaning up. "Morning exercises, first. Then I will see what else needs to be done. Alejandro said that the goat fence has some loose boards."

Carlotta raised a brow at his sudden industriousness, but didn't say a word. "We will be in the sanctuary, if you need anything." Estéban nodded, and disappeared into the house after dropping the dishes off in the sink. His mother sighed softly, allowing some sadness into her dark eyes for the first time since we arrived. "He feels he must step into his brother's place...and his father's."

"It's what we do." I gave her a small smile and a shrug, and after a moment, she smiled back.

"Foolish men. Taking on the world alone, when we would gladly do it beside you. Come then. I need to gather a few supplies and then we will see what can be seen." She paused, looking at Terrence. "Señor Zelenko said you would be helping with this?" There was no mistaking the skepticism in her voice, no doubt put there by the faint odor of gin that followed the old man like a cloud.

Terrence harrumphed, pushing his way to standing with a screech of the wooden bench. "I'm not so old that I can't sling a few spells when called for. You just lead the way."

"And you have training?"

The old man paused, then drew himself up stiffly. "I can promise, I've been doing this longer than you, young lady." It should have been a compliment, almost flirty, to call Carlotta a young lady. Instead, it came out snide, and her dark eyes flashed dangerously.

"We shall see."

So that's how this was going to go. I was
going to be the guinea pig in the middle of a magical
pissing match. Sveta didn't even try to hide her
smirk. I threw a bit of tortilla at her. "Oh shut up."

With a chuckle, she stood as well. "I will
walk the perimeter, do some reconnaissance."

"You realize we're probably in the safest
place in the entire world, right?"

"And I will be certain that it remains so."

There was a strained silence between Carlotta
and Terrence when they returned from gathering up
whatever it was they needed, and as we left the main
house for the sanctuary – whatever that was – I spied
Estéban in driveway, working his way through his
morning katas. For a moment, I stopped to watch,
trying to look at him with a teacher's critical eye, but
really, he looked good.

I wasn't the only audience, either. The kid-
pack had materialized, forming a wide-eyed ring
around my protégé as he went through the motions of
a fighting style that was completely alien to them. As
far back as history could remember, before their name
was even Perez, the men of this family had fought
with everything they had at hand. They fought with
machetes, shovels, and crude stone weapons. They
had been farmers, and ranchers, and the occasional
soldier, but they had no formal training in combat.
Their style was simple and brutal, at once rustic and
completely lethal.

Compare that to me with my extensive martial
arts background. While I wasn't above a down and
out street brawl, the basic motions of my fighting
style were on the opposite end of the spectrum from
what Estéban had learned at his father's knee. There
was grace there, and control. We'd blended his

teachings, and his fury was tempered now with calculation, his rage with a rock-steady patience.

He slipped into a sword kata, one of my favorites actually, though we'd had to modify some of the moves to account for his shorter blade. A machete just wasn't going to be a katana, no matter how we tried. And while he'd practiced with my sword a bit, for the sheer logic that being confined to one type of weapon was never safe, the thicker blade of the machete was where he found his comfort. It had been his brother Miguel's, and before that, their brother Joaquin's, and before that, their father's. I had no idea how many generations that weapon went back, but there was as much Perez sweat and blood on that blade as there was demon blight. It was part of their DNA.

"He has learned much from you." Carlotta's voice was soft, but still, I jumped a little. I hadn't heard her come up behind me. "He seems...calmer, than when he left."

"He's a good kid." I deliberately turned my back on the scene. Estéban didn't need me watching over him anymore. He could do this on his own, and that included his morning exercises. I offered my elbow to the lovely woman at my side, and she slipped her hand into the crook with a small smile. "Mira and Anna are heartbroken that he's gone."

"He could have stayed. If he wanted." It was the right thing for a mother to say, as she prepared to let go of one of her newly-adult sons. The right thing, but that didn't make it any less painful.

"No, he really couldn't. We all know that bad things are coming for me, and...he needs to be clear of that. He needs to be somewhere that he can go on and do good things, while the world goes to shit elsewhere."

"Language, Jesse."

"Yes, ma'am."

The sanctuary was nothing more than a small, well-built building located on the very edge of the Perez property. It had four wooden sides, a roof, a door, a couple of windows. It could have been a tool shed, or a small storage unit, except for the fact that Terrence waited just outside with a look of speculative caution on his craggy old face. Oh, and the fact that the entire structure glowed and writhed with magical wards. Just drawing in sight of it made the tattoos across my back crawl, some of them twisting in a decidedly unpleasant fashion.

My breath hissed between my teeth, and my steps faltered a bit. Carlotta stopped and turned a concerned eye on me. "It hurts?"

"A little. I don't know why."

"Let me see." With quick, officious mom-hands, she stripped me out of my T-shirt in a heartbeat, then circled behind to look at my back, making clucking noises in the back of her throat. "There is…what is this…darkness here?"

She never touched my skin, but I felt one finger trace a searing line across my shoulder blades, cutting a line through Axel's concealment spell. It almost dropped me to my knees, and I sagged, gasping. "Leave it! Gah, leave it!"

"Here now, what're you doing to the boy?" Stars danced in my vision, so I couldn't see Terrence bustling to my rescue, but I could smell the moment he arrived. "Poking at things you don't understand, causing problems…" His gnarled hand clamped down on my elbow, pinching hard, but oddly, the mundane pain allowed me to focus, to breathe.

"There is a spell laid upon him, something filthy and nasty. Was this your work? Did you do this?" Accusation dripped from Carlotta's lips, the sound of a mother wolf about to do battle for her cub.

"No, that was done before I arrived." Terrence sniffed, offended at the implications. "Boy won't let me remove it either, and it sets the souls all aflutter if you try to touch it. You have to work under it, or around it."

As the pain subsided, Carlotta's face appeared in my swimming vision. "Jesse? What is this spell? It is not Mira's work."

"A...friend did it. It serves a purpose, so just leave it. Please." Raising my head, I looked again toward the sanctuary, and the same few souls coiled up tightly somewhere in the vicinity of my lower back. It felt like someone had kicked me in the kidneys. "That's not the problem. They...some of them don't like the building. They don't like the magic there."

"Hm. Just a few, you say?" Again, she disappeared out of my field of vision, and Terrence squeezed my elbow again just to remind me that he was there. "Here, do you see?" Obviously, she wasn't talking to me, since I'd have to pull an Exorcist to get my head around that far. "This grouping here. The skin is red, angry."

"I see it. What's it mean? We've never seen them do this before." Terrence prodded me in the ribs with one thick finger and I jumped in spite of myself.

"I think...perhaps...these are the souls of someone who knows *brujeria*. The magic calls to them." A palm lay flat against my skin, and soothing cold spread out from the touch. Quietly, Carlotta murmured in Spanish, and the riot of action in my back calmed, then stilled entirely. The knotted muscles relaxed, and Carlotta chuckled softly. "How interesting."

"What did you say? That was no spell." Terrence was right, I realized. I smelled no cloves, the tell-tale marker of a magic user at work.

"I simply told them that I was a *bruja blanca*, a white witch, and they had nothing to fear. Whoever they are, they have known *la bruja negra*, and they were afraid that I was one."

I'd only ever seen one person that I thought might qualify as a *bruja negra*, a black witch. I'd never seen her cast a spell, or even do anything more than smile and chat with me, but that tiny Korean woman in her college sweatshirt and worn jeans still scared me more than most of the demons I'd ever faced. I had to wonder what I would feel if I encountered Mystic Cindy again while hosting these two hundred and seventy-five souls. Probably best not to find out.

"All right, enough of this twaddle. We have work to do." The old British curmudgeon gave me a shove toward the small structure, but he waited until he was sure I was steady on my feet before he did it. I could almost think he cared.

The small structure should have been stifling hot in the early summer heat, but once they got the windows opened up and a breeze flowing through, it was actually quite pleasant. I found a spot on a small bench against the wall, and watched as Carlotta and Terrence unpacked the implements of their respective trades.

Terrence's gear looked most familiar to me.

Salt, a mortar and pestle, a silver bell, some other things. I'd even seen him employ his heavy cane in some of his casting, using it to set the borders of his personal protective circle.

Meanwhile, the first two things Carlotta pulled out of her bag were an ornate silver cross, and a vicious obsidian knife, the black stone gleaming like it was wet. She made that clucking noise in her throat again as she sorted her things, placing bundles of dried herbs just so, laying out a large skein of coarse red cording. Next to that went a coil of black cord, and beside that, a rosary that looked to be carved of amber.

"Before we begin, perhaps you can tell me what has already been determined, so that we are not covering the same ground again." Carlotta's gaze fell on Terrence, and the pair of them started talking magic and things that went right over my head.

I quit listening, just leaning against the wall and concentrating on the faint swirl of movement beneath my skin. They had calmed, but they weren't still, and wouldn't be so long as I was inside this building. While they may have destroyed my danger sense, there was no way someone could hide any magic from me now, as the souls reacted to even the tiniest spell.

I had to wonder if they had moved like this for Gretchen, the previous host. We hadn't exactly been BFFs or anything, but she'd never mentioned it. She didn't say whether or not they responded to her moods, or if some of them would react to memories their physical selves had made. How much of their living counterparts were still in there? The question only served to remind me that these were real people I was carrying around, living breathing people, and if these souls were destroyed in some fashion, those lives were over.

I already had one death on my conscience. One soul, burned up to power a magic I hadn't even realized I was using. Someone, somewhere, dead to save my life. It ate at me, coming back to nip at the edges of my thoughts at inopportune moments. Didn't matter that I hadn't known what would happen, or even what I was doing at that moment. Soul-drunk, I'd started calling it, high with the sheer amount of life force that had surged into my body upon Gretchen's death.

It had eased up in the time since, but sometimes, when my guard was down, they'd flare up into my eyes again and I could see everything in that moment. Things like air currents, and infinitesimal imperfections in a flat surface. Water pulsing through plant leaves and the exhales from sleeping garden rodents, well hidden from normal sight.

It was hard to pull myself out of that, too easy to get lost in the minute wonders of the world. The first time, it had scared Mira to death. She had to slap me to bring me back to myself, and then she cried for an hour. I think she was afraid that one day, my mind would go walkabout, and wouldn't be able to wander back. I was afraid of that too.

Realizing that my eyes had fixated on a knot in a board for the last five minutes, I squeezed them shut and pressed the heels of my palms against them. I had to watch it, or I'd drift off, just like I feared.

"You all right?" Something nudged my boot, and I nodded at Terrence's gravelly question. "C'mon then. Herself wants you standing."

I got to my feet, dropping my T-shirt on the bench, then moved to the center of the room as

Carlotta indicated. "I get to keep my pants, right?"

"Hm. So far." Both practitioners walked slow circles around me, looking me over from head to toe, so I just rested my hands atop my head and held the pose. Occasionally, one of them would reach out to touch my back, getting a couple of good jumps out of me. "Hold still."

"I'm ticklish!"

Terrence snorted at that, then took over my former seat on the bench, leaning both hands on his cane. "You can see that they're dug in hard. Not just sitting on the surface, no, they're soaked all the way in to the muscle and bone." Well that didn't sound encouraging.

"I've never seen the like." Carlotta's voice was a mixture of awe and serious contemplation. "I have no idea how to remove them, let alone remove them without harming them, or Jesse."

"Well, what I'm thinking is, they need a vessel. We can't just return them to their homes, because they were given up willingly, and because we don't know who they all belong to, so we can't just go askin' them to take their souls back pretty please." Terrence's accent got thicker, I realized, when he was truly concentrating on what he was doing.

"Hm. Yes. A new host of some kind, willing to keep them safe."

"Or maybe somethin' non-livin'. A talisman to bind them to, or some kind of holy relic."

Again, they lapsed into talking amongst themselves, and left me just standing there feeling poked and prodded. A lab rat, that's what I was. "Uh, can I put my shirt back on?"

"No." From both of them, in unison, and they didn't even miss a beat in their conversation.

"Perhaps we are thinking too large," Carlotta finally remarked. "Perhaps it would be easier to extract them one at a time, rather than all at once."

This was gonna hurt. I just knew this was going to hurt.

Terrence snorted again. "If you can figure out how to get even one of them out, you're a better spell-worker than I. Honestly, I'm not sure we can get them out unless they actually *want* to leave."

Now that was an interesting thought. The souls had left Gretchen and come into me because of the terms of her demon contract. Those circumstances had been laid down and cemented long before I'd ever met her. However, with no deal on my part, no rules and regulations set, what was going to govern the passing of these souls on to someone else, if the souls themselves weren't willing to be passed?

"What…what happens to them if I die while I still have them?" I hadn't asked that question before, and I was pretty sure neither of the casters with me had the answer, but it was one of those things that needed to be out in the open. What *was* going to happen, upon my death, if I still held these two hundred and seventy-five lives?

As expected, neither of them answered me, but I could feel the weight of the looks they exchanged behind my back. Finally, I felt Carlotta's warm had come to rest on my shoulder, just above the highest of the shiny white marks. "That is not going to happen."

Her voice sounded a thousand times more confident than I felt.

7

I'd like to say that Carlotta and Terrence put their heads together and magicked me up a cure, but it quickly became apparent that the only thing they were going to put their heads together for was to lock horns. About three hours into their experiments, my back was burning like fire from the constant mystical poking and prodding, and my head was pounding from the incessant bickering. Terrence had dubbed Carlotta "you old bat" and Carlotta only muttered darkly in Spanish at him in return. I knew those words. Those weren't polite words.

I honestly couldn't even tell you what they were fighting about. It started when Terrence tried to use gin and his cane to mark out a protective circle around me on the floor, and just got increasingly ridiculous from there. They disagreed about everything, up to and including basic tenets of Christianity –and trust me, Anglican versus Catholic wasn't even that much of a stretch, they just wanted something to argue about – and how it applied to working magic. When they finally got around to bickering about the type of bees that made the wax in the candles, I'd had enough.

"Oh dear God, get a room." I scuffed my foot across the chalk line on the floor – Carlotta had won that argument – and the magical circle broke with a faint pop of pressure in my ears and the scent of cloves. I went to slump on the bench, letting my head rest in my hands. "I'm calling a break here, folks."

"Working the boy too hard. Old bat." Terrence hobbled over to sit beside me like he was my long lost best friend, and glared at Carlotta.

"*Idiota borracho*," she grumbled at him in return, and took a seat on the bench opposite us, arranging her long skirt neatly. "We are getting nowhere, and honestly, I do not know if the pain we are causing you is worth the effort. It may be more beneficial for us to work on the theory of this for a while, without your presence."

I looked skeptically between the two of them. "Do you really think you can play together unsupervised?" The absolute lack of amusement on both faces was identical, and if I was a bit more suicidal, I would have laughed.

Before we could hash out any more details, there was a knock at the door, and Rosaline's voice. "Mama Carlotta?"

"Come inside, Rosaline." The door swung open, and Rosaline gave us all a bright grin before setting her gaze on Carlotta. "Señora Alvarez. She is calling for you."

Carlotta heaved herself up off the bench with a decisive shake of her skirts. "Well, that ends this for today. Babies do not wait. Fetch my bag, Rosa." She glanced back once, to fix Terrence with a stern look. "Do not touch my things, I will gather them up when I return."

"As if I'd want to touch anything of hers…" The old grouch muttered at Carlotta's back, but I noticed it wasn't loud enough for her to actually hear him. "All right, you, go make yourself useful elsewhere. I've got work to do."

You don't have to tell me twice. I bailed before anyone could change their minds, yanking my T-shirt on as I beat a hasty retreat. The burning sensation in my skin eased as soon as my back was covered, as if the souls knew they weren't going to be assaulted anymore for a while.

The Perez compound was bustling with life as I made my way back toward the main house. Children ran across my path, playing games and shouting to each other. A few of them even paused to give me grins, then darted off again. There were women at a few of the other buildings, hanging out laundry on lines, or shaking dust out of rugs. I nodded and waved when they noticed me, but I couldn't have told you any of their names. There were just so many people.

No one was in the kitchen when I sauntered through, so I grabbed a stray orange out of the bowl and headed out the back door to keep looking. Wasn't hard to locate Estéban, all I had to do was follow the sound of a pounding hammer.

As promised earlier, my protégé was working on the fence for the goat pen, nails sticking out of his mouth as he carefully hammered the loose boards back into place and replaced a few that had gotten too chewed or rotten to be of use anymore. He didn't even hear me coming until my shadow fell across him, and he looked up, blinking against the sun.

"You need some help there?"

He spit the nails out into his hand before answering. "No, I'm almost finished." Standing, he stretched with a grimace, proving that he'd been at it a long time. "I do not understand why it was allowed to get like this. Paulito could have made repairs, or anyone really. This didn't need to wait for me."

"Maybe they just didn't think it was important. I mean, it looks like the goats are all still here, right?" One of the furry beasts, all wiry black fur and gnarled horns, looked at us and gave a disgusted "blaaaah!"

"Only because of Pueblo."

"Who's Pueblo?"

"That's Pueblo." He pointed toward some scrubby shade trees across the lot, and at first I didn't see anything. Then, the shadows shifted a little, and I realized I was looking at a dun colored donkey, the creature's ears perked and his gaze fixed on us as if he knew we were talking about him. Standing under the low hanging branches, the dappled light broke up the tan form and made him almost invisible if he remained still.

"That's a donkey."

"Mhmm. Best guard dog you can have. He will not let the coyotes get to the babies, and he keeps the goats together if they get out."

"But...that's a donkey." Despite my rural-ish origins, I am so not a farm guy.

"*Burro*."

"Whatever."

The kid chuckled at me, gathering up his tools. "Come on. We will wash up and then find lunch."

I offered him a few sections of my orange as we walked to the tool shed. "Your mom had to run off on a baby thing, so looks like I'm free for the afternoon. Any more repairs need to be done?"

"I haven't had a chance to look around yet. Probably. Where is Sveta?"

I shrugged, my mouth full of orange, then helpfully added, "Dunno. Said she was going to walk the perimeter or something, but that was at breakfast." If I had to wager, she wasn't too far away. She struck me as the lurk-in-the-shadows-and-watch type. That thought made the souls across my shoulders ripple uncomfortably, and I had to remind them (and myself) that Sveta was on our side.

The tool shed was more of a small barn, and as we went in to store the hammer and a few other things, a tarp-covered shape caught my eye. If I didn't know better, I'd say that looked like... "Is that a motorcycle?"

Estéban glanced to where I was pointing, and tensed up so hard he almost tripped over his own two feet. I caught his elbow until he could find his balance again. "Hey, you okay?"

"That is Miguel's motorcycle." Ah. Oops. I watched him as he tucked his tools away, noting the uncomfortable hunch to his lanky shoulders. His eyes kept going back to that dusty tarp in the corner, and his jaw was clenched so tight I thought he was going to grind his teeth to powder.

I just stood silently, watching him struggle with whatever it was going on in his head. After a few moments, he sighed, resting his hands on the workbench in front of him and hanging his head. "He was working on it, you know, before. He didn't get to finish it. I don't think it even runs."

"Can I look at it?" He nodded his permission, so I went over to strip the tarp off the bike, sending clouds of dust swirling into the air. Crouching down, I examined what I had revealed.

It wasn't anything special, just an old dirt bike in a state of semi-disassembly. Looked like it had been red and blue at some point in its life, but it had been used hard, and the paint was more scuffed and scraped than solid color. A small box of parts rested behind the front wheel, obviously a project in mid-completion that someone had expected to come back to shortly. He never made it.

"Miguel was teaching me about engines. He said once we were done with this one, we would find one for me." I could hear a ghost of a smile in his voice as he came to stand behind me. "Mamá would have freaked out, so we weren't going to tell her until we were done."

Secret plans, promises between brothers. I knew how that was. Cole and I had made a few of our own, back in the day.

"Didn't know you knew about engines." Funny how you can live with a guy for over a year and still know so little about him.

He crouched down beside me, hand resting on the handlebars to hold his balance. "I don't know it well. Like I said, he was teaching me."

"Maybe you can finish this yourself, then. If you can find someone to help."

"Maybe." Absently, like he wasn't even aware of what he was doing, he picked up a small socket wrench, twirling it between his fingers. "We spent hours out here. We'd go in for dinner, covered in grease, and Mamá would yell at us for not washing up. Miguel would just give her this grin, and then it was all okay. I think he was her favorite."

"Parents don't have favorites," I lied, because it was what you are supposed to say. Cole was my mom's favorite. We'd always known it, and I never really thought about it anymore. Cole was the good son, and I'd been the hellion she was always pulling out of trouble. It wasn't until I was an adult that my mom and I had truly gotten to know each other.

I quickly jotted down a few mental notes for things to do (and not to do) when my own second child arrived. I didn't want either of my kids to ever feel like I favored one over the other.

Estéban reached out and tweaked something with the wrench in his hand, the ratchet making a clicking sound that was loud in the quiet barn. Whatever it did, it wasn't want he wanted, because he frowned and started digging through the box on the ground for something else. Hey, what I know about engines is confined to my ancient Mazda pickup, and largely revolves around making sure I'm not walking home. Finally, he fished out a different socket, and leaned in close to fiddle with something else.

"Hey, could you hand me that…?" He gestured vaguely to my right, and when I offered him an allen wrench I found lying there, he seemed satisfied.

With a small smile, I settled down on the pile of tarp, watching as my student started fiddling with the motorcycle engine. I could totally imagine him in here, with Miguel, both their dark heads bent close together as the older brother explained this or that about what they were working on. Miguel's presence seemed to linger here, even though I knew very well that his soul had passed on to wherever good people go in the end. (Despite the fact that I'd recently met an actual angel, I still wasn't completely sold on the idea of heaven. Hell, on the other hand, that I believed in whole-heartedly.)

I don't know long we sat in that dusty, dimly lit barn while Estéban tinkered and fussed over the motorcycle. I handed him things when he needed, but other than the occasional request, we sat in companionable silence. When the sun wandered around to where it wasn't beaming in the door, I found a work light and plugged it in to give us more illumination.

We only realized we'd been missed when a small head crowned with dark pigtails poked in through the door, and a little girl's eyes lit up in triumph. "Señor Smythe! *Los encontré!*"

"Aw crap, we're in trouble, kid." I muttered before the doorway was filled with a large, grumpy frame.

"Well it's about goddamn time you two turned up! Scare an old man to death, why don't you!" Despite his bluster, Terrence patted the little girl on the head, and slipped her a toffee candy when he thought no one was looking. Giggling, she ran off. "What the hell are you doing, all holed up in this dustbin?"

"Working on Miguel's motorcycle." Estéban leaned back to show off his efforts, and Terrence shuffled closer, leaning on his cane as he bent to peer into the half-finished engine.

"Hmph. Not bad. Needs a bit of tender loving care, is all." Without even looking, Terrence leveled a gnarled finger in my direction. "You. Find me a seat."

"Sir, yes sir," I mumbled, but managed to locate an overturned bucket that would suffice. I reclaimed my nest on the tarp and watched in amazement as Terrence proceeded to school Estéban in the finer elements of small engine work. Hunh. Who knew?

Watching that grizzled old curmudgeon quietly and carefully explain the mechanics of your basic dirt bike made me realize that Terrence wasn't exactly everything he wanted people to think he was. Old and grumpy, yes. Drunk, quite often. But he had a keen mind for a lot of things, and very little slipped

past him when it came to true observation. I could
tell by his attitude that he had fully grasped the
importance of "Miguel's motorcycle," and that he
possibly even cared that the kid was taking this very
seriously.

Under Terrence's tutelage, the engine shaped
up pretty quickly. The pair of unlikely mechanics
figured out that all the parts were present, at least, it
was just going to be a matter of getting them all
functional before the bike would actually run. We
were about to go in search of things like gasoline and
motor oil when the kid's stomach growled loudly,
echoed quickly by mine. Then I remembered that
we'd only had about half an orange each since
breakfast. Lunch had obviously gone the way of the
dodo.

"Think that's our cue to call it a day,
gentlemen." I shoved up off the ground, brushing the
dust off my clothes with little-to-no success. "We
need to get something for dinner, or I'm going to eat
Pueblo."

Estéban snorted at me, while Terrence gave
me a puzzled glance under his bushy eyebrows.
"What the hell is a Pueblo?"

We meandered toward the main house with a
feeling of accomplishment that only comes from
working with your hands. Hell, I even felt pretty
good about myself, and all I'd done was watch and
hand them things.

Dinner was well underway in the Perez
kitchen, but Carlotta was conspicuously absent.
Instead, a rather lovely woman – "My cousin
Alejandro's wife, Veruca," Estéban reminded me
quietly – scolded us all in rapid Spanish until we
lined up at the sink to scrub our hands. While we

lined up at the sink to scrub our hands. While we cleaned up, the first wave of the dinner crowd – Estéban's younger siblings and several cousins I hadn't met yet – scarfed down their food and then scattered to the four winds, leaving the long table ready to be filled again.

By some unspoken signal, my roommates appeared about the same time we sat down, the adolescent boys jostling each other and conversing in loud, joyful voices. Like most teenage males, they didn't seem to care what food they shoved in their faces, so long as there was a lot of it. With most of the conversation in Spanish, I could catch maybe every fifth comment, but that didn't keep me from enjoying the meal. There was something about being absorbed into a large family that just made things all right. I even caught Terrence chuckling and shaking his head a time or two, though he'd probably deny it.

Sveta showed up shortly thereafter, with no hint as to where or how she'd spent her day. She simply stared at one of the boys – Thing 1, I thought – until he squirmed under her gaze and scooted over to make room for her. After that, the conversation came to an awkward halt, more than one pair of dark eyes fixating more on the beautiful woman at the table than the plates of food in front of them.

"Have a good day, Sveta?" I raised a brow at her.

"Mmf." Fine. Whatever she'd been up to, she was going to keep it to herself for now. She fished her boot knife out, using it to spear some sliced mango, and the boys decided to make themselves scarce in a mass exodus that was usually reserved for things like shouting "Fire!" in a theater. I didn't miss the faint smirk that curved her lips as she nibbled delicately at the fruit impaled on her blade.

"*Oye, Estéban!*" Paulito's shout preceded him, and even then he only hung his head inside the back door, grinning rakishly. I only got about half the words in his question, but Estéban turned to look at me.

"The older boys are going down into town. He wants to know if I want to go." There was uncertainty in his dark eyes, as if he wasn't sure he had permission to just *be* a teenager. That made me sad. I'd worked real hard when he was in Missouri to make sure he got to do kid things, too.

"You should go. Have fun." When he hesitated, I bopped him on the nose with a rolled up tortilla. "But I'm not saving you any food, so you're going to starve."

He gave me a smirk and snatched the tortilla out of my hand, devouring it in two bites. "Not if you don't move faster." He gave Paulito a nod indicating that he was coming, and then disappeared out the door to answering whoops of excitement from the crowd of guys waiting for him.

"It's good, you know." I glanced over at Terrence's interjection, and he gave me a firm nod. "He's too young for these things, these messes we get into. Not right to offer to give up your life before you've even lived it."

I was inclined to agree with him, for once, but I knew that Estéban would fight the notion that he could have a normal life. Lord knew, I wasn't the best example either.

I tried, oh sure, I tried. I had Mira, and Anna, and a baby on the way. One point five kids and a dog, right? I had a normal job working in retail, and I mowed the lawn and cooked dinner and did laundry, just like anybody. But in the past year I had been mauled by a hellhound, chased by spider-monkey zombie things, and nearly squashed flat by a monster made of living clay. My house was ringed with the most powerful magical wards created by multiple casters.   I currently carted around two hundred and seventy-five souls that weren't mine, and I truly believed that at any given moment, a demon was going to pop out of nowhere to take them, any way it could.

Poster boy for normal I was not.

But I'd made that choice when I was an adult. Well old enough to know better, sure, but able to give informed consent. Estéban wasn't, despite his efforts to prove me wrong.

Part of me wanted to go talk to Carlotta, to really plead the case that the kid was simply not ready to take on the duties they wanted to assign to him. Surely, if they seriously *needed* an active champion, one of the older boys could, one of the cousins. It was in their blood, too.

I knew, though, that Estéban would never forgive me if I did. He'd see it as me, doubting his abilities, which I didn't. The kid could fight, and he wasn't going to turn tail and run at the first sign of trouble. I knew that. I'd seen it, and he'd saved my bacon. I just wanted him to know that I had faith in him, but that I didn't want to see him turned into demon chow before he ever hit twenty.

With a sigh, I pushed my plate away, no longer hungry. If this was what being a father was like as your child grew up, the years ahead of me were going to suck.

The sound of the old pickup truck carried through the evening air, and there was a chorus of excited childish chatter, followed by Carlotta's unmistakable soothing voice. When she and Rosaline came through the back door, she smiled to see the three of us still at the table. "Oh, good, there is some dinner left."

I stood up to let her take my seat, and took the big duffel bag away from Rosaline who thanked me with a grateful smile. "How was your...thing?"

Carlotta chuckled and shook her head as she fixed her plate. "It was a false alarm. A new mother tends to fret over things that are quite normal." Yeah, I remembered a few of those with Mira when she was pregnant with Anna. They weren't always her false alarms, either. I think I did more fretting than she did. "I do not think the baby will come before next week, but I have been wrong before, so we will see."

Rosaline glanced around the room with a puzzled frown. "Where is Estéban?"

"He went out with Paulito and some of the older boys. Cousins, I guess?" I shrugged. "Boys' night out or something. Said they were going down into town."

Carlotta paused in the middle of raising her fork to her mouth. "How long ago did they leave?"

"Um...twenty minutes? Maybe?" I glanced to Terrence for confirmation, but he only shrugged. When she continued to frown at her food, I asked, "Was that okay? Should I have made him stay?"

"No, no. It is all right." She smiled, but it was obviously forced.

"Do you want me to go down and find him?" At the word that we might be leaving, Sveta shoved the last of her food into her mouth and stood up, ready to go.

Carlotta offered us both a smile again, this one slightly more genuine. "No, I am certain he will be fine. They will just be coming in very late, is all. They wake up the little ones, when that happens."

Sveta looked back and forth between Carlotta and I, then sat back down, filling up her own plate again. "Then I will take his bed, and he can sleep with the *visljuk*." We all stared at her, and she frowned. "The animal. The brown animal that is not a horse."

"The donkey?"

"Yes!" She pointed her knife at me, and since she was smiling I was going to assume she wasn't about to kill me with it. "The donkey."

I raised a brow at her. "You slept with the donkey last night?"

"It was warm. He is pleasant." She shoved her plate away again, and wiped her knife blade off on her jeans before slipping it back into her boot. "I will go walk the perimeter again. Good evening."

We all just watched her go for a moment, before Carlotta broke the silence. "But…the *burro* bites."

Well apparently, he bites everyone but Sveta. Or maybe she bites back.

8

I spent the rest of the evening completely immersed in the large, boisterous Perez family. Everyone around me had a story to tell about Estéban, and I even added a few of my own from the time he'd lived with me. The only thing we were missing was the kid himself. I hoped he was having a good time. He'd earned a bit of rest and relaxation.

We talked and ate and laughed until even the adults were yawning, and Carlotta finally issued the edict that it was bed time. Obediently, we all wandered off to our assigned bunks.

True to her word, no sooner than I'd made myself as comfy as possible on my cot, Sveta sauntered in and hauled herself up into Estéban's bed with one arm and a graceful swing of her leg. Thankfully, she wasn't dressed just in a T-shirt and panties, but the faded sweat pants she had on looked suspiciously like… "Hey, those are mine!"

The smirk she gave me very clearly dared me to take them back from her, and I really couldn't do anything but glare. God, it was worse than having a little sister.

The peanut gallery was suspiciously silent as we flipped the lights off, the banter of the previous night obviously being stifled by the presence of a female. There were some faint coughs, a few sounds of rustling blankets, and the overwhelming feeling that every pair of eyes in the room was fixed on that upper bunk.

After a few moments of that, Sveta chuckled softly. "I do not bite, young ones. Nor will I grow a second head while you sleep. Close your eyes."

That led to more shuffling, more uncomfortable squirming, and then one brave voice rose out of the darkened room. "Is it true that you are a champion, *señorita*?"

"It is true."

Thing 2 was the next brave one. "Why do you fight? You are a girl."

My eyes had adjusted to the darkness enough that could see when Sveta rolled over to fix the young man with a serious look. "Why should I not? I have the ability, the skill. My sword is as sharp as his." She pointed across the room to me, and I held up my hands.

"Hey, you leave me out of this." Thankfully, they ignored me.

"Who taught you to fight?" They were sitting up now, every single one of them, all pretenses of sleeping tossed to the wayside.

"My father taught me. From the time I was a very small girl. Smaller than you, there." She indicated the youngest of the pack, who couldn't have been more than ten or eleven.

"What about your brothers? Did he teach them too?"

"Or did they die?" It happened. They all knew it.

I kept waiting for the moment that Sveta would grow tired of the questioning and snap at one of them, but she simply rolled over, resting her chin on her pillow as she talked. "I have no brothers. I am alone."

"What about your mother? Did she fight too?" It was clear that the concept of a female champion was about to short-circuit their little brains.

Stood to reason, when only the males of the Perez clan were trained to be champions. I had to wonder if that was by design, or if none of the girls had ever wanted to.

"No. My mother was a…a fine lady. Very…gentle. Delicate." There was no mistaking the fond smile in Sveta's voice. "She was not like me."

"Is she dead?" Funny how children can get away with questions that would be rude coming from anyone over the age of about fifteen.

"Oh yes. Many years ago. But I still feel that she watches me, and it makes me smile." When they continued to look at her expectantly, she went on. "Sometimes, when I am afraid, I think of the songs she used to sing me when I was a very small girl, and then things are better."

"Can you sing one of them for us?"

For that, I sat up too. If Sveta was going to sing, I wasn't about to miss it.

"They are in my native language. You would not understand them." They quickly assured her that it was unimportant. "Very well then, but if I do this, you must lay down, and try to sleep. I will sing you a lullaby of my home, it will help."

Quickly, dark heads met pillows, even the eldest of the boys who was no doubt too old for such nonsense if someone had asked him. Once they were settled and still, Sveta started singing quietly in her native Ukrainian. She was right, it didn't matter what the words said. Lullabies are another universal thing that crosses cultures and borders.

When the song ended, she started another one, and then another, and I could hear the breathing around us evening out as the boys drifted off into dreamland. Finally, she pointed a finger at me, then pointed down. "You too. Sleep."

"Yes, ma'am." I settled down on my cot, laying my arm across my eyes, and allowed her voice to lull me into sleep. As drowsiness crept in on me, I marveled a little that a Ukranian demon slayer was singing me to sleep. How was this my life?

Somewhere around dawn, the dream came. It was the tunnel dream, as I'd come to know it, as frustrating and vague as it ever was. On an endless loop, I stepped out of a concrete tunnel onto a vast field of hard packed dirt. The stars above me shown with piercing clarity, but offered no light to see by. The far end of the field was cloaked in shadow. Sometimes, there was a figure there, waiting, and other times it was gone. Never enough light for me to see who it was, and nothing to tell me if it was friend or foe.

Behind me in the tunnel, someone else was waiting. Always silent, always unseen, but the reek of desperation and panic tainted the very air I breathed. Every time I stepped out onto the empty field, I knew that the fate of whoever it was behind me lay in my hands. And every time, whether the mystery figure was there or not, I felt a sense of…inevitability. Like, even if my shadowy visitor was there or not, nothing was going to change the outcome. What was going to happen was going to happen, regardless.

It wasn't a frightening dream. I'd had some of those, ones that brought me up shouting and sweating, ones that brought me up swinging. Ones where old enemies ripped out my insides and laughed as I choked to death on my own blood. No, this dream was not one of those.

But it did disturb me, mostly because it felt prophetic. There was no reason for something like this to plague me, unless it was a warning. I just had to hope I'd figure out what it all meant, before the day I *really* found myself stepping from that tunnel, wherever it may be.

The light in the room was faintly pink as the sun crept over the peaks of the mountains, spilling down into the houses that sprawled across the mountainside. I watched the room grow brighter for a few moments, knowing that I wasn't about to get back to sleep again, and finally got up. I felt Sveta's eyes on me as I left the room, but she didn't move to follow me. I guess she figured I couldn't get into too much trouble inside this particular house.

The kitchen was dark still, though I knew it wouldn't be long before Carlotta herself roused to start making breakfast for the unwashed masses. I left the lights off, only starting the coffee pot, and found a seat where I could see out the window, watching the world come to life just behind the glass panes.

As it happened, that was the only reason I caught Estéban sneaking back in. There'd been no sound of a vehicle in the driveway, so God only knew how far the kid had walked, but he slipped in the back door, shutting it very carefully to avoid the betraying click of the lock. He turned and drew up short to find me sitting at the long kitchen table, raising a brow at him. "Um…"

Even in the dim morning light, there was no missing the black eye, the blooming purple bruise on his jawline, his skinned up knuckles. Immediately, I was on my feet, looking him over with a critical eye. "Shit, kid, what did you do?"

"Nothing." He hissed and jerked his chin out of my grasp. "I am fine." His dark eyes were shuttered, revealing nothing.

Stepping back, I crossed my arms over my chest, giving him that look. All parents know how to give that look. They come home from the hospital with the skill, the nurses give you a manual along with the baby. I myself copied mine from my own mother, who could still turn me to jelly with that look. "What happened?"

"Nothing! Leave it alone!" And now his eyes begged, and I knew that look as well. I'd used that one myself, too.

Stuff happened, when you were a teenage boy. You did stupid things, tempers flared, insults were hurled, fists flew. Most of the time, it was a scuffle and done, with both parties deciding they didn't really hate each other within moments of it being over. I knew that. It was worse with family, even. I knew that too. Some of the worst fights I'd had were with Cole, and I honestly couldn't even tell you what any of them were about. Sometimes, they were just about the fact that we both had too much testosterone flowing at the same time.

This was the moment, I realized, when the parent had to decide what to push and what to let go. Did I scold the boy, or just accept that the young man could handle his own shit? Hell, he wasn't even my kid, what right did I have anyway? If Carlotta wanted to take him to task later, she could.

I sighed. "And what have we learned?"

A bit of wariness crept into his gaze, like he was afraid it was a trick. "I…."

I reached out and lightly cuffed him upside the back of the head. "Move faster. *Entiendes*?"

Some of the tension went out of his slender shoulders as he realized I wasn't going to make a federal case of it. "*Entiendo*. Sorry I am so late."

"Don't apologize to me, tell your mother." I walked over to pour myself a cup of coffee, and at his nod, poured him one as well. "I wouldn't try to claim your bed, though, Sveta's in it."

He winced, but I couldn't tell if it was the thought of the Ukrainian psycho in his bed, or the heat of the coffee on his split lip. "It is all right. I will find a place to sleep elsewhere."

"She said you should try the donkey. She's his new best friend, apparently."

Estéban gave me a baffled look as we both took seats at the table again. "Pueblo? He's a vicious little bastard."

"Watch your language. If your mom catches you, she'll skin us both."

He made some agreeing noise, and we both nursed our black coffees in silence. There were faint noises in the back of the house, the sounds of people slowing coming back to wakefulness. We weren't going to be alone much longer.

"You clean those cuts on your knuckles?"

"Yes."

"You know when your mom sees you, there's going to be hell to pay, right?"

"I know."

"Does the other guy look worse?"

A ghost of a smile flashed across his face, but he only shrugged.

"You need me to step in or provide backup?"

"No. Thank you." He sighed, finally, resting his elbows on the table. "*Familia*, you know?"

"I know. But you're my family too now, kid."

That earned me a genuine smile, which faded
quickly into a flinch as the split lip opened up again
and trickled blood. "I know that, too." I passed him
a paper towel for his lip, and we sat there in
companionable silence again, listening for the
footsteps coming down the hallway, the ones that
would herald his mother and the storm that was going
to descend when she saw what shape he was in.

It happened sooner rather than later, Carlotta
appearing with an apron already tied around her
waist. Her eyes only glanced over the pair of us at the
table, smiling to see Estéban, who had carefully
turned his head just enough to conceal the shiner.
"*Buenos dias*, gentlemen."

"Good morning, ma'am."

"Morning, Mamá."

She went about rustling up breakfast,
producing pans and bowls out of seeming thin air.
"What time did you get in, *mi hijo*?"

The kid glanced at me, I think trying to guess
if I was going to bust him. "Uh…a few hours ago? I
sat here, I did not want to wake the boys."

"That was thoughtful of you." Deeper in the
house, the morning noises were growing louder, no
doubt prompted by the clatter and clank of impending
food. "And how was your evening with Paulito and
the others? What did you all do?" That question was
the prying kind, the kind moms are supposed to ask.
Carefully phrased to sound casual, but pointed in the
direction of the information she wanted to know.

"We went down into town. We hung out."

"Oh? That sounds nice." Carlotta had her
back to us, stirring up something in a large metal
bowl, but I could tell that her mom-senses were
tingling. What she really meant was "that doesn't

sound like nearly enough information, please elaborate." He didn't, just falling silent and staring into his coffee, and I could have told him it wasn't going to go well for him. "Where did you hang out?"

"I don't know, some place Paulito knew." Inwardly, I winced. That was basically a giant neon sign that said, "I don't want to tell you where we were." Estéban was sinking fast.

"More coffee?" Before he could think of a reason why not, she was at the table with the coffee pot in hand, and the kid had no place to hide. Her eyes spotted the skinned and bloodied knuckles, and her gaze locked with his, his black eye and bruised jaw now fully on display. "*Que pasó*?"

"*Nada. Estoy bien.*" Inwardly, I cringed. Not the right thing to say, kid.

Thunderclouds gathered in Carlotta's dark eyes, and the paranoid part of me started looking for cover. "*Fue Paulito, verdad*?"

"*No! No pasa nada. Estoy bien!*"

I admit, that's where I lost the thread of the conversation. The Spanish flew fast, and thick, and way past my abilities. It was easy to guess the gist of it, though. I'd been a teenage boy, I'd had this same argument myself more than once.

Carlotta demanded to know who Estéban had been fighting with, and the kid refused to tell. Then, she demanded to know where they were last night, but it was like she already knew and was just daring him to lie to her. He stood up, pointing out that he wasn't a child anymore, all the while sounding more and more like one as their voices rose. There were sweeping arm gestures, and shouting, and it all ended with the kid throwing up his hands and stomping out of the room.

"Estéban! *Regresa*!" When he obviously had no intention of coming back, Carlotta put her hands on her hips and swiveled her head to look at me. "This is what he learns in the United States? To disrespect his mother?"

I held up my hands, there was no way I was getting involved in this battle. "Don't point that finger at me. You know as well as I do that this was coming. You've raised boys before. He's stuck between being a kid and a man, and neither one of you knows which way to shove him."

Her glare lasted a few more seconds before it folded into defeat, and she sank down onto the bench next to me, twisting her apron in her hands. "He is very much like his father, you know. Headstrong, willful. Miguel was gentler, calmer. Joaquin, too. Miguel was younger than Estéban, when he took up the machete, but he was older on the inside. Estéban…he is so very young."

I reached out and took one of her hands in mine, because it seemed to be what she needed. "He's a good kid. Smart like you would not believe, and he learns so fast. Trust me when I tell you that he *can* do this, if he has to." Crap. This was the exact opposite of the speech I really wanted to give, but I couldn't sell the kid short. He'd earned every bit of the respect I had for him. "But he can't do it if you're still clinging to his sleeve the first time he goes."

She gave me a smile that was more than a little tearful, but the glimmering drops caught on her eyelashes and didn't fall. "I know. I do. But… I have buried two of my sons already. A parent should not ever have to bury a child."

On that point, I couldn't agree with her more.

The herd descended for breakfast in waves,

without any sign of Estéban. With Sveta's promise to look out for him as she prowled the property during the day, I was surrendered to Terrence and Carlotta's tender ministrations again.

We didn't get very far. At the first touch of Terrence's magic, the souls under my skin made it very clear that they were not pleased to be subjected to more poking and prodding, and they framed their protests in the form of brain-scrambling muscle spasms across my shoulders. Every muscle I had – and some I think I must have borrowed – clenched up and twisted into impossible knots, contorting my torso in ways it was never meant to go. Any more, and I was afraid my head really was going to spin around like the Exorcist. "Enough! God, enough, just stop touching them!"

Carlotta and Terrence both withdrew to a corner of the small building, conversing in hushed whispers as I tried my damnedest not to curl up into the fetal position on the floor. I breathed through my teeth, concentrating on the feeling of the barely contained life force throbbing along my spine. It felt like they'd moved, the line of fire continuing up the back of my neck right into my long hair, and tracing a path all the way down the back of both thighs.

"You guys gotta quit this, you're killing me here," I told them, not sure if I was talking to the souls, or the spell casters. The coiling, churning pain across my back seemed to relax a bit, and I stretched, trying to loosen up something enough that I could sit up straight. "Just settle down, ease up. No one's going to hurt you. Or me, for that matter." Bit by bit, the pain died down, and the sensation of the iridescent tattoos retreated to their proper locations, stopping just at the top of my shoulders and the waistband of my jeans. Relieved, I took a few deep breaths, offering them silent thanks.

"I despise admitting this, but I fear that Señor Smythe may have been correct yesterday," Carlotta finally said, including me in their little secret magic conversation.

Terrence was as surprised as I was. "I was? About which?"

Carlotta nodded toward me. "They listen to him. They react to his situations, they react to threats to themselves and to him. They are not simply spells bound to him, they are living entities, even separated from their true hosts. It may be that they will *not* leave him, unless it is their will to do so."

"So…what? I just ask them nicely to go away?" I stared at them both, incredulous. If this was seriously that easy, I thought I might go and beat my head against a convenient wall.

"No…no, they must have a home, a vessel."

Terrence nodded his agreement. "You can't just have bits of soul floating around unattached, it doesn't work like that."

I think I liked it better when they were fighting. "So we're back to square one, then. No place to put them, and even if we find somewhere, we can't be sure that they'll migrate willingly."

"Possibly. Though I have to wonder, if you spent some more time fostering a relationship with them, if they might be more accepting of your request, when the time came. Terrence and I can then spend our efforts trying to devise a receptacle."

"You want me to make friends with them? Take them out on a date, maybe? Seriously?"

She gave me that mom look. "Think of it as meditation. This is something you were teaching

Estéban, yes? It is good for you."

And just like that, I was dismissed. Like, go away kid, you bother me. I blinked at the door as it shut in my face, then turned around to find myself alone in the Perez wilderness. Or something.

"You gotta be kidding me," I muttered, rubbing my hands over my face. "See what you guys got me into?" The sensation that rolled across my skin can only be described as bubbly, like someone had poured fizzy soda pop down my back. They were amused. "Not helping."

Whether or not I thought relating to my inner souls was an option, Carlotta had been right about one thing. I hadn't meditated in months. It used to be something I did every day, rain or shine. It kept me centered, it kept my mind clear, it let me truly ponder the *bushido* code that I held in such high esteem.

There hadn't been time for meditation, lately. There was Estéban to teach, and my family to take care of, and my real job, and then that whole demon slaying thing that seemed less about slaying demons than it did just trying not to die on a regular basis. There were demon wars and spying angels and hitchhiking souls. Who had time to just sit and stare into space?

Well, I did, dammit. I'd make time, I decided right then and there. Time to get back to my roots, time to remember who I was and why. Maybe that would help alleviate this feeling of bleak helplessness that choked me every time I thought about all things I could *not* do to get myself out of this mess. And if the souls in my back wanted to get all zen with me, then maybe we could come to some kind of arrangement. I wasn't going to hold my breath for that, but stranger things had happened.

With my new mission firmly in mind, I marched off to find myself a quiet place to get in touch with my inner samurai.

9

You would think that finding a quiet place in a family the size of Esteban's would be difficult, but there were actually lots of nooks and crannies where someone could lose themselves if so inclined. My nook happened to be behind one of the smaller houses, a place where I could rest my back against a tree, but still hear the children playing just out of sight. Women called to each other, there was a hammer pounding across the way, life was going on unimpeded. People were within shouting distance if I needed them, and judging by the feeling of invisible insects scampering up and down my arms, I was still well within the Perez family wards. It should be safe.

While my environment seemed fairly conducive to meditation, the rest of me really didn't want to cooperate. I sat and let the sun trickle over my skin through the leaves, just breathing into my core and trying to find a balance point in my own brain. My mind wasn't exactly a restful place anymore, but with a little concentration, I thought I could at least tie up the worst of the distractions and stuff them in a dark corner.

Yeah, not so much. Everything was irritating me, from the tiny bug that decided my ankle looked like a snack, to the musical but incessant bird chirping somewhere over my left shoulder. The air was too warm despite the occasional breeze, the sun felt dry and prickly on my arms, and my nose itched. A lot. I shifted my position, trying to find a better place to sit, but there were pebbles and sticks digging into my backside and obviously that one tiny bug had told all his buddies, 'cause there was suddenly a horde of flying bitey things trying to make a meal of me. After about the third slap, I gave up on trying to defend myself.

This wasn't like me. I normally prided myself on my ability to focus, to drown out the world and get myself centered. Sure, I hadn't actually had time to sit and try to meditate for…a while…but it wasn't like I'd forgotten how. It just wasn't working for me, this time.

I knew why, of course. I had two hundred and seventy-five really big distractions, and they were marching up and down my back like the world's worst pins and needles. Two hundred and seventy-five lives, tied inextricably to my own, but with feelings and instincts all their own. Hard to get centered within myself when I was so seriously unbalanced. Top heavy. How in the world was I supposed to find some harmony with those things when it was next to impossible to be heard over their 'shouting'?

Honestly, I could tell you about the hours that I sat there, trying to figure out what was actually communication from mystical life forces, and what was just my body saying "Hey, dummy, you have to pee!", but nobody wants to hear that. Suffice to say that by the end of it, I was tired, hot, frustrated, hungry, and had mosquito bites in places I don't even want to talk about. I can honestly say that I don't think I've ever had a more unproductive meditation attempt.

Mentally growling at myself, and the souls, I opened my eyes to find Rosaline not three feet from me, an anxious look on her face. "Christ! You scared me to death!" There was a faint twitch from the marks on my back at my tiny adrenaline surge, but they settled again as I pushed myself up from my seat, brushing leaves and grass off my jeans.

"I am sorry, I did not mean to." She bit her lower lip, glancing back toward the big house, then seemed to come to some decision, nodding to herself. "You must go get Estéban."

"Wait, what?" There was no mistaking the tension in her shoulders, anxiety practically oozing out her pores. "Where's Estéban? What's going on?"

"I am not supposed to tell you this. Mama Carlotta says that it is family business and that we should not involve you, but Estéban will listen to you where he will not the rest of us. You must go and fetch him."

"Rosa, you have to slow down. First, where is Estéban?"

"He left an hour ago or so. With Paulito and the others again."

"Is this about the fight he got into? Is that why you're worried about him? The kid will be okay, he can handle himself." I reached to pat her arm soothingly, but she jerked out of my reach, giving me a fierce glare.

"You do not understand. It is not what you think, and it is no good for him. Please, just go down into town and bring him home."

I sighed, running my fingers through my hair. "Rosa, he's not going to be happy to see me if I come busting in there, trying to save his butt like he's some little kid."

"Please, Jesse. Please, believe me and trust me. There is a warehouse on the west side of town. That is where they will be. Estéban should not be there." Her dark eyes begged me, and what can I say,

I'm a sucker for a pretty girl.

"Okay. And I'm guessing I shouldn't tell Carlotta where I'm going, yes?"

"Oh yes. Oh, thank you Jesse!" The worried lines vanished from her face instantly and were replaced with a beaming smile. "Thank you so much!"

"Yeah yeah, it's what I do." I couldn't help but chuckle. "Don't suppose I could borrow the keys to a truck or something, could I?"

She fished a set of keys out of her pocket and dangled them in front of me. "I came prepared."

"I see that. All right, go on. And pack some dinner away for us, okay? If anyone asks, I went down into town to get some cell reception to call home." Which wasn't a bad idea, actually, while I was down there.

I had no sooner settled into the driver's seat of the old pickup truck than something heavy landed in the bed, and there came a tap-tap-tapping at the back window. I turned to see Sveta giving me a raised brow, and I just leaned over and unlocked the passenger door with a sigh. She joined me without even asking where we were going, or why.

Cosalá seemed oddly quiet for so early in the evening. Sure, there were a few tourists around, with bags of loot over their arms and snapping photos at every vaguely photogenic spot. But that was it, just a few out-of-towners. Maybe everyone was hurrying home to their own dinners, but the days were getting longer with the advent of summer, and you would think there would be more people out in the streets. Running errands, coming home late from work, chatting with neighbors, something. The few locals we did see eyed the truck as we rumbled past quickly averted their eyes, minding their own business so hard it had to be hurting their heads. Nothing like a billboard-sized sign advertising "SOMETHING IS NOT RIGHT HERE!"

"This feel weird to you, Sveta?" She only grunted in reply, but she shifted in her seat and I caught a glimpse of the gun tucked away at the small of her back. "Yeah, me too."

"Warehouse on the west side of town" would seem like a rather vague designation especially considering that there were at least a dozen warehouse occupying a small industrial area just past the town proper. However, at this time of evening, only one of them had a parking lot full of vehicles, so I figured that was our best bet.

The two huge guys standing watch on either side of the big rollup door were also a key clue, and told me that our company might not be welcome. "Shoulder holsters," Sveta noted, "Keep driving." Didn't have to tell me twice. *What the hell did you get into, kid?* The next lot over was empty, and out of line of sight for Tweedle Dee and Tweedle Dum, and that's where we parked.

"What is this place?" Sveta fixed me with that icy blue gaze of hers, and I could only shake my head.

"Guess we're gonna find out. The kid's in there somewhere. Try not to shoot anyone."

There were doors on the backside of the warehouse, every single one of them padlocked shut. Inside, we could hear raised voices, shouting, chanting, cheering. Sounded like a helluva party, so it was pretty much guaranteed that they weren't going to hear us when Sveta grabbed a piece of broken concrete and smashed the lock off the nearest door.

We waited for a moment to see if there was any break in the din, but it continued on without pause, and we slipped inside.

The interior of the warehouse was mostly dark, at least where we were, and lined with crates and pallets of dry goods as far as we could see. Bags of rice, beans, cases of canned vegetables, grocery stuff. Not exactly what I'd expected, given the firepower at the front door. Sveta, pistol in hand but pointed at the floor, gave me a raised brow, and I just shrugged in return. I had no idea.

The noise, and what few lights were lit, were off to our left, and we maneuvered through the tight stacks in order to get closer. One of the very few times I was grateful for being as skinny as I was. A bigger man wouldn't have fit through some of the close quarters.

Sveta, taking point, held up a closed fist as the narrow alley gave way to flickering fluorescent lighting and the view of many backs facing our direction, the crowd surging and chanting in Spanish. The voices rang off the metal roof high above us, doubling and quadrupling the output until my ears wanted to ring with it.

There had to be a hundred people there, at least. Mostly men, from what I could see, but there were a few women sprinkled throughout, waving their fists in the air and screaming just as loudly. A few of them stood out to my senses, glimmering with faint magical talent, and I mentally pegged them as Perez relatives, though probably distant. Not one person turned around, though, and no one noticed when Sveta and I slipped into the very rear of the crowd, trying to spot what had them all so transfixed.

They'd formed what was probably a loose

circle to start, but had pressed closer and tighter as their fervor rose. It was hard to see past the sheer wall of shoulders that blocked our way, or find a line of sight through the churning, screaming throng. Somewhere under the noise, though, at a different pitch than the rest of the voices, I started to hear grunts and groans, and the unmistakable sound of fists on flesh. A particularly loud hit reached my ears, and the crowd responded with a roar that nearly deafened me. The men directly in front of us slapped each other on the backs, a few exchanged money, and one voice rose above the others, quieting the cacophony.

I didn't understand all the words in all the shouting, but I recognized the voice, pitched to carry to every person in the warehouse. "Paulito," I mouthed to Sveta, and she nodded her agreement. Whatever the Perez cousin was doing, he sounded like a sports announcer, his words big and broad. Putting on a show.

Now that I knew for sure he was here, I started searching the crowd for Estéban, trying to locate the tall, slender kid in all the mess. Like hunting a needle in a haystack. Nearly every person there was dark-haired, dressed in T-shirts and jeans, and identifying the kid from just the back of his head was proving to be a futile effort.

The people in front of us shifted, suddenly, the crowd loosening up as whatever event they'd been watching came to an end, and I got a clear look into the center of the circle. Paulito was there, sure enough, his arm around the shoulders of another young man that looked like he'd just gone ten rounds with a bulldozer. Blood ran freely down the strange guy's face, and his eyes were so swollen I knew he wouldn't even be able to find his own feet, let alone walk with any certainty. On Paulito's other side was another man in similar condition, bent over and panting as blood and spit poured from the massive gashes in his lips.

Neither of them was Estéban, I was relieved to note, and Sveta and I edged closer as Paulito congratulated what appeared to be the winner and handed him a small stack of money. Both men staggered away to be swallowed by the crowd, and then Paulito raised his voice again, obviously calling for the next participants.

Two men stepped from the crowd, stripping off their shirts as they came, and I finally realized what was going on. "Shit. It's Fight Club."

"It's what?" Sveta's eyes never left the crowd around us, but if anyone noticed the two critically Caucasian people in their midst, they let it slide.

"First rule of Fight Club, you don't talk about Fight Club." I smirked, watching as the two new combatants squared off facing each other. Neither of them was Estéban either, so I was content to just see how this played out.

That fight was over in seconds. The bloodthirsty crowd never even had time to work themselves into full voice. The bigger of the two men tried a jab, and the little one feinted and came in low, throwing the sweetest uppercut I think I've ever seen. Big dude toppled over like he'd been poleaxed, his head bouncing when it met the cement floor. The unexpected triumph was met with an equal number of cheers and boos, the underdog no doubt costing quite a few people some money.

"This is stupid," Sveta muttered close to my ear. "If Estéban wishes to get his brains bashed in, that is his prerogative. We should go, you should not be here."

I was actually kind of inclined to agree with her. If this was what the kid wanted to do with his free time, more power to him. Hell, I even kinda wanted to see him fight, just to see what would happen. But Rosaline's worried face lurked at the back of my mind, and I couldn't go back to the house without at least trying. "See if you can find him, get his attention subtly."

I couldn't hear her growl in all the noise, but the look she gave me was enough. She was done with this foolishness, and was about ten seconds from dragging me out by my ponytail.

Paulito, obviously taking the role of emcee to this lunacy, called out again, and the crowd fell nearly silent, stilling to the point that Sveta and I didn't dare move or someone was surely going to notice. There was a palpable tension in the air suddenly, a hungry anticipation. They knew what was coming, it was what they'd all been waiting for.

It was clear, whatever he was introducing, this was going to be the big finale. He did a lot of talking, a lot of sweeping gestures, and with one sweep of his arm, the crowd on the far side parted willingly to reveal a bigger section of the floor, this one marked with dark lines and squiggles that I couldn't quite read from my vantage point. From a distance, it looked like some little kid had gone nuts with finger paints on the warehouse floor.

"Y ahora! *El demonio*!"

A chill ran down my spine, and the souls in my skin fluttered along my muscles in unease. Had he really said what I thought he'd said? I mean, my Spanish a work in progress, but demon sounded a lot alike in many different languages. *It's a name, a fighter's nickname, surely. He can't really mean...* "_____!"

Yup...yup, he really did.

The demon name rang out into the stillness, echoing for way longer than can be explained by bad acoustics, and several things happened simultaneously. The guy directly to my right doubled over, barfing all over his shoes (he wasn't the only one, by the sounds of it), Sveta took in a sharp breath, and the souls in my skin tried their damnedest to crawl out of me by taking the front of me through the back.

I hit my knees, swallowing a scream of pain, my vision blacking out completely. I could feel the swoops and whorls of the iridescent tattoos turning into a writhing, agitated mess, every single occupant sending the same clarion alarm call through my tortured muscles. Iron bands wrapped around my chest, refusing to allow air into my lungs, and for just a second I thought I was actually having a heart attack. I was faintly disappointed that something so lame could do me in, and then I realized that it wasn't cardiac arrest, it was a panic attack and it wasn't mine. Two hundred and seventy-five souls were having simultaneous meltdowns. The message was very clear, Do Not Want!

After a while, I realized that Sveta's voice was low in my ear, urging me to get up, to retreat with her to the safety of the stacks. "Come. On your feet. We must go now." I blinked the blackness away from my eyes, forcing my way up through sheer stubbornness. Sveta slipped her free arm around my waist, and I fully admit I was leaning on her more than not.

No one noticed the spectacle we were

creating, everyone else also caught up in their bodies' very natural reactions to the abomination that was demon speech. At least two had fainted, that I could see, and several others will still revisiting their lunches. It took a strong stomach to dabble in the demon tongue on a regular basis, and it didn't escape my attention that Paulito was way too comfortable with it. Hell, the one time I'd spoken a demon name aloud, I'd ralphed up my sneakers. But he stood calmly in the cleared circle, a small smile on his face as a roll of black fog started oozing out of nowhere.

It seeped between people's feet, coiling sinuously through the crowd like a living creature. Twining, twisting, it all ran into the circle of painted symbols, assembling into a rolling, bubbling ball of black smoke. *Blight.* I don't know what it really was, but on the real world side of the divide, it was everything that made up a demon. Blood, bone, flesh, all of it was formed from blight, and as the insidious substance poured into the circle, the ball got bigger and slowly started to take shape, creating itself a body.

I ignored Sveta's urgent tugging at me, sick dread freezing me to my spot. I had to see. I had to know what it was.

Ultimately, it wasn't the scariest demon I'd ever seen. The roil of blight spun faster and faster until it resolved itself into something no taller than my knee, pale-skinned, all scrawny arms and bony legs. Its ears looked like batwings, larger than the head itself, and the eyes were big enough to take up most of its face. It looked kinda like that thing that sat next to Jabba the Hutt, but before I could find amusement in that, it smiled. The mouth was full of shark's teeth, jagged and black, and each finger and toe was tipped with a viciously curved claw. Tiny did not mean harmless. Right. Got it.

The luminescent eyes fixed on Paulito, flashing a violent red, and the thing hissed, charging at the young man. I tensed, ready to...do what? I couldn't even stand up on my own, and I was totally unarmed. The woman beside me, however, was not, and Sveta leveled her gun at the thing, already squeezing the trigger at the moment that the demon bounced off an invisible barrier not a foot from Paulito, and sprawled on its bony little ass. Quickly, Sveta lowered her weapon, tightening her grip on me. "Come *on!*"

The audience seemed to be recovering, finding their voices at once as they hooted and jeered at the angry little demon. That only pissed it off more, and it shrieked its fury at a pitch that had everyone wincing in discomfort. It pounded its fists on the invisible wall that held it trapped, and when that was unsuccessful, it raked its claws across the barrier over and over again. Blight rolled off the tips of its nails, scoured away by whatever was holding the demon in place.

Paulito laughed, almost fondly, crouching down to look the demon right in the eyes. "*Sabes que no puedes escapar.*" *You know you can't escape*, my mind translated. The thing only hissed in response, growling something in its own language that was definitely not an endearment. "*Estás listo para intentar ganar tu libertad?*" *Are you ready to try to win your freedom?*

"Yesssss.... Free me...." I thought for a moment that the thing was speaking English, which just seemed stupid given the circumstances, but after a moment I realized that whatever it was speaking it was something we could all understand. Made sense. What demon wanted to waste its time doing mail order language classes?

The souls shuddered under my skin at the sound of the demon's voice, and I swallowed away the oil slick taste that it left at the back of my throat. *Look, you guys have to calm down. I can't walk out of here if you've got me all tied up in knots like this.* Almost instantly, the pain ceased, my 'companions' stilling abruptly. Leaving was obviously high on their list of things they wanted to do right fucking now.

The crowd was pressing closer now, crowding the magical circle in fevered anticipation, pulling Sveta and I along with it like the tide. Her hand was like a vice on my arm, firmly intent on dragging me the opposite direction.

"We have to get the kid," I insisted. "I don't know what's about to happen, but we can't leave him here with that thing."

Whatever she said, I'm pretty sure it would have gotten my mouth washed out with soap, but she finally relented, releasing her hold on me. "I have not seen him yet. We must circle around to the other side."

"*Y el retador!*"

"Wait," I hissed at Sveta. It was suddenly important to see who else was going to step into that ring. My danger sense may not be functioning as intended, but you just kinda know when something really bad is about to go down.

There was a scuffle on the far side of the cleared circle, and the crowd parted to reveal two men manhandling a third into view. Whoever the challenger was, he obviously wasn't a willing participant. His captors had his arms twisted behind his back, and one of them had a hand fisted in his hair, controlling his head. Only when the big thug yanked back brutally on his grip did I get a look at the prisoner's face.

Estéban. Of course it was. It couldn't have been anyone else. His shiner from the night before had darkened into a nasty shade of black, and there was a new cut across the bridge of his nose, proving that he'd put up a fight tonight as well. His dark eyes flashed with contained fury when they landed on his cousin, and he spit blood, the mess landing at Paulito's feet. "*Vete a la mierda.*" Definitely not language his mother would have approved of.

"*Now* may I shoot someone?" Sveta started elbowing her way through the crowd before I could tell her no, and I wasn't sure I wanted to. I just followed in the path she cleared, noting the exclamations of surprise as she roughly shoved people out of her way. Our presence was definitely being noted now.

Paulito hadn't seen us yet, and he patted Estéban's cheek with one of those vicious smiles that is all teeth and no genuine emotion. "*Y ahora, campeón, muéstranos cómo se hace.*" *And now, champion, show us how it's done.*

"*No voy a pelear.*" The kid shook his head. *I won't fight.*

"*Esto es lo que aprendes en los Estados Unidos?*" Paulito sneered. "*Para ser un cobarde?*" *Is this what you learned in the United States? To be a coward?*

Inwardly I winced. If I knew the kid at all, I knew he wouldn't stand for that. Sure enough, the kid's lip curled in a snarl, and when Paulito leaned a bit too close to leer into his cousin's face, Estéban jerked against his captors, their surprise earning him enough slack to slam his forehead into Paulito's grinning face.

The crowd went nuts, screaming and hollering, and the last few rows between us and the open area surged together tightly, ignoring Sveta pushing at their backs. With a growl, she pointed her gun at the ceiling and fired off three shots, the sound deafening even amidst all the shouting, which immediately went from blood-thirsty to terrified. People hit the ground to take cover, or blatantly turned and ran, and suddenly there was a wide circle of empty space around Sveta and I.

Most of the audience scattered in panic, but I was willing to bet that the people remaining were all of Paulito's flunkies. Definitely not a welcoming committee I wanted to deal with. I even caught a glimpse of Reina, Paulito's girlfriend, watching us from the shadows . Her dark eyes showed no fear, only an odd sort of curiosity, and I had to wonder just what all this girl had seen that a gun-toting maniac didn't elicit even the slightest bit of fear.

With a blank expression on her face, Sveta lowered the muzzle of her gun to point directly at Paulito's head. "Release him."

He sneered at her around the blood dripping from his nose. *"No hablo Inglés."*

She marched forward without hesitation, until she could press the barrel of the gun directly between his eyes. "You speak gun. Release him."

After a moment, Paulito made a motion with his hand and the two thugs let go of Estéban's arms. The kid worked the aches out of his shoulders, but he made a show of walking slowing away from his captors, his head held high. Our eyes met for a moment before he dropped his gaze to the floor, wiping blood off his face.

"Time to go, Sveta." We only had moments before the remains of the crowd realized that they still greatly outnumbered us.

She tilted her head, so I knew she heard me, but she kept her gun pressed against Paulito's forehead, and from his grimace, I knew she was digging the metal into his skin. "Sveta, we have to go. Now." Again, she refused to respond, and I started to worry that maybe this was going to be the thing that tripped her, the thing that proved she was the stone-cold killer I'd always suspected her of being. "Svetlana!"

The line of her shoulders shifted ever so slightly, a tiny bit of tension going out of them, and she stepped away from Paulito, gun still leveled, but no longer touching him. "We will not see you again this night."

"Come on, kid," I muttered. "Let's get out of here before she really does kill somebody." Silently, he followed at my side as I turned to retreat into the stacks.

"I seeeeee you!" The screech brought us to a dead halt, the oil slick taste of a demon voice instantly coating the back of my tongue. "I see you, soul-bearer!"

We'd forgotten about the little demon, but it hadn't forgotten about us. The creature flailed against its invisible bonds in its excitement, its enormous eyes gleaming bright red. "I seeeee you!!!! I see you! I see you!"

Only then did I realize that the souls in my back were doing their spotlight into the heavens bit. I could feel them shining like a beacon, brought to the very surface by my own adrenaline rush. There was only so much that Axel's spell could do to conceal them, and if they were in full display mode, there was nothing that could hide them.

The trapped critter did backflips and cartwheels in demonic joy, bouncing from its feet to its hands and back. "I see you, I see you!" Over and over, it chanted, and finally Sveta gave me a push toward the stacks again.

"Go. What's done is done. We cannot stay here."

Boy, didn't I know it. Guess the cat was out of the bag now.

10

The ride up the mountain to the Perez home was a tense one. Sveta rode in the back of the truck, watching for pursuit, and the kid stayed hunched into himself, refusing to meet my eyes again. We wended our way up the road in painfully uncomfortable silence, broken only by the occasional wince as I plowed over a particularly nasty bump.

For my part, I wasn't sure what to say to him. I was pissed, probably angrier than I'd been in a very long time. The kid knew better. He damn well knew better! What the hell was that year he spent with me *for*, if he was just going to throw it all away with something stupid like pit fighting against a demon? I was going to smack him upside the head. Twice. I might even dump him on his scrawny little ass just to get my point across.

Being angry with Estéban and planning how I was going to kick his ass when we got home was easier than letting my mind mull over the other development of the evening. My secret was out, just like I'd feared for the last few months. Everything I'd dreaded was about to come true. Sure, the little rat in the summoning circle was low down on the demon ladder of power, but that only meant that what he knew could be taken from him. Some bigger demon was going to roll up on that little bat-eared piece of crap and squeeze him until his head popped, and then they'd all know. Things were about to suck. A lot.

The second we parked in the driveway, Estéban bailed out of the truck, heading for the house at a nice clip. I was out right behind him, not even bothering to slam the door shut.

"Stop!" He froze at my barked command, probably more out of ingrained habit than anything else. "Get your ass back here." Reluctantly, he turned on his heel to face us. "Just what the hell was all that?"

"It was nothing."

"Nothing? Summoning demons is nothing? How long have you been doing it, Estéban? How many demons did you bring into the world?" I grabbed him by the front of his shirt and gave him a good shake to make sure I had his full attention.

"None!" His eyes flew up to mine, and he grabbed my wrist in both hands, but didn't try to escape. "I didn't summon them, I swear to you. That is why they beat me, last night. Because I would not give them any demon names. They know only a few, and they thought that I would know more."

"You don't know any names." The one demon fight the kid had actually been in, the demon had been on scene before the kid arrived. He'd missed the traditional calling, so while that particular demon's name swam around in my head as I thought about it, the kid was clean.

God, if he'd known, though… What that bunch of rank amateurs would do up against something like the hell hound we'd fought… The thought sent a chill over my arms, and the souls swirled lazily in response. It had taken two of us to bring that hulking beast down. That monster would tear through that fight club like they were made of wet tissue paper.

"I know. They didn't believe me."

Sveta hopped down out of the truck, landing

lightly on her feet as always. "If you knew this is what they wanted, why did you go with them again?"

He sighed and ran his fingers through his hair, parts of it stiff with matted blood. "I thought if I went with them, I could stop this. Find a way to end it. But this time, they wanted me to fight it. I refused. And…well that's when you showed up."

"You should have said something, kid. You know that, right? There's no shame in calling for backup for something like this." I gave him one more shake and released him, scrubbing my hand off on my jeans. Damn, my skin still felt oily from just being within earshot of that ratty little demon.

"I thought… He is family, Jesse. I had to try." I got it. I truly did. Didn't mean I was happy about it.

"What were you supposed to fight for? Someone's soul?"

The kid shook his dark head. "No, there was no contract, no wager. The demon fights one of the men, and if it wins, it is freed from the circle. That is all. Last night, he called the same one, and the man defeated it."

I exchanged a look with Sveta. "Something doesn't smell right. It could just poof out of that circle any time it wanted, why would it need to be freed?"

"But the barrier was real," she pointed out. "It scraped its nails on it, and was damaged."

"I don't know the spell he used to bind it. The symbols weren't familiar to me, they're not ones that Mamá taught us."

I filed that away as something that would definitely need more investigating, sometime when we weren't barreling toward the darkest part of the night. Before I could pry anymore, however, the light over the kitchen door flicked on, momentarily blinding us all.

"What is happening out here?" Carlotta stepped into the courtyard, her robe covering her nightgown. "Estéban? Jesse?"

The kid cast me one pleading look, and I just snorted. "Oh hell no. This is on you, you tell her."

"Tell me what?" Carlotta's 'mom' look was instantly focused on her son. The kid, easily towering a foot taller than his mother, just ducked his head and started a mumbled explanation in Spanish I couldn't really follow.

Sveta took that moment to touch my elbow lightly. "I will begin packing our things, and wake Terrence. We should leave once the sun comes up."

I nodded. She was right. We'd be safe where we were for the night, behind the Perez family's formidable wards, and dawn would chase the demons back to their own world. When the sun spilled over the mountains in a few hours, we had to be ready to go.

"*Qué hizo*?!" Ooh, I knew that tone of voice. Estéban had obviously just gotten to the good part of the story. "Jesse! Is this true, what Estéban tells me?"

I leaned against the truck, crossing my arms over my chest. "Depends. Did he get to the part about Cousin Paulito summoning a demon for the kid to fight, yet?"

"He did." Carlotta fixed the kid with a glare that threatened to melt him into a little pile of guilt-goo. "I cannot believe such a thing. Paulito, of all people…"

I gave a small snort, and then her glare turned

my way. "Hey, don't look at me like that. You knew
what they were doing down there. You and Rosaline
and probably everybody, 'cause why else would Rosa
ask me to go after the kid? Don't try to act all
shocked and offended now."

Her jaw clenched, and anger flashed through
her dark eyes. I saw so much of Estéban in her at that
moment, it was almost uncanny. Finally, after a few
moments of uncomfortable silence, she gave a short,
sharp nod. "I was aware of the fighting. The boys
have always gathered to test themselves. Miguel
would go, and Joaquin before that. But it was
foolishness. Brawling, you call it. Young men
blowing off steam. I did not stop it, because it was
helpful for them to experience fighting in a…safe
environment." Once again, she fixed her son with the
death glare. "This business of summoning demons,
this is new, and I should have been made aware."

"You're aware now, and I trust that you'll put
an end to it." I shoved off the truck, and headed for
the door. "I've got bigger problems right now, and
we're going to have to be gone at sunup."

"What? Why?" Carlotta followed me inside,
with the kid right behind her, and while she didn't
actually have him by the ear, he still looked like he'd
been swatted on the nose with a rolled up newspaper.

Terrence was just shuffling into the kitchen,
gray hair standing out at manic angles to his head as
he rubbed his stubbled face. "Why is the crazy bint
saying that we're leaving? Rousted an old man right
out of his warm bed, she did!"

"We're blown here. Sveta's packing our
stuff." I sank down on the bench as the reality of it
all hit me. We were blown. The demons knew where
the souls were. Where the hell could I go that I

wouldn't be putting someone in danger? I damn sure couldn't go home. "The demon saw me. He saw the souls. They know I have them now."

Terrence rubbed his nose with one gnarled finger, making way more noise than that gesture should normally make. "Was bound to happen sooner than later. Been a miracle you got by this long."

"Yeah, the honeymoon is obviously over. Best thing we can do is vacate, try to buy some time."

"Jesse…" It was Estéban who spoke up first, a frown darkening his young face. "What good do you think running will do?"

"You heard the thing, kid. It saw me clear as day, and that little critter isn't strong enough to keep that knowledge to itself. If something bigger and badder doesn't know already, it's a matter of hours, days if we're lucky, and then they'll come for me. Best place for me to be is 'not here.'"

"You don't know that. Besides, where will you go?" I hated to have my own thoughts echoed back to me out of an eighteen-year-old's mouth, but he wasn't wrong.

"I don't know. Maybe… Italy. Maybe the Knights Stuck-up-idus can help." I didn't have a great opinion of the Catholic order of demon slayers, the Order of St. Silvius, but if there was anywhere that was truly going to be demon-proof, I figured the Vatican had to be it. Judging by Terrence's dismissive snort, he didn't really like them either. "Or…hell, just stay on the move, maybe. One step ahead of them." Stay on the move, don't go anywhere near my wife, or my children. Christ. *Mira*…

Someone pressed a cup of steaming coffee

into my hands, and I looked up into Carlotta's very calm, very serene face. "There is nowhere in the world safer than this place, Jesse. Even if an army of hell-spawn came charging up the mountain, these wards would hold. They have stood in place for more generations than you can imagine."

"The whole charging demon army image isn't exactly comforting, Carlotta."

She patted my hand. "Regardless. You have time to make plans. There is no reason to go rushing off into an uncertain situation. You will stay for the *fiesta* tomorrow, and the ceremony honoring Miguel. Señor Smythe and I will attempt again to devise a vessel for the souls. We will proceed as we had planned in the beginning."

I sighed and sipped the coffee. "I don't want to put your family in danger."

"It is what we do, Jesse." That from Estéban, his hands resting on his mother's shoulders and his eyes looking way older than he had any right to.

I glanced to Terrence, who just shrugged his shoulders. "I just want to go back to bed."

With a sigh, I threw up my hands in defeat. "Fine. Then someone better tell Sveta before she gets everything loaded in the truck."

"That'd be me then." Terrence shoved away from the table and went shuffling into the back of the house, muttering again about the crazy bint.

"You too, *mi hijo*. To bed. You have an important day tomorrow." I guess it spoke to how exhausted Estéban was that he didn't protest being treated like a wayward child. He kissed his mother on the cheek, then stumbled toward the back of the house, his arm wrapped around his ribs. That told me he had more injuries than I'd previously noticed. Oh well. If he thought he was man enough to take it, he was welcome to it.

Carlotta settled down on the bench next to me, her own cup of coffee cupped in her hands. "I should not drink this at this time of night. I will never get to sleep. But I find the heat soothing."

I made a small noise of agreement, nursing the dark liquid in tiny sips. It was good just to have something to do with my hands. We sat together in companionable silence for a long time, just listening to the clock over the kitchen sink tick away the night hours. Finally, I sighed, pushing the cup away from me. "What are you going to do about Paulito?"

"I do not know." Carlotta stared into her cup as if all the answers would appear there. "I do not know this boy who has taken my Paulito's face. He may not be my son, but I have always treated him as one of them, like I would any of my nephews or nieces. My Paulito, he would not have committed this crime."

"But he did. I heard it from his own mouth, and he said it real easy. It wasn't his first time. Estéban said he knows more than one demon to call. You need to figure out where he's getting this information."

She nodded, weariness and sorrow deepening the faint lines around her eyes, her mouth. "He will tell me, I think, if I ask. Surely, someone has placed this evil into his mind. I cannot believe that he would seek it out on his own."

"Sometimes, people aren't who we think they are, Carlotta. Even people we've loved for a long time."

A ghost of a smile twitched at the edges of her mouth. "You know, my husband's father was named

Paulo. That is why so many of the boys bear that name now. Even Estéban. But when Paulito was born, everyone said that he looked just like his *abuelo*, and so he became Little Paulo. Even now, as a grown man, he remains Paulito."

"Little Paulo is dabbling in things that are going to get him killed, and that's if he's lucky. I couldn't see his arm, to know if he's given up his soul or not, but if he's gone this far, it's only a matter of time." I reached out to take her hand, squeezing it a little. "Once that happens, I have seen the truly terrible things they can do to him. It will be bad."

Somewhere in the mountains of Colorado, there was a creature wandering around with only half an arm remaining, no voice of her own, and a hunger that had no way to be satisfied. Neither living nor dead, that thing that I'd left up there was just one punishment that a demon could inflict on a person when they owned their soul. The last thing in the world I wanted to see was Estéban have to go put his own cousin down because Paulito tried to eat someone's face.

After a moment, she squeezed my hand back. "I will speak to him tomorrow at the *fiesta*. I believe that he will allow me to help him. We will have it sorted quickly and there will be no more of this." Patting me on the hand, she deposited her cup in the sink and went to return to the room she was currently sharing with Rosaline.

That left me all alone in the kitchen, a cup of cooling coffee on the table in front of me. Wearily, I just lay my head down on my arms, feeling the grain of the wood under my skin. Immediately, I could feel the soul-drunkenness setting in, and I was too tired to stop it, letting it wash over my senses. The humming started in my ears, the sound of the very air around me, and my skin prickled with the feeling of tiny particles of dust landing on me.

The surface under my face was an old table, and it had fed countless members of this family. If I trailed my fingertips across the surface, I could almost feel the dips and crevices in the wood, like canyons to my heightened senses. I could smell traces of dinners and breakfasts like there were platters of food in front of me, and the faintest sounds of laughter and voices tickled at my ears, the ghosts of long-forgotten conversations.

It would be so easy to close my eyes, to just lose myself in the overwhelming feelings. No more worries about souls, or demons, or champions or anything. Just drifting along from one sensation to the next.

You'd waste away. Just shrivel up and blow away on the wind. I knew the little voice in my head was right. I think there was even a myth like that, a guy who starved to death because he just couldn't quit staring at beautiful stuff.

As my gaze followed one curl of steam from my coffee cup swirl up into the air, I felt like I could follow the individual water molecules as they cooled and dispersed into the kitchen air. I could have watched them forever.

With effort, I pushed back the stars in my vision and sat up. The clock on the stove said that I'd lost two hours in that little episode, and I shivered a little. Dangerous. The power I was currently hauling around was too damn dangerous for any one person to have. They needed to be somewhere else, and soon, 'cause honestly, I wasn't sure that I was strong enough not to get lost in it. Maybe more importantly,

I wasn't sure I was a good enough person not to use it if needed.

Though my body knew it was hungry – I hadn't eaten for hours, I realized – my stomach felt unsettled. Not to mention it was somewhere around the darkest armpit of night, and clanking around in the kitchen was the surest way to wake up the family. And I already knew that sleep wasn't going to come easily, if at all. That left just one thing to do.

Outside, the night was mountain-air cool, though we really weren't at a very high altitude. Still, I stripped off my shirt, hanging it over the side mirror of the pickup truck, and did a few stretches to warm up my muscles. I unlaced my boots, feeling the dry dust and gravel under the soles of my feet. For just a moment, I wanted to stop and examine that, catalogue the different textures, the high crags and low valleys of the tiny pieces of rock I stepped on, and ruthlessly I bit the inside of my cheek until it bled. The pain helped, and the fuzziness around the edges of my vision receded.

The katas were easy. After so many years, so many repetitions, my body flowed through the forms without any conscious direction from my brain. I honestly couldn't even tell you how many I actually know, but I made it my mission to get through as many as I could. There was something simple in feeling how my muscles moved and bunched, stretched and flexed. There was power there, my own power that had nothing to do with magic or souls or spells. Sheer kinetic energy, and I could use it for something good, like exercise, or something wholly destructive. I could kill, just as easily as not, but other than demons, that had never been my choice. And it was the choice that made the man. I had to remember that.

The night birds, once they became accustomed to my presence, set up their usual cacophony of calls, and a small family of bats darted and whirled just out of my reach, drawn by the insects that were clustering around the single light I'd left burning. It would have been easy to drift into their dance, just standing and watching how they darted and twirled above me, but every time my mind started to stray, I brought my *bushido* teachings to mind.

The first thing that popped into my head was from the *Hagakure*. If you are caught in a rainstorm, it doesn't do any good to go running and hiding under shelter. You're going to get soaked anyway. Okay, maybe it's a bit obscure, but it was what spoke to me. See, the basic idea is, if you know the outcome is inevitable, then railing against it isn't going to do you a bit of good. The demons were going to come for me. That much was a given. It could be in a few hours, it could be in a few days, hell, it could be twenty years from now. Time really didn't mean a lot to them, not like it does to us. I needed to just man up and go walking in the rain. It can't hurt you if you know it's coming.

The second thing that floated to the surface of my mind as I worked was a comment on marriage. See, the samurai believed that you should always treat your wife as you did when you were first together, and then you would always be happy. Man, I really hoped I did that one. Mira was the brightest light in my very dark world. Even when I couldn't be with her, I hoped that she felt treasured. I didn't deserve her, and I knew it. She put up with so much crap because of me, ranging from my blatant disregard for my own personal safety to the very real possibility that she would do herself serious harm casting a spell to save my life someday.

I'm sure I looked like a crazy man, spinning and kicking and punching all by myself out in the darkness, my only company being my very long shadow cast by the kitchen light. I worked until my muscles gave up burning as a lost cause, and even the tattoos on my back seemed to have stilled out of sheer exhaustion.

It was the last teaching that kept me out there, the one that I just couldn't get out of my head. Ironically, it is also the first teaching of *bushido*: the essence of the *bushido* is death. To do nothing, and live, is a worse disgrace than to die trying.

It was one of those things that I knew, but I couldn't say that I honestly *knew* until recently. A tiny part of me always thought I'd find a way out of most of the dangerous shit I'd done. That little part of me believed I was immortal, like all dumb young males ever. I'd come close to death before, sure, but until I stood there in that driveway, chest heaving and skin full of more life force than I could ever possibly contain, I don't think I'd ever *felt* it close before. Death was near. It was just a matter of time.

11

I think the sun was coming up by the time I snuck into the room I was sharing with the Perez boys. Estéban was curled up snoring in his bunk, so I had to assume that Sveta was once again snuggled up with the donkey, which was just too much weird for my brain to even handle at that state of tired.

Even as my head hit the flat little pancake they were calling a pillow, I heard Carlotta's house slippers whispering down the hallway and knew that breakfast and the chaos that went therewith would be occurring soon. My stomach gave a half-hearted growl at the thought of food, but the rest of me said "screw you, I'm sleeping," and I didn't really think about anything after that for a while.

The smell of a fried pork product of some type woke me, and I opened one eye to find Estéban waving a plate full of food back and forth in front of my face. He gave me a small smirk, marred only slightly by the bruises on his face and sat the plate down on the floor. "The family is starting to arrive for the fiesta. You have about twenty minutes before Mama comes to wake you herself and presses you into chores."

I snorted at his retreating back, but rolled over and helped myself to a couple of strips of bacon. Chores. I could do chores. Chores were going to be the easiest thing I'd done in days. After a few moments of munching on my breakfast-in-cot, I sat up, stretching out muscles that were still protesting my treatment of them last night. I guess it said something that I'd slept through the mass exodus that morning, though the boys usually sounded like a herd of stampeding wildebeest.

Fed and dressed – Mira had confiscating my best T-shirts, but I'd managed to smuggle one out that said "I'm not perfect, but parts of me are excellent" – I girded myself to face whatever the Perez clan could hope to throw at me.

Okay, there were like a hundred people there already, and more arriving every few minutes. I gave up trying to remember everyone's names after being introduced to the third Jorge and fifth Maria. Carlotta latched onto me the moment I appeared and I was set to work with the older boys, layering firewood into the huge pit out behind the main house. I got the idea there was probably going to be some kind of roast beast issuing from the pit later, but for now, all we had was the grunt work.

On one pass through the courtyard, I caught sight of Sveta teetering on top of a tall ladder as she helped drape strings of lights through the overhanging trees. Terrence was off to one side, surrounded by a circle of ancient Mexican grandmother types, the women cackling at something the old man said like he was the second coming of James Dean.

Somewhere around midmorning, Carlotta collared both me and Estéban again, directing us to go take showers and get ready for the ceremony with the same drill sergeant voice that she'd ordered everything else.

"Is she going to follow me into the shower and make sure I scrubbed behind my ears?," I asked the kid as we gathered up our nicer clothes.

"She might. Better scrub just to be sure." And y'know, I wasn't sure if he was joking or not. Don't laugh, but I scrubbed behind my ears.

I'd brought the one good suit I had, and I tried not to think that this was the same suit I'd worn to Miguel's wedding, just over two years ago. I didn't believe in bad omens or jinxes, I reminded myself firmly. With my long hair still damp, I bound it into a tail at the nape of my neck and seated the knot of my tie properly at the opening of my collar. Damn, I clean up pretty good if I do say so myself.

I was passing by the boys' room again when I caught a glimpse of Esteban standing at the window, staring out into space and definitely not completely dressed yet. "Hey, kid." He flinched, proving that wherever his mind had just been, it wasn't there with us. "You better get that tie on, or your mom is going to skin you."

He looked at the strip of silk in his hands with a sigh, shaking his head. "I don't even know how to tie this stupid thing. Miguel always did my tie for church."

"C'mere… Christ, can't take you anywhere." My jab got a little bit of a smile from him and he handed the tie over obediently. "You gotta learn to do this yourself, y'know. Women like a guy who doesn't wear a clip-on."

"Yes, because there are so many girls around right now. I'm related to half the mountainside, you realize." I raised a brow at him, realizing that I had to look up just slightly to do so. Damn kid needed to quit growing. He just shrugged his shoulders. "Just saying."

I got his tie all knotted up neatly, then patted him roughly on the cheek until he swatted my hand away. "You learned bad habits in America. Where'd all this attitude come from?"

He smirked and gave me a pointed look. "I

had a good teacher."

"Yeah, well get your jacket on, or we'll both be in trouble with your mom."

With a sigh, he collected the jacket, but touched my arm when I went to leave the room. "Jesse, I want to thank you."

"For what, kid?"

He kept his eyes fixed firmly on the floor. Neither one of us were what you'd call expressive with our emotions, which meant that even this much effort was important to him. "For teaching me all that you did. And not just the fighting stuff, everything. I mean, I know I was only there a year, and there's still tons that I have to learn, but... I'm glad for the time we had. I think Miguel would have been really happy, knowing that I was with you and Miss Mira."

"I'm glad you were there too, kid. I learned at least as much from you. If you ever need *any*thing, anything at all, you just get on the phone and I'll be there. And I don't just mean champion stuff. If you just want to share a beer 'cause some girl broke your heart, you call me. Y'know, when you're old enough for beer."

He gave me a small grin. "In Mexico, I *am*."

"Oh lord, we're doomed." We shared a chuckle, and then one of those awkward man-hugs that nobody wants to talk about later, but means so damn much at that exact moment. "Okay, kid. Let's go get you made all official."

The tiny chapel on the Perez land wasn't even remotely big enough for the entire clan to congregate, so most of the distant family remained in the courtyard, catching up on family gossip and working to get the party food ready for later. It was a small procession that followed the pebble-lined path to the chapel, now decorated in wreaths of aromatic flowers. The priest led the way, followed by Carlotta and Estéban, the boy's machete and studded leather armor cradled in his arms like they were made of glass. The stained weapon and worn hauberk seemed so out of place with the rest of us all dressed in our Sunday finest, and yet they were the reason we were here. They took up a rather odd seat of honor, all eyes repeatedly drawn to the slender young man and his strange burden.

Estéban's siblings came next, from his older sisters on down to the youngest girl who was around twelve, and too young to have actually known her own father or eldest brother. Behind them came cousins and aunts and uncles, most of whom I knew lived at the compound. Once, I caught a glimpse of Paulito, his arm lent to an older woman for support. His mother, I supposed. Later. There would be time to talk to that little shit later. I wasn't uncouth enough to make a scene at a funeral.

Bringing up the end were Terrence, Sveta and I, even the Ukranian woman looking finely coifed with her dark hair up and in a retro forties-style dress and jacket suit in steel gray. She gave me a small smile and slipped her hand into the crook of my elbow, pressing close enough that I could feel the knife sheath on her forearm. I wasn't even going to bring it up. If that's what it took for her to feel comfortable, so be it. Terrence himself was dressed in a neatly pressed kilt and formal suit jacket, hobbling along with his cane as if he wasn't just as capable of walking without it. We made an odd trio, but I knew that Estéban was glad for our presence. It was the least I could do for the kid.

The chapel itself looked like something out of

a post card. The white stucco walls gleamed in the midday sun, and garlands of flowers dripped from the eaves and lined every window. Inside, a central aisle led the way between the pews to the altar, a statue of the Virgin Mary and Jesus standing in each corner. Around the walls, though, was the feature unique to this particular chapel.

Starting at the doors and wrapping around almost all the way to the front were tiny shrines, each sporting a tiny flickering candle. The ones closest to the doors had only small, yellowed cards, neatly printed with a name and dates. Some of them were adorned with items of obvious age, everything from a wooden club to an ancient farmer's hoe. At some point, the pictures began, starting with painstakingly hand drawn images, progressing up through the very first attempts at photography. Each man – and every one was male – stared out with the same dark eyes and hair, something unmistakably alike about such a disparity of faces.

The images went past tin-type into faded black and white photos with curling edges. At some point, color was introduced, first hand painted, then in the film itself as technology advanced with the years. The weapons, scattered and varied, became steel blades and axes. Every champion was there, as far back as the family's collective memory could recall. They claimed that there were more, predating written record. All of them were catalogued, the span of their lives noted on neat little cards, their weapons cared for and cherished once they were truly retired from use.

Along the left-hand wall, the last three photos were the ones that drew most of my attention. Three eight-by-ten glossy photos in neat frames, each man smiling at the camera, the stamp of blood clear between the three.

The oldest of the three, a man with salt and pepper at his temples and a vicious scar following the line of his jaw, was Estéban's father. He'd been older, when he died, a rarity for a champion. His oldest son, Joaquin, had already largely taken up the family mantel, when a stray call summoned the father out of retirement. It was his last challenge.

Joaquin himself graced the next frame, a charm to the smile that reminded me so much of Miguel. I hadn't known Joaquin. He had fallen and Miguel had stepped into his place years before I knew the family. Miguel had been so young, younger even than Estéban, when he'd stepped up as head of the family. His was the third photo, and one I recognized as being from his wedding day. My eyes found Rosaline, standing at the first pew next to Estéban's sisters, her head covered by a dark lace veil, and my heart hurt for her. Too soon. It had all happened too soon.

The three of us, all outsiders, claimed seats in the very last pew, leaving Sveta on the aisle where I knew she'd be happiest. Clear line to the only door, y'know, wouldn't want her feeling trapped.

The priest gestured for everyone to sit, and we did, obediently. I wasn't sure what to expect from such a ceremony which was part funeral, part celebration, but I'd seen enough Catholic masses to guess at most of the words, even if it was all in Spanish. The padre spoke for a while, the congregation responding quietly at times, and then Estéban stood, bowing as he presented the machete and armor to Rosaline, whose shoulders were stiffly proud as she accepted her fallen husband's weaponry.

Standing, she walked to her husband's shrine and laid the leather hauberk and stained machete down in front of the picture. She kissed her fingers and pressed them to his smiling photo, and I pretended that there was no knot in my throat and that my eyes were stinging because of allergies. Stupid Mexican pollen. With a thin taper, she lit the candle in front of him, and as one we bowed our heads to pray.

I'm not really a prayer kinda guy. Still not sure how I feel about God-with-the-big-G. In light of my recent discovery that his angels were going to stand by and do nothing while the demons went to war and destroyed everything in their path, I'd probably have to have a long talk with the Guy about that if I ever met him. But for Miguel, I'd make an exception. *Take care of him.* It was all I wanted, and I hoped that someday, someone would have the same thought for me.

Once the prayer was over, Rosaline took her seat again, and Carlotta rose, facing Estéban. The priest looked between the two, his gaze settling on Carlotta. "*Este es el hombre que será un campeón ante los ojos de Dios?*" *Is this the man who will be a champion in the eyes of God?*

She inclined her dark head. "*Sí.*"

The priest looked next to the kid, who didn't look much like a kid anymore at all, if I was forced to admit it. "*Y voluntariamente viene ante Dios para ser un campeón, mientras viva?*" *And do you willingly come before God as his champion, so long as you shall live?*

Estéban answered without hesitation, and I was a bit proud of him for that. "*Sí.*"

The priest gestured for us all to bow our heads

and pray again, resting his hand atop Estéban's dark hair. This time, I prayed. I prayed my ass off. *God, you and I may not get along, but you better watch this kid's ass. He's a good kid, and this war isn't his. Keep him safe.* The skin along my back warmed as the souls I carried responded to my vehemence. Sveta elbowed me lightly and gave me a subtle "what the fuck?" look when I glanced her way. I just shook my head, and willed my strange passengers into calm. I think God got the message.

After that, the ceremony was over in pretty quick order. The single bell above the chapel pealed with a high, joyous sound, and we all filed out of the tiny church, Estéban escorting his mother on his arm. The family broke into loud chattering the moment we were outside, as if the sheer level of noise they could create could only be contained for so long, and from that moment on, the party was on. Someone in the courtyard struck up the band, and mariachi music filled the afternoon air.

The kid got his back slapped, his shoulder slugged, his hand shaken, and through it all, he kept a tight smile on his face. Only someone who knew him really well would have seen the unease behind his dark eyes, and I had to wonder if anyone in his family really *did* know him that well. He was doing his duty, but it didn't sit well with him.

Through the packs of darting children, the gossiping clusters of family members catching up on news, and the occasional circle of dancing that broke out, I prowled the crowd, looking for Paulito. I knew he was there, and I fully intended to snatch the little bastard and present him to Carlotta once I could lay hands on him. Sveta followed along behind me, close enough that I could feel her presence but not so close that she was smothering me. I had to admit it, I liked having backup close at hand. Sure, I could take Paulito on my own, but there'd be less of a disturbance if Sveta and I could corral him quietly. (It may make me a bad person, but I kinda wanted to watch Sveta beat someone's ass with a high-heeled shoe. 'Cause that would be hilarious.)

Unfortunately, I couldn't find him. We made three circles of the packed courtyard, ducked into the kitchen and made two sweeps through the main house, and even went to check out the stable once, and there was nary a sign of him. I spotted the woman he'd escorted, presumably his mother, several times, but Paulito himself had vanished the moment we left the chapel. No doubt, he'd known that we had cooked his proverbial goose, and he was trying to delay the inevitable.

Sveta's fingers curled around my arm as I raked my fingers through my hair in frustration. "He is not your concern, you know. They will deal with their own."

"I know. I just wanted this done with, before we left. Don't want the kid having to handle this crap on his own."

She gave me a small smirk. "This 'crap' *is* his to handle. He is not yours to protect any longer."

"I don't like you very much."

She chuckled and slipped her hand into the crook of my arm again. "I know. Now let us go find punch. These things have punch, yes?"

Yes, the party had punch, though I'm pretty sure one bowl was eighty-five percent tequila. A very stern looking older gentleman was guarding that one closely, herding the small children toward the bowl at the other end of the table. There was enough food to feed three armies, though the family was going to put a pretty decent size dent in it by the time the evening was done. We grabbed plates where we could, finding a seat near Terrence just to make sure he wasn't causing trouble. The old geezer was holding court with the same gaggle of women that might have been old enough to be *his* mothers, proving that he could be a charming old sot when he put his mind to it.

I elbowed Sveta at one point, jerking my chin in Terrence's direction. We watched as his gaze left the group around him to follow someone across the dance floor. Carlotta was out there, whirled along like a girl of twenty by one of the younger cousins. The old man's eyes followed her, and I swear a tiny smile curved the corner of his mouth. Several times, her gaze found his, and she flashed him a flirtatious grin that I never would have expected from Carlotta. Sveta and I just grinned at each other. Old people falling in love are cute, especially when they don't realize it themselves.

It was nice, I decided, just drifting along with the party atmosphere. I could sit and watch the people, just listening to the joyous voices and it didn't even matter that I only understood about one word in five. Happy translates well. At one point, Terrence threw a napkin at me, and pointed toward a group of young men all clustered and whispering and glancing our way. Finally, one of them was elected, and I bit back a smirk as one of Estéban's older cousins got up the nerve to ask Sveta to dance. To my surprise, she said yes, and to my greater surprise, she was actually really good.

The souls in my back didn't matter, for just a little bit. The demon war that I knew was brewing just out of human sight didn't matter. The fact that my secret was out was irrelevant for just these few precious hours, and the only thing that really dimmed the day for me was the fact that Mira wasn't there. For her, I'd have gotten up and danced, even though I suck at it.

It was a good day. And there was cake! The kid finally found a moment to come collapse near us, and our odd little team of champions just sat and devoured like half a pound of icing a piece. Even Terrence, and I shudder to think what buttercream icing tastes like, mixed with gin.

"You've got icing in your hair. How the hell does that even happen?" I grinned and nudged Estéban's leg with my foot, while he self-consciously wiped a bit of blue frosting out of his hair.

"One of the little ones wanted a hug, it was probably from her hands."

"Sure it was." He kicked me back with a roll of his eyes. "So, I was thinking–" I promptly forgot whatever it was I was thinking as the pack of younger children came boiling into the courtyard, yelling at the top of their lungs.

"*Tía Carlotta*! *Tía Carlotta*!" They jumped up and down around her like a pack of frantic puppies, tugging at her skirt. "*La iglesia*! *Alguien ha destruido la iglesia*!"

Estéban's face went pale. "No…the church…" And he was on his feet and running before I could even figure out what had happened.

"Come on." Sveta didn't need to be told twice, and we followed the river of people as everyone went to investigate. It took some elbowing and shoving, but we managed to make it through the doorway as everyone else peered inside with hushed whispers of horror and awe.

Damn, someone had really done a number on the place. The shrines had been wrecked, every single one, the placards and photos scattered all over the floor and the weapons tossed into corners without regard for their value. The altar was knocked over, and a few of the heavy pews had even been shoved out of place.

Carlotta pressed her hands to her face, just staring in shock, and Estéban knelt to retrieve one of the picture frames from the floor, the glass now shattered beyond use. It was Miguel's, and it had obviously been stomped on after it was tossed on the floor. His gaze found mine, helpless and bewildered, and I didn't have any comfort to offer him. "*Ave María purísima...Quién haría algo así?*"

Terrence shoved his way in behind us, having caught up, and hobbled his way to Carlotta's side, putting a comforting arm around her shoulders. She turned and hid her face against his shoulder. The old man surveyed the destruction, then looked to me. "Whoever did this was right peeved. Look at which pictures were damaged the most."

He was right, when we looked. The three pictures that had been completely destroyed were the last, Estéban's brothers and father. Beyond just being thrown to the floor, they'd been stomped on and ripped up. There was anger in that action, with a specific aim.

"The armor...the machete. They're gone." Once Estéban said that, we all looked closer, ducking down to peer under pews, moving things aside, even walking a circle around the outside of the chapel. He was right. Miguel's gear...*Estéban's* gear was gone.

Yeah, I hated to be the guy to say it, but...

"Has anyone seen Paulito?" A murmur ran through the crowd, but it quickly became clear that no one had seen him since the ceremony.

"No. No, he wouldn't do this." Carlotta sounded more like she was trying to convince herself than anything. "He is family." Estéban and I traded looks over her head as Terrence patted her back comfortingly. We both knew damn well Paulito was fully capable of doing this.

A group of women armed with brooms and dust pans finally shooed us all out of the way so they could start cleaning up the mess, and I gave Sveta and Estéban a look that had them falling in step beside me. "Change clothes. The first moment we can slip away, we're going hunting."

12

Unfortunately, we didn't get our chance to sneak out until well after dark. The Perez clan firmly refused to let the vandalism put a damper on their fiesta, and the music was still playing when Sveta slipped me the pickup keys that she'd managed to pocket.

The three of us looked like we were wearing some kind of odd uniform, all of us in jeans, black T-shirts and heavy boots, but I knew we were all capable of fighting in those clothes, so it was necessary.

We almost made a clean escape, until Terrence cornered us as we loaded into the pickup truck. He gave us a once-over glance, and raised an eyebrow at me. "You shouldn't be leaving the safety of the wards, y'know."

I wasn't about to admit he was right. "We're going to go take care of this issue, then I'll be right back here, safe and sound. Besides, I've got Sveta with me."

He snorted. "And you're going unarmed? Take this, at least." He tossed something at me and I caught it before I realized it was my own sword in its scabbard. I took a moment to trace the kanji carved into the bone hilt, the same ones that tattooed my biceps, then nodded my thanks to him. "If we're not back by dawn, get worried." That earned me a grumble, and he hobbled off toward the house again.

I carefully stowed The Way behind the seat of the truck, and slid behind the steering wheel. "Okay, kid. Where do we start looking for him?"

Estéban, crammed into the middle seat, just looked straight ahead, his jaw tight. "Head down into town. He wouldn't try to hide with family, so he'll go to one of his usual places. We should try the warehouse first."

"You got it."

The ride down the mountain was bumpy and silent, and I could see Cosalá lit up like Christmas long before we drove into the empty nighttime streets. Even the tourists had vacated, though with the windows rolled down, I could hear the low bass beat of music throbbing from a few cantinas as we passed. The town wasn't entirely asleep yet.

The warehouse was dark, and the parking lot was completely deserted. "No fight club tonight?"

Estéban shook his head as we slid out of the truck. "They won't come back here again. They'll find someplace else."

"But you think your cousin will be here?" Sveta had her gun out already, I noted, though it was pointed safely at the ground.

"Probably not. But it is a place to start."

The door where we'd broken and entered the night before was still unlocked, and we slipped in that way, the kid producing a flashlight out of the old pickup. Sveta took point and I brought up the rear, and we slowly made our way toward the open end of the warehouse. The packed aisles of grocery staples were still as tight and claustrophobic as before, but there was something about the echoing silence of the place that made it worse. I determinedly kept my gaze from drifting up, not thinking about how someone atop the tall towers of pallets could easily shove a stack over on us, ending all our worries in a second.

The fighting arena looked like one would expect after an illicit party. Beer bottles and food wrappers were strung everywhere, and broken glass crunched under our boots. With no ventilation in the enormous building, the smells of sweat and blood and…other things hung heavy in the air, almost solid enough to form their own shapes. The kid muttered under his breath at the stench, and Sveta cast him a withering glare. "Quiet!"

The three of us stood in the open, an easy target if someone were so inclined, straining our ears for something, anything, that might say there was another living creature in the building. After long moments, I was willing to concede that we were alone. Even the rats seemed to have vacated, probably scared off by the sulfuric demon stench that lingered.

Still, rats weren't the only vermin that could linger in such a place. "Keep the light still, kid, I wanna check something."

My rune-etched mirror was always on my keychain, and it buzzed softly against my fingers as I fished it out and angled it to give me a view of the warehouse.

Watching my surroundings in the tiny glass, I turned a slow circle, paying close attention to the dark areas just outside the range of the flashlight beam. What I was looking for would be hard to see in the shadows, but that's where they liked to hide. Sure enough, I caught a flicker of movement off to our left, near the stacks of pallets we'd just cleared. I waited a few moments to see if it happened again, then turned my head to double check that what I was seeing was only in the mirror. "When I say, Estéban, point the light at this pallet of rice over here."

"Okay."

I tilted the mirror so that I had a clear view of the pallet's corner, then said, "Now."

The kid swung the light around, illuminating absolutely nothing but a pallet of rice, at least in the real world. In the mirror, a dark mop-like shape froze for a second, then scurried deeper into the shadows on four insectile legs. "Knew it. Nasty little buggers gotta be crawling all over this place.

It was what I called a Scrap demon, a parasite of the demon world, and while I'd only seen the one, I was willing to bet there were more. They liked to attach to people, sucking their energy and will to live until the host just faded away. A place like Paulito's fight club, where stronger demons were already hanging out, would be a prime breeding ground for the filthy little things.

Sveta frowned. "Should we try to kill it?"

"No, let it go. We don't have time to clear a place this size, if the infestation is large. We mostly just need to make sure none of them latch onto us." I flipped to another item on my handy-dandy keychain, a small canister of demon mace. "Step back, don't breathe this in."

The kid and Sveta both covered their mouths with their T-shirts, and I did a quick perimeter sweep around the cleared arena area, spraying a fine mist of cumin and cayenne in my wake. Demons hated the stuff (wasn't real fond of it myself, truth be told), and hopefully it would keep the Scraps at bay until we could get out of there.

That accomplished, Esteban slowly panned the beam of light around us, even up into the rafters, then sighed. "Paulito's not here."

"It was a long shot at best." Something in the beam of the flashlight caught my attention, and I gestured for him to give it over. "But since we're here, I want to take a look at this magic circle he's got going."

The symbols had been slapped haphazardly on the cement floor with blue paint. They formed a full circle about ten feet across, but other than that, they made zero sense to me. I traced one with my finger, waiting for the tell-tale tingle that would mark lingering magic, and got nothing. Odd. "Do you recognize these at all, kid? Sveta?"

The Ukrainian woman came to crouch at my side, tilting her head as we surveyed the messy scribbles. "They are of no system of magic that I know. Neither pagan, nor Christian."

"They're not *brujería*." The kid knelt down too, peering across the floor. "If I had not seen it work, I would say it is just gibberish. Nonsense."

"I have to wonder if we really saw what we thought we saw." There wasn't a hint of magic in the place, I would bet my life on it. Sure, I wasn't a wiz at it myself, but the souls in my skin hadn't been wrong so far, and they'd pegged traces much fainter than I'd have ever sensed myself. Now, they were totally quiet, not stirring in the least. I actually found that comforting. If they weren't upset, then we were probably safe here, at least for the moment.

"The circle worked. Both nights, I saw it hold that small demon. It pounded on the barrier and could not escape."

"You can't hold a demon, kid, unless it wants to be held. That thing could have just poofed back across the veil anytime it wanted." Rocking back on my heels, I tried to see the bigger picture, tried to figure out what we were missing. "Did you actually see him cast the circle?"

"No. It was already in place when we arrived, both times."

"A permanent structure would have to be bound to something more than these symbols, and there would be traces left. I find none." It was good to hear that Sveta found no leftover magic either. Made me feel better about myself.

Taking the flashlight with me, I stood and started walking a slow spiral out from the painted circle. "He had to know we'd come back here. Maybe he dismantled whatever it was." A few yards out, I caught something shiny in the edge of the light. "Here. What's this?"

This proved to be a tangle of very thin wire, wadded up in a useless ball and kicked into the corner. There were shreds of cellophane tape stuck to it in places, and as I unwound bits of it, I could see that it was long enough to encircle the symbol-covered area. My fingertips tingled very faintly as I ran the wire over them. "Tricky, but it's been done before…"

"What has?"

"Portable ward." I showed them a length of the wire with tape attached. "Bless the wire, circle the area, tape it down. The symbols are for show, they did nothing."

Sveta held the wire up to her face, sniffing it with a disdainful wrinkle of her nose. "There isn't enough magic here to light a candle, let alone cage a demon."

"Paulito was never that strong," Estéban offered, looking uncomfortable when we both turned to look at him. "When we would practice our casting, his spells were always the weakest."

I dropped the tangle of warded wire and stood up, taking one last glance around the empty warehouse. "It wasn't enough to cage one, just enough to put on a good show. Which means that the demon *wanted* to be held. And that worries me more than anything. Your cousin was way too buddy-buddy with that thing for my comfort."

The kid's face looked creepy and grim in the shadows cast by the flashlight. "We have to find him, Jesse. We have to stop him."

"I know, kid."

"Where do we look next, then?" Sveta was all business, all the time.

"What about the girlfriend? Where does she live?" If Paulito was like every other red-blooded male I'd ever met, he wouldn't be far from his girl.

The kid shrugged his shoulders. "I don't know who she is. I've never seen her, until the other day. But he told me about this cantina in town that he likes. He was going to take me, later. Even if he's not there, we could ask if anyone knows where Reina lives."

"Better than nothing. Saddle up."

The cantina itself gave a whole new meaning to hole in the wall. Like, the door itself was literally a hole in the stone wall of an old building, covered with only a decorative curtain that did nothing to stifle the horrible canned music playing through tinny speakers.

Inside was worse, if possible, with tiny round tables packed in so close that making a path to the bar was an event in and of itself. There was a ratty dart board in the corner, currently occupied by a couple that was...well, not playing darts. It was the kind of

place whose main asset was obviously the fact that
they were still open. Y'know, that place where the
drunks go when their usual bar boots them out.

Heads came up and conversations stopped as
we entered, and I was painfully aware that I'd left
The Way in the truck this time. There were at least
twelve men in there, several of them sporting wounds
that placed them at Paulito's fight club in their very
recent history. Either that, or they were just guys who
liked to get in fights. Neither possibility bode well
for us. Sveta and I stood out like sore thumbs, to say
the least, and none of the three of us were going to
pass for tourists. The back of my T-shirt rippled a
little as the tattoos adjusted themselves, not
distressed, just aware.

"*Oye.* You lost, *gringo*?" The bartender
leaned on this bar, giving me a challenging look.

"I'm with him." I pointed at Estéban who was
just stepping through the doorway behind me. The
kid came up on my left, and I felt Sveta flank right,
just behind my line of sight.

A scruffy man at the table immediately to my
right laughed into his beer, an ugly, wet sound.
"*Apoco ya está mayorcito el bebito como para
tomar?*" I didn't quite catch it all, but it was
something about "Is the baby old enough to drink?"

Ignoring him, Estéban's eyes swept the bar,
and he shook his head with a frown. "He's not here."

"*Oye, chico! Qué te crees demasiado bueno
para hablar tu propio idioma o qué?*" *You too good
to speak your own language or what?* A round of
ugly chuckles rippled around the room. Sveta pressed
close to my side then, giving the pretense of being a
timid female, but I felt the butt of her gun snug
against the back of my thigh, and I knew that the

drunk assholes here had no idea where the danger was about to come from.

Esteban focused on the bartender. "*Dónde está Paulito Perez*?"

The bartender snorted. "Oh now he speaks Spanish." He swiped a filthy towel over the top of his bar nonchalantly. "He is not here, *niño*. We have not seen him tonight."

"His girlfriend, then. Reina. Where does she live?"

"Reina?" The man pursed his lips thoughtfully, taking his sweet time. "Don't know no Reina. *Oigan, vatos. Alguien conoce una tal Reina*?" A chorus of negatives answered him, but their sneers and chuckles said otherwise.

"They are useless," Sveta snarled in my ear, but Scruffy at table two heard her.

"Hey, *chica*. I gotta use. You come on over here." He leaned back and patted his lap with a leer.

Sveta's eyes fell on him, and I knew we were screwed. She tilted her head slowly to one side, examining him thoroughly, and a slow smile spread over her face. To anybody else, it looked inviting, but up close I could see the cold blankness to her blue eyes. This was going south, real quick.

"Don't do it…" She ignored me. Women do that.

With some extra sway to her hips, she sauntered in his direction, her gun hand carefully concealed behind her leg. If I didn't know her and fear her so thoroughly, I would say she was an attractive young woman. She caught her bottom lip between her teeth, ducking her head playfully, and I saw the guy's eyes dilate, even in the murky light of the bar. Her new best friend had obviously had too much to drink to sense the imminent threat. "And how might I best make use of you?"

Scruffy smirked at his companions and patted his lap again. "Sit down, we can talk about it over a beer."

Without looking, I reached to my left and found Estéban's arm, firmly pulling him behind me as I pushed us both back toward the door. With all eyes on Sveta, no one else noticed.

The dark-haired woman straddled Scruffy's knees, settling down on his lap and slipping her free hand around his neck. "Like this? I am a stranger to your country, I am not sure of the proper etiquette."

"Your etiquette is just fine, *chica*. Very good." One big, greasy hand came to rest on her ass, and that's when it all went to hell.

Faster than anyone could see, she brought the gun up and had the barrel pressed up under his chin hard enough to tip his head back awkwardly, the smile never leaving her face. It took Scruffy a few moments to process his sudden change in fortunes, and then the color drained from his tan face, leaving him a strange, ashy color. "What? Is this not also very good?"

"Well that escalated quickly," I muttered under my breath, trying to figure out how to best defuse the situation.

One of the guys near the dart board twitched toward something at his belt, and somehow, without even looking up, Sveta put her full attention on him. "Move again, and you will wear his brains. *Entiendes*?" When the man held up his hands and backed up a step, she smiled at her would-be suitor once more. "What is your name?"

He had to try twice to get the word out.

"Enrique."

"I am Svetlana, Enrique. I am glad that we are going to be friends." She settled in his lap firmly, in a way that might have been enticing, y'know except for the giant freaking gun between them. "Now, we are looking for Paulito Perez, and his lovely lady friend, Reina. Are you able to help us?"

Scruffy shook his head slowly. "Like he said, Paulito hasn't been in tonight. I don't know where Reina lives, she doesn't come in here." He swallowed hard, his Adam's apple bobbing in his throat, and Sveta gave him a smile that I'm sure should have been encouraging, but instead looked like she was going to eat him with some fava beans and a nice chianti.

"And your friends? Do any of them know where she lives?"

Scruffy cast beseeching looks at his buddies, but one by one they shook their heads to the negative. If possible, he went paler.

"Wait, let me get this straight. Not one of you knows where she lives? This town isn't that big. Someone has to have seen her coming and going."

The bartender gave me an uncomfortable shrug, but his eyes never left Sveta. "She just turned up one day, you know? Don't even know her last name or anything."

Sveta sighed and stood up, but her gun stayed firmly against her new friend's chin. "I am disappointed. I believe you all, but I am still disappointed."

"What are you going to do?" Scruffy looked like he maybe didn't want the answer to that question, but felt compelled to ask.

"I think I will go spend some time alone, and

be sad." She patted his cheek gently, then leaned down to press a kiss to his forehead, leaving a smudge of light pink lip gloss there. "You were correct. You were very useful to me. Thank you, Enrique."

Backing her way toward the door, she kept the gun leveled at the room in general now. "Pardon us for interrupting your evening. You may continue."

"Go, kid," I muttered, making sure Estéban was out through the curtain before I followed. I held the fabric aside so that Sveta could step through without losing her aim. She backed up a few paces then jerked her chin in my direction, and I let the curtain drop. "Move, both of you."

Okay, we didn't exactly *run* back to the truck, but we moved with definite purpose. "Have you ever considered some therapy for your obvious social interaction difficulties?" Sveta just gave me a bland look, eyeing the night as the kid and I climbed into the truck, and only then did she follow us. "You realize that every guy in that place probably had a gun on him, right?"

"So? I am faster."

I threw the truck into drive and got the hell out of Dodge before Scruffy Enrique and his buddies got over wetting themselves and came after us. "What were you going to do, shoot someone? You can't just go around shooting people, Sveta. It's not what we do."

"It's not what *you* do, you mean." She gave me a cool glance across Estéban, who was doing his damnedest to shrink into a tiny, not-there ball between the two of us. "I do not always have the luxury of some of your moral choices. I have been in places like that before. Force is the only authority they recognize."

"And the fact that the guy pissed you off and groped your ass had nothing to do with it?"

A slightly feral smirk crossed her face, visible in the dash lights. "They discounted me because I was female. It is their weakness."

"It's not a mistake they'll make again. That trick only works once, and they'll be looking for you now." Getting around in town was going to be a helluva lot harder, from now on.

Our avenues of investigation were obviously exhausted for the night, so I pointed the truck up the mountain. "Think, kid. If you wanted to live somewhere here, and you didn't want anyone to see you coming and going, where would you shack up?"

He sighed and shook his head. "I do not know. Perhaps one of the homes in the mountains, but most of those have held the same families for generations. Reina does not belong to any of them that I know of."

"Would any of them shelter Paulito?"

He frowned, the crease between his brows looking deeper in the dim light. "At one time, I would have said no. But there were men at the warehouse that I have known since I was a small child, families that we have lived near for years. I would not have believed them capable of such actions either, and yet there they were."

The frustration practically dripped from his voice, and I let the silence stretch out, hoping that he would go on. Finally, he did, smacking his hand against the dash. "I do not understand why these things are happening. Everyone on the mountain, in town, they all know what my family does. They used to respect the name Perez. Now... I do not know what has caused the change. I do not know why Paulito would do these things. He is one of us."

"But he is not." Sveta's eyes watched out the window as the dark trees whizzed past. "You are the champion, Estéban. And your brothers and father before you. Paulito is only a cousin, he is not in line to be a champion."

The kid frowned even harder, if possible. "That… That doesn't matter. The title has passed through cousins before, it doesn't have to only come through our line."

"Then why did it not go to him when Miguel died, hm?" Sveta finally turned to raise one delicate brow at him. "He is older. Physically, he is larger than you. He has trained alongside you, yes?"

"I… His casting ability is weaker, I suppose? Maybe that is why Mamá decided that it should come to me instead."

"And why is it her decision? She is not a Perez by birth."

"Because…because it just is. Papa would have wanted it this way. Mamá is strong, and smart and no one knows more about magic than she does." Esteban blinked at us both as if we'd just asked him to explain what the number nine tasted like. His mother's authority was an unquestionable absolute in his world.

"Jealousy is a terrible mistress, kid. And I have a feeling that Paulito doesn't give two shits that his magic isn't as strong as yours. All he sees is that he got passed over for something that should have rightly come to him, even if he's the only one who thinks so."

"So…do you think he took Miguel's weapons because he is going to use them to become a champion?"

"No. No, I think he took them because he's a petty little shit and he didn't want you to have them." I gave him a small smile. "He doesn't understand that the weapon doesn't make the champion. You could pick up anything and be ten times the man he will ever be."

Even in the darkness, I could see the blush color his cheeks, and he dropped his gaze to his hands. "Thank you, Jesse."

"No problem, kid."

13

Somewhere on the dark road between town and home, Estéban sat up and tapped my arm. "Stop the truck. Stop!" Turning in his seat, he eyed the empty night behind us.

"Did you see something?" Sveta, permanently wary, already had her gun in her hand, and I honestly couldn't say that she'd ever put it away after the cantina incident.

"No, I just…" After a moment, his shoulders sagged, and he turned to face front again. "Never mind. It was stupid."

"No, you had a thought, what was it?"

He ran his hands through his dark hair. "You asked where a person would go, if they didn't want to be seen. And it occurred to me that there is one place that no one goes, and it would be perfect, except that it's crazy to go there in the first place, which is why no one goes. Even Paulito wouldn't."

"Sounds like a perfect place to check out. What is this place?"

"The ruins. There's a small trail, just back down the road a bit. But the ruins are dangerous, that is why no one goes there."

I tilted my head at him. "Ruins? Like Mayan or Aztec or whatever? There aren't any ruins near here."

"Not flashy, tourist attraction ones, no. But they're there, all the same. Well, what's left of them. They're not even really ruins anymore."

I exchanged looks with Sveta across Estéban, and she gave me a firm nod. "Sounds like we're going exploring. Where's this road, kid?"

I threw the truck in reverse and backed slowly down the empty road until the headlights caught a faint opening in the trees that might have been a cart path, back in its ambitious younger years. "Thought you said there was a road."

"I said a trail. You said road. The truck should fit."

Quite certain my night was going to end up with me pushing the truck out of some forest mud hole, I slowly eased the pickup off the gravel road and into the trees. Me and my brilliant damn ideas.

"Cart path" had been generous. It was a game trail at best, and the tree branches made horrible noises as they scraped over the sides and roof of the truck. Even at low speed, the rough terrain bounced us all in our seats, and I had to white-knuckle the steering wheel just to keep us from jolting right off into a tree. "I think we could get out and walk faster than this."

"At some point, we'll have to. You can't drive all the way."

I gave the kid a raised brow. "If no one comes up here, how do you know you can't drive all the way?"

He shrugged as best he could with his hands braced against the dashboard. "Sometimes we have to come."

"'We' meaning champions, or 'we' meaning the Perez family?"

"It depends."

After ten minutes of the most excruciatingly obnoxious drive I'd ever made, we were confronted with a large tree down across the path, which was going to definitely impede our progress. There happened to be just enough clear area that I felt I could turn the truck around and point it facing out, so it seemed as good a place as any to leave the vehicle.

"Take The Way," Estéban said, tossing my sword at me as he slid out of the truck.

"You think I'm going to need it?"

"Better safe than sorry. Sveta, keep your gun out." If she thought Estéban's order strange, she said nothing.

As we clambered over the fallen tree behind him, I finally thought to ask, "Uh, kid? Just what kind of danger is up here? I get the idea you're talking more than just falling rocks and poisonous snakes."

The flashlight beam bounced down the trail ahead of us as we walked, like some will-o-wisp from a children's story. The night birds fell silent as we passed, but picked up again as soon as we were out of sight, all things that were right and normal in the midnight wilderness.

"No one remembers what the ruins use to be. If it was a pyramid, or a building, or what. There are only old stones left now, scattered in the grass. They are very old, and the symbols on them have been worn away with age. But there is a legend."

We had to pause a moment to maneuver around another batch of deadfall across the path, and I started to wonder if the obstacles had been put there deliberately. Seemed convenient that every tree in the place wanted to fall across this narrow, three-foot trail.

"A legend?" Sveta prompted, once we were back on track again.

"Yes. The legend says that many, many years ago, before the Spanish came, one hundred ancient priests gave their lives at this spot to defeat a great evil. No can remember what people they were of, and the line died here, with them."

"What evil?" Legends often had a grain of truth behind them, I'd found.

"No one remembers." Abruptly, we stumbled out of the trees into a large clearing covered in tall grass. The waist-high weeds provided a smooth surface against the forest fabric, looking like a grass-filled lake probably thirty yards in diameter. "But we know it is true, because of what they left behind."

"And what did they leave?"

Estéban turned to face us, and flipped the flashlight off, sinking us into total darkness in a split second. "Magic."

For a second, I was really annoyed at him for what I thought was a prank, but then I realized that I could still see his face, illuminated by a soft green glow. Sveta on my right was similarly visible, and I saw her frown as she tried to find the source of the light.

"Here, look." The kid advanced a few feet and bent down to clear the tall grass away from something. Upon further examination, we found nothing more than a smooth rock. It might have once been square, but the passage of unfathomable amounts of time had worn away the angles and corners, and left behind only a stone, gray and unremarkable except for the faint green glow emanating from its surface. "Some of them still shine. Most have gone dark by now. The spell is older than anything anyone remembers."

My skin prickled across the back of my neck, and the souls stirred a bit. Old magic wasn't always the most stable thing in the world. Though spells usually faded with time, sometimes the magic lingered, warping and going stagnant beyond its original purpose. Sticking your hand in a puddle of that was...unadvisable. "Think you should be touching that thing, kid?"

He stood up and flipped the flashlight back on. "This one is fine. There are a few, further in, that I would avoid."

"This is why no one comes here." Sveta prowled a few paces to my right, parting the grass to reveal another stone. This one glowed as well, though it was much fainter than the first. "Because of the corrupted magic left behind."

"Right. It's dangerous to stumble into it. It...does things."

Only a lunatic would wander around this clearing, Estéban was right. You'd never be able to see the pocket of bad mojo until you were in it, and then it would be too late. "Don't go too far, Sveta." She gave me a scathing look that I could see even in the dim light. "You know this place best, kid, do you see any signs that anyone's been here lately but us?"

We all looked, Esteban playing the flashlight slowly over the tall grass. There were places in the weeds, empty spots that concealed another stone, and I realized that there wasn't a single sapling or tree growing anywhere in the large open circle. Whatever had happened here, the land remembered.

Where we'd entered, the grass was broken and flattened, marking a clear trail into the trees, but if someone else had been here, it hadn't been recently. The odds of someone making camp at this exact place were slim at best.

"Do you smell that?" Sveta, having ranged farther than I was comfortable with, stood as a tense silhouette at the corner of my vision. "Something is dead." Well that's never good.

"Careful," I muttered, as we all three proceeded to be stupid and go exploring. Once it was pointed out, the thick stench of decaying meat was obvious on the night air, and grew stronger as we circled the outside of the clearing. It didn't take long to trace it to its source, another of the glowing rocks.

This one was the largest we'd stumbled across, and flat, providing a nice working surface for whoever had been here before us. Because someone surely had. The chicken carcass that had been left dismembered on the stone could attest to that.

Sveta crouched down, wrinkling her nose against the stench. The kill wasn't recent, by its advanced state of decomposition, and the putrid smell hung like a thick cloud around the stone. "Its head is off, cleanly, and the meat was left. This was not an animal kill."

Estéban frowned. "Someone killed a chicken here?"

"A sacrifice," I murmured, because it felt like saying it louder would make it worse.

Sveta nodded her agreement with me, and spat off to one side. I felt like spitting too. Sure, there were people in the world who used blood and sacrifice to fuel their magic, but they weren't the kind of people anyone wanted to talk about. Or to.

Again, I recalled Mystic Cindy, and the impossible lifespan she claimed to have lived. If she was telling the truth, I had to wonder if magic like this was how she managed it. *One day, you will ask how I did it, and if you are very, very unlucky, I will tell you.* I shivered and closed my eyes for a second, willing the voice away before it could develop into a full-blown flashback.

"Nothing came to eat it, later. If it was just a dead chicken, some coyote would have had a meal by now."

"I must tell Mamá. Whatever spell this was meant to power, it cannot be allowed."

Ah, now that was the question, wasn't it? What exactly had this dead chicken been meant to conjure up? "Can you feel any spells at all around it? Anything more than the stone itself?"

After a moment's thought, Sveta shook her head. "Nothing recent. Perhaps it failed, or it was something done by an uneducated caster."

I crouched down as well, and Sveta stood up, keeping watch over us as I extended my hand toward the gore-stained rock. *Hey in there, you guys see anything here that I can't?* If there was one thing I'd learned in the last few months, it was that the slightest trace of magic was guaranteed to set my passengers off. May as well make use of it.

My back had been buzzing unpleasantly since we entered the clearing, but they suddenly quieted, almost like they were pondering the situation. Feeling brave, I leaned closer to the stone, palm outstretched. In response, goosebumps travelled down my arm – just one arm, and didn't that feel weird – and my hand grew warm for a moment. Before I could examine the novelty of that, the sensation retreated, and the souls were quiet again. Whatever was here, it wasn't enough to warrant their interest, apparently.

"Maybe it was just a bunch of kids, playing at casting spells. Saw one too many movies or something." I gathered my sheathed sword up again and stood, shrugging to Estéban. "That stuff happens, right?"

"Sometimes." His gaze roamed the circle again, and he frowned. "They're supposed to know better, even the people in the town. Everyone knows this is a dangerous place. Tourists, maybe? Though I don't know who would have shown them the way up here."

"Well, there's nothing else we can do here now, and I'm tired as hell, so let's get moving. Sveta…?" I turned to look at her, only to find her back to us, her arms up in a perfect shooter's stance as she aimed at the dark treeline. "Uh…Sveta?"

"We are being watched."

The words froze me in my tracks, and I strained my eyes to find what she'd seen. "Where?"

"I…do not know. Something is here, though." Slowly, she tracked her line of sight along the edge of the trees. "I can feel it, but I see nothing."

"She's right." Estéban's voice was barely more than a whisper. "The birds have gone silent."

Oh hell, why couldn't a walk in the woods just be a walk in the woods? Slowly, I drew my katana from its scabbard, feeling the spells on it as they sent my senses tingling. "Backs together, keep an eye out. Douse the flashlight." There was a faint snick as the light was extinguished, leaving us in only the green glow from the ancient spell stones.

There was nothing. No sound, no scent save the decaying chicken. The night air was oppressively still, and the only thing I could detect was my own heartbeat and Estéban's quiet murmuring next to me. Even in Spanish, I recognized Psalms 23:4. *Yea, though I walk through the valley of the shadow of death, I will fear no evil.* Yeah, I'm not religious, but I had a T-shirt that ended the phrase with "Because

I'm the baddest sunofabitch in the valley." See?
Educational.

The odor of cloves burst into the still air
suddenly, and the souls in my back surged toward my
left, toward the kid. Whatever he was casting, they'd
noticed.

Long moments passed. Very long, tense
moments. Finally, even Sveta was forced to lower
her arms, frowning in confusion. "And it is gone.
Whatever was here has vanished."

"Perhaps I frightened it off?" There was a
note of hopefulness in Estéban's voice, but we all
knew his tiny little prayer hadn't been enough to
scare a flea.

I finally forced the muscles in my shoulders to
relax, rising out of my fighting stance. "Or maybe it
just got bored." Glancing to my left, I looked Estéban
over critically. "You okay, kid?" His spell, whatever
it had been, was tiny by casting standards, but that
didn't mean that he wouldn't be feeling the effects.

"I'm fine." It was hard to see the pallor of his
skin in the darkness, but he seemed steady on his feet,
so I dropped it. "We should go now before it comes
back."

I wholeheartedly agreed.

We followed the bouncing flashlight beam
back through the trail we'd already broken in the
grass, all of us keeping a wary eye on the trees around
us. I think I only truly relaxed when I heard the first
of the night birds resume calling. Whatever had been
with us, it was gone now.

The walk back to the truck seemed shorter
than the trip in, and I was inordinately relieved to see
it sitting right where we'd left it. Maybe I'd seen one
too many horror movies, but I'd half expected it to be

gone, or the tires slashed or something. Still, there was the chance that something horrible was going to jump out of us right as we reached the safety of the vehicle, and I tightened my grip on my sword. Because movies, you know?

Right on cue, the brush to our right rustled, and all of us spun to point weapons and flashlights in that direction. *Too small*, my brain was telling me as the bushes shook and rattled at knee level, *too low to be human*.

What finally broke cover was…well, I'm not sure just what it was. I think it had been a raccoon once. There was something left of the roundish shape, the gray fur, the waddling walk. That was about all that was identifiable, however. A row of spikes had sprouted from its spine, glistening with wet scales, but as it passed under a low hanging twig, the protrusions bent aside, soft and floppy. The lower jaw had grown grotesquely outsized, sharp pointy teeth curving up to form a cage around the upper part of the snout until the thing couldn't even open its mouth anymore. The eyes were milky white and filmed over, but tears of something dark stained the fur beneath them. One back foot had become twisted around to face the wrong direction, and the thing hobbled with a labored wheezing to its breath.

It should have been terrifying, but instead it was unspeakably pitiful and sad. The creature staggered vaguely in our direction, its feet moving it along without any real purpose or direction.

"What the ever loving fuck is that?" At the sound of my voice, the beast stopped, trying to raise its head only to find its attempt hampered by the pseudo spines growing out of the base of its skull. It could hear, then, if nothing else.

"This is why we don't come up here. This is what can happen if you wander into a pocket of the old magic." The kid shook his head a little, sounding grim. "There have been more and more of these in the last few years. Animals horribly changed. They wander out to the farms, or into town, and we usually get called in to take care of it. Mamá thinks that something here is breaking down, barriers are weakening that used to keep the creatures out, or maybe just more of the magic is going bad."

"Kill it." Sveta's voice was choked, and a small part of me marveled that we'd finally found something that could rattle the hardened killer. The other part of me totally agreed with her.

"May I?" The kid held his hand out for my sword and passed me the flashlight in exchange. I held the light steady as he advanced toward the pathetic creature, the thing managing a respectable hiss of warning as he approached. Estéban paid it no mind, though, and with one clean swing of the blade, lopped its head off. The body twitched for a bit where it lay, and then was still. After he was certain it was dead, he knelt to wipe The Way off on the grass and handed it back hilt first. "Let's go home."

It was a quiet ride back up the mountain. Oddly, I think that pitiful little former raccoon disturbed me worse than the rest of the evening's events. The ability to use magic wasn't common in the overall population, but it wasn't exactly rare, either. And the thought that so many people were wandering around the world, callously wielding powers that could eventually turn into *that* was sobering to say the least. Not for the first time, I wondered at the price the human race would have to pay for dabbling in things like that. Years, even centuries later, one spell could still linger, wreaking havoc on people who might never even know it had been cast.

I don't think I want to live on this planet anymore.

14

The kitchen light was still on when we pulled into the drive, and Estéban sighed. "We're in trouble."

I snorted as we all piled out of the truck. "You mean *you're* in trouble. She's not my mom."

"You really think that's going to stop her?"

As if on cue, the kitchen door slammed open, revealing Carlotta wearing a bath robe and a look that could have melted titanium. "And just what did you think you were doing?"

"I had to try to find him, Mamá." As the kid tried to argue his way out of whatever trouble he was in, Sveta slipped off into the shadows, abandoning the kid and I to our fate. Gee, thanks. "I had to try to get the machete back."

She smacked him upside the back of the head, and he just hunched his lanky shoulders. "They are things, *niño*. They are not special in any way. You can pick up any weapon and be a champion." I must have twitched or made a noise or something, because she rounded on me next. "And *you*! What on earth possessed you to leave the safety of the wards? Do you know what happens if they find you undefended?"

"No, and neither do you." That seemed to take the wind out of Carlotta's sails and she just blinked at me. "I don't think the demons have any more idea how to get these things out of me than we do, else they'd have been at your door already. Now can we please go inside? We've got some things to talk about."

It took us a few minutes to get settled around the kitchen table, and involved the kid going to roust Terrence out of his bed, too. The old champion grumbled as he shuffled out into the bright kitchen, but did manage to mumble thanks when Carlotta pressed a cup of tea into his hands. When did she learn to make his tea?

"We didn't find Paulito," Estéban started, "but we found the ward he was using to bind the demon."

"Oh?" Terrence raised his scraggly head and looked to me.

"Yeah. It was pretty much nonexistent. A show, nothing more. Which means…"

Carlotta sighed, inexplicable sadness in her eyes. "Which means that he is working with them."

"Yeah." And because I didn't know what else to say… "Sorry."

Estéban wrapped his arm around his mother's shoulders and leaned his head against hers, the pair of them sitting in silence for a few moments. Finally, she patted his hands, took a deep breath, and drew herself up straight. "In the morning, when we are all rested, we will do a scrying to locate him. He cannot hide from that without more magic than he possesses."

I'd seen Mira do scryings before, but they required something intensely personal from the person being sought. "Do you have something of his? Some way to track him?"

Carlotta gave me a ghost of a smile. "We keep hair from every member of this family, just in case it is needed. Finding him will not be difficult."

Estéban leaned his elbows on the table again. "There is more. We went to the ruins tonight."

The look his mother gave him was nothing

short of horrified. "You did what? At night? You could have walked into anything, up there!" At that point, she switched to Spanish, because apparently English was not sufficient to express what a very bad, very stupid idea it had been to go walking around those glowing stones in the dead of night.

The kid took it for a while, then placed his hands on hers. "Mamá! English, please. Our guests can't keep up."

Carlotta pressed her lips together firmly, but gave a short nod. Her eyes fixed on me sternly. "I can excuse you, because you did not know. But *he* knew better. It is *dangerous* up there, even in broad daylight. There is an evil in those stones."

I raised a brow at the kid, and he just shrugged. "Look, I don't know what the history of the place is, but someone else has been messing around up there. We found a sacrificed chicken."

That drew grim looks from both Carlotta and Terrence, and the old man made a disapproving noise in the back of his throat. "Blood magic..." I think he might have spit, too, but he didn't want to make a mess in Carlotta's kitchen.

"Neither Sveta nor I could feel any spell work around the carcass."

I nodded my agreement. "The...*they* didn't even twitch." I lifted my shoulders in illustration. "Whatever someone was trying to do with the chicken, it failed." When Carlotta continued to look deeply disturbed, I went on. "It was probably just some dumb kids, trying to do something they'd seen in a movie or something."

She shook her head quickly. "Even untrained, even without any magic behind it, every death has power. Even a small death like a chicken. I will need to go there soon, and see if anything has changed. The ancient spells there have become unstable in the last decade or so. They are decaying."

Terrence winced. "You be careful, missus. Old magic isn't anything to trifle with."

Carlotta cast him a quick smile, and there was no mistaking the fondness behind it. "All right, everyone to bed. After breakfast, we will scry for Paulito's location. Estéban…" The kid paused in mid-motion as he was standing up. "I would like you to help with that. The more power we have behind it, the more precise it will be."

"*Sí*, Mama."

"I would like your help as well, Señor Smythe, and Sveta's."

"Yes mum." The old curmudgeon levered himself up out of his seat. "Best get myself some rest then." Together, he and the kid wandered off down the hallway.

Carlotta and I sat in silence for a bit. Most of me really wanted to go fall onto my rock hard cot and get some shut-eye, but she looked like she needed to talk. Sure enough, after a few minutes, she sighed. "He has not sold his soul."

"No," I agreed. "He doesn't have the look."

"Then what is he *doing*?" There was anguish under her words, the kind that mothers get when their kids have wandered off the right road. "I cannot fathom what has possessed him to behave like this. His poor mother will be devastated when she finds out. Paulito was not raised this way."

"The human heart is a weird thing. You never know what's gonna settle in like a little thorn and get all infected. Something's eating at that kid, and it's just all blowing up now. Festering to the surface."

She sat there, looking all distressed and I had to say something else, something that would give her hope, even if I didn't really believe it. "Maybe…maybe it's for a good reason. My own brother sold his soul to save his son's life. It's possible to do bad things for good reasons." Did I believe it? Hell no. But for Carlotta, I'd say just about anything.

She finally looked up at me. "What will you do when you find him?"

"What do you want us to do?" That was an excellent question, actually. We couldn't exactly arrest him. We couldn't keep him tied up and gagged so he couldn't summon any more demons. In fact, bringing him back into his family's stronghold while he still had that ability might be…inadvisable.

"I don't know. I honestly do not know what to do." She twisted at the wedding ring on her finger. "I wish Estéban's father were here. He always knew the right thing to do. I feel as though I am simply inventing things as I go along."

It was hard to remember that Carlotta was not a Perez by blood. She had married into the powerful family, and was doing her best to see that it continued in its proud tradition until one of her sons could take the helm. Until Estéban was old enough to take over. If he survived that long.

"That's what we're all doing, Carlotta." I patted her hands as I got up off the bench. "Just making shit up. See you in the morning. Don't stay up too late."

I left her there, staring at her hands, and went to collapse onto my cot. Estéban wasn't asleep – I could tell by the stiff way he was laying on his bunk – but he didn't say anything, so I didn't either. We could talk in the morning.

The sounds of young boys' soft snores lulled me into sleep, but it was uneasy. I dreamed the tunnel dream again, stepping out into immense space over and over again, always watching for the dark figure at the other end. Sometimes it was there, sometimes it wasn't, and I was never sure when I was more relieved.

Breakfast, when it rolled around, seemed more subdued than usual. I mean sure, there was the usual stampede of ravenous teenage males, the typical roughhousing and taunting, but the adults in the room all had a bit of a gloom hanging over them and the kids picked up on it. They scarfed down their food and scattered in record time, leaving me with the spell casters and a plan to work a scrying.

"What are we going to use, Mama?"

Carlotta pursed her lips for a moment, then nodded decisively. "Salt, I think. I want a clear picture of what he is up to."

There are different kinds of scryings. Some of them involve a pendulum and a map, others can involve something akin to dowsing rods that will swing in the direction of the sought item. The only one I'd actually seen performed involved a giant basin of salt water, and if it went as expected, would provide us with an actual picture of where Paulito was and what he was doing at that given moment.

Oddly, the last time I'd seen a salt scrying performed, it had been Mira, searching for the kid's brother Miguel. He'd already been dead by that time, and all we'd seen was the moment of his death, caught in an endless loop. It was…unpleasant.

Like a line of ducklings, we followed Carlotta across the compound to her little sanctuary. The souls in my shoulders prickled a bit as I crossed the threshold, but at least they didn't drop me to my knees again. I found a seat on one of the benches and stayed out of the way as the four casters laid out their tools for the spell.

At one point, Carlotta looked at me thoughtfully. "I am unsure if you should be present, given how strongly you react to magic."

"I can go back to the house, if you want." Not being in this tiny building with massive amounts of magic swirling around was a brilliant idea as far as I was concerned.

"We need someone outside the circle," Terrence grumbled. "In case." After a few moments of thought, Carlotta nodded her agreement.

A large metal basin – nearly big enough to be called a cauldron – was placed in the center of the room, and Carlotta dumped the entire box of salt into the bottom of it. Esteban and I got drafted to haul in buckets of water from a nearby hydrant, both of us making four trips before we got the vessel filled to Carlotta's liking. She stirred the water slowly, until the salt had dispersed enough to make it a uniform milky white, then nodded to her son. "Fetch the box."

The box turned out to be a small cigar box, nondescript in appearance, unless you happened to have the ability to see spells. On the magical spectrum, the thing shone like a tiny little floodlight. It had been overlaid with so many sigils and marks that my eyes watered, and the souls in my shoulders swirled around in sudden interest. I backed my way into a corner, putting as much distance between myself and that box as I could.

The reason for such strong protections on it became clear once it was opened. Inside were locks of hair. Hundreds, probably, each neatly tied and labelled with a name. Here was a link to every single living member of the Perez family, something that would allow an instant magical connection. The only thing more powerful than hair would have been blood, but I was willing to bet that didn't store well.

Carlotta sorted through them until she found the one she wanted, holding the clipping of raven black hair by the tag as the kid put the rest of the box away. "Sveta, Estéban, if you could step inside the boundaries while Señor Smythe closes the circle, we will begin. Jesse, if the souls become too agitated, you can step outside."

There was a faint pop of changing air pressure in my ears as Terrence closed the circle around them with barely a wave of his hand. The four of them got comfortable, Carlotta facing Sveta across the vessel, and Estéban mirroring Terrence. Sveta and the kid both rested on their knees, I noticed, fighters ready to spring to their feet at a second's notice. The older pair were more solid in their seats, legs crossed as best they could, and I had to wonder if it was a magical thing, or just the necessity of older bodies.

"We will begin now. I will take the lead." Carlotta waited until everyone had nodded their understanding, then she closed her eyes, breathing deeply. The other three regulated their breathing as well, until they were all aligned with hers.

If it weren't for the overwhelming scent of cloves that billowed into the air, it would have looked like nothing was happening. Carlotta and Terrence both sat with their eyes closed, while the younger pair watched everything with intense concentration. My skin prickled in response, like an army of fire ants crawling all over me as the souls roused themselves

for such a blatant display. My vision flickered
dizzingly between regular sight and that strange state
where I could almost see molecules drifting in the air.

    I could actually see magic pouring off of
them, drifting upwards like tendrils of steam.
Carlotta's energy was a pale gold, delicate and warm,
and there was a scent of something like warm
tortillas. The magic rising from Terrence's shoulders
was an olive green, and there was a faint hint of
something old and mossy beneath the cloves. The
kid's power was red and tasted like chili peppers,
which didn't surprise me a bit, though there were
hints of his mother's gold threaded throughout.
Sveta's was ice blue, like her eyes, and if there was a
flavor to it, it was lost underneath the burn of absolute
cold. The thin bands of energy wafted to and fro for a
moment, twining in amongst each other above the
casters' heads, creating a solid rope of magic that then
plunged into the depths of the cauldron. With every
moment that passed, the braided cord grew thicker,
stronger, almost pulsing with four matching
heartbeats.

    I'd never seen a group cast a spell before. I
don't know what I'd expected. Maybe a lot of
chanting or robes or something. This went beyond
just a joint ceremony, though. This was a true
melding of their powers, three of them willingly
giving their magic over to Carlotta to be used and
guided as she saw fit. And the woman herself glowed
in my strange vision. Carlotta's power – her soul –
seemed boundless, shining bright enough that my
eyes stung and watered. I couldn't have looked away
if my life depended on it. Some guardian I was
turning out to be.

    The feeling of pressure in my ears was

building, almost to the point of pain, by the time Carlotta stretched a hand out over the cauldron and dropped a few strands of Paulito's hair. Instantly, there was a disturbance at the surface of the water, the dissolved salt coming to the top like hungry guppies. It bubbled and churned there, and when Carlotta began making a circling gesture over the water, the salt followed. Soon, there was a whirling vortex of white streaks in the water, the salt solidifying, coming together with purpose.

"Show us." They spoke in unison, though only Terrence's words came out in English. Everyone else spoke their native language as they said, "Reveal him."

I leaned forward as far as I could without disturbing the circle, anxious to see what the salt scrying would reveal.

The water continued to swirl in the confines of the cauldron, but the whiteness of the salt coalesced into shapes, amorphous at first, then taking on purpose and definition. What finally appeared was a vision of Paulito in negative, his black hair stark white, the tan of his skin showing as a light gray. His shirt, which must have been white, was marked by patches of perfectly clear water, which read as black against the depths of the giant bowl. The image was so clear, we could see individual strands of hair that hung down over his forehead, the wrinkles at the edges of his eyes as he opened his mouth to laugh at something.

The clove odor that I associated with spells took on a faintly charred smell, and the souls in my skin surged in Estéban's direction. The edges of his power were frayed, pieces flaking off in spiky, brittle bits in response to his anger. Where his energy fed into the joined spell, the edges of the other strands browned and blistered with the heat, and instinctively, they tried to recoil from the damage.

Carlotta's jaw grew tense with strain as she tried to hold the scattering powers together.

"Easy kid...You gotta hold it together, or your mom's gonna lose connection." Carlotta couldn't spare the attention to chide him, but I could, and as I'd hoped, the sound of my voice reached wherever he was. He closed his eyes for a few deep breaths, and the thorns on his magic tendrils smoothed out.

In the cauldron, Paulito's mouth moved as he talked to someone out of our sight. We wouldn't be able to see his companion, the salt of the spell attuned only to the salt in Paulito's own body. But we might be able to get an idea of his location if we could just discern what he was doing.

Sitting, obviously, that was the first thing. He was lounging back in some kind of low chair, one hand drifting to his mouth and away as he idly smoked a cigarette. The chair was vaguely visible where he touched it, as was the floor where his feet rested. He gestured with his other hand as he spoke, dismissing something with a sneer and a roll of his eyes. At some point, someone handed him a bottle, which only appeared in the vision once he held it in his hand. It was disturbingly like he had just willed it into being. He swigged out of the bottle, then gave another wave, obviously bidding farewell to whoever was in the room with him.

We needed him to get up and move, that much I knew. A snapshot of the room he was in was going to be next to worthless unless we could place just where it was. *Come on, get up...move...* I didn't realize that I was thinking it so hard until the skin of my back grew warm, and I started to feel the lines of every single tattoo that decorated my shoulders. In the salt picture, Paulito paused for a moment, his head tilted like he'd heard something, and then with a thoughtful frown on his face, he slowly got to his feet.

"Jesse! Stop!" Carlotta hissed at me, and I tried, I really tried.

Down, guys, back off. This isn't our show. They didn't want to listen to me, I could tell that much. The muscles around my shoulder blades cramped as my passengers lodged a formal protest. They could help, why wouldn't I let them help? The message was plain as day.

Paulito turned his head to his left, obviously speaking to someone else. He was still frowning, and he shrugged in response to their unheard question. At some prompting, he held his hand out to the unseen person, and there was a ghost of a shape there as another hand took his. It wasn't enough to see the person, but the fingers were delicate, the skin the same shade of light gray as Paulito's. *Reina.* Had to be.

The moment their hands touched, Paulito jerked upright, his spine ramrod straight, and his gaze whipped to the right…straight at us. Almost like he could see right through the water and salt, watching us as we watched him.

That's not good… Paulito gave a sneer and mouthed a few words with exaggerated care. Estéban whispered, "He says he sees us." *That's really not good.*

A knife appeared in his other hand, and with a smirk, he turned away from us and very deliberately ran the blade over his palm. A plume of bright red blossomed in the bottom of the basin, the white of the salt quickly overwhelmed by the sudden burst of color.

The souls in my skin went crazy, and for once I totally agreed with them. "Drop the spell. Carlotta, drop it!" When she couldn't respond, I tried to barge in, fully intent on kicking the basin over. I was brought up short at the edge of the circle, slamming into a wall that smelled like Terrence's mossy magic. *Dammit!* I bashed my fist on the barrier, but knew already that there was simply too much magic in me to allow me to cross. "Carlotta! Kid, snap out of it! Sveta!"

The red water swirled, faster and faster, and I could only watch as a shape rose up out of the depths. A head, vaguely human-shaped, but with a mouth full of fangs and eyes that gleamed the blood red of an angry demon. It dragged itself out of the depths of the water, rising a foot, two feet into the air. A clawed hand appeared, clamping down on the edge of the basin, and I knew, just *knew* that if this thing crawled its way out of that water, we were in deep shit.

I shouldn't have worried. I was in the presence of two of the strongest spell casters I knew, and they had the strength of two younger folk thrown in on their side. With a grim frown, Carlotta made a gesture with her hand, and the rope of combined power looped around the creature's neck. Terrence motioned, and the rope grew taught, strangling the thing. The sound that rose from its throat was a choked snarl, but the single clawed hand abandoned the edge of the basin and instead scrabbled at the cord around its throat.

"You are not welcome here." Again, the four spoke in unison in their respective native tongues.

"Begone, and do not return."

It was working, I realized, the blood-salt thing melting slowly back into the cauldron. The lips curled back from its fangs in impotent rage, the coil of combined magic dragging it back down into the water. The water itself bubbled and churned, boiling with the force of all the power that was running through it.

The thing wasn't done, though. With one last thrash, it managed to sink its teeth into the rope that bound it, and what followed could only be described as an explosion. The basin erupted, boiling water splattering in every direction, and the force of the blast knocked me off my feet, completely blasting through Terrence's protective circle.

I may have blacked out for just a second, the ache at the back of my head clearly revealing where it had met the hardwood floor. What few lights we'd had were out, but I could hear movement as the other four slowly stirred. "Sound off... Who's hurt?"

"I am here." The kid's voice came first, followed quickly by Sveta's. "Here."

"Bloody hell." Terrence was conscious, then, but there was no response from Carlotta.

Something hit my foot and I kicked out reflexively, but it was only the metal basin, now blasted into shards like a wicked metal flower.

"Mamá? Mamá!" By the time I could crawl over to them, Estéban had found his mother, her head cradled in his lap. "Jesse, she's not waking up." There was barely contained terror in his voice.

I found her pulse easy enough, rapid but steady. Her skin was clammy under my touch, but we were all splattered with rapidly cooling water, so it was hard to tell what was what. "We need to get her into the house. Spell sickness is going to kick in any second, and we don't know what is going to happen."

Terrence was on his feet already. "You boys carry her, I'll get some things that may help."

The kid and I managed to carry Carlotta with as little jostling as possible, Sveta following along to support her head. By the time we'd crossed the compound, the older woman's body was shaking with chills that were enough to almost knock us over. "Hypothermia…we gotta get her warm."

I glanced at Sveta and Estéban, and they were both gray around the edges too. We had about ten minutes before they dropped, they just hadn't realized it yet. I'd seen this before. It was hard to tell how the body was going to react to a massive spell, to a giant chunk being cut out of the soul. I'd seen Mira suffer from dangerously high fevers and equally life-threatening drops in body temperature. Cameron had suffered a seizure strong enough to stop his heart.

This was how spell casters killed themselves, I knew. Most magic comes from the soul, the caster using their own to power their spells. Most things were like taking tiny slices off the surface, and the wounds healed over fairly quickly. The bigger spells – things like scryings and explosions – were more like taking an ice cream scoop to the soul, dipping out big hunks, and those injuries took more time to fill back in. Sometimes, the high of working magic overrode the spell worker's need to rebuild what they were ripping away, and they would just cast until they keeled over dead.

"Get her on the bed. Get blankets, hot water bottles." We obeyed Terrence without question, though I kept an eye on the old man too. He'd expended just as much energy as any of the others, and he was older… So far, the only sign of his exhaustion was leaning heavier on his cane, but it was just a matter of time.

Estéban was the first to go down. He abruptly whirled and ran out of the room, and we could hear him retching into the toilet down the hall. Sveta just sank into a chair in the corner of Carlotta's room, her skin gone paper white. I checked her temperature with my hand, and she didn't even have the strength to bat my touch away. Her skin was cool to the touch, but not dangerously so.

"And…I'm done for, boy." Terrence found the other chair, dragging it over next to Carlotta's bedside, and collapsed into it. With a sigh, he rested his head on the quilt next to her.

"What do you need?" Christ. With all four of them down, this was the most undefended this place was ever going to get. And there was no way to know how long it would take them to recover.

"Nothing. Just rest. See to the boy. Me and the crazy bint, we can watch here. Come back in half an hour to change out the water bottles."

Sveta's eyes were open, staring blankly ahead through sheer force of will, but I wouldn't have counted on her to be able to do much of anything. Still, she gave me a small nod, and what else could I do?

"Kid?" I poked my head into the bathroom to find Estéban curled up on the floor, knees doubled up to his chest in pain. "Aw shit, kid."

"Go…go away…" He tried to protest as I took a seat near him.

"Nah, I'm gonna stay right here." I rubbed my hand up and down his back, just like I would for Annabelle if she were sick, and despite himself, he relaxed a little. Hey, I'm a dad. We know this stuff. "It's okay, kid. It's all gonna be okay."

I sure hoped I was right.

15

What followed was like being witness to the most epic hangover after the most colossal alcohol binge ever. I managed to get Estéban shuffled onto my cot – there was no way I was going to be able to manhandle his lanky butt up into his top bunk – and left him there with a bucket in case he found anything else to ralph up.

I checked on Terrence and Sveta frequently, both of whom seemed to be dozing off and on, if you can call it dozing when Sveta's eyes never closed. Carlotta herself seemed stable, her temperature slowly climbing every time we replaced the warm water bottles under the pile of quilts. It was late afternoon when she finally opened her eyes long enough to ask, "*Mi hijo*?"

"He's fine. Resting. You rest too, okay?" I think she tried to smile before her eyes fluttered closed again. At her side, Terrence sighed quietly, never raising his head where he was leaned over on the bed. "C'mon, Terrence. You need to find a bed. Your back is never going to forgive you for this."

"G'way." He swatted at my hands half-heartedly, but finally allowed me to get him to his feet. With a mental note to apologize to Rosaline either, I deposited him into her bed, and came back out in time to see Sveta lurching her way down the hallway.

"Whoa, whoa… Hey." I quickly put my shoulder under her arm, taking as much of her weight on myself as I could. "Where do you think you're going?"

"Someone must patrol the perimeter."

"That's fine, and someone will, but not you. You're going to patrol your way into the boys' room and thoroughly examine the bottom half of a bunk bed." She gave me a withering look that might have been more intimidating if she could actually stand up on her own. "Yeah, yeah, kick my ass later. I look forward to it."

With the invalids cared for as best I could, Rosaline and I managed to wrangle the kid-pack together and set them at the task of preparing the evening meal. I'd expected more resistance, or maybe just more screwing around, but the boys set in with the precision of a team of line cooks who had worked together for years. I was actually pretty impressed with the group of hooligans.

Carlotta was propped up on pillows when I brought her a small plate of food, and she smiled fondly when I told her who'd done the cooking. "I made sure my boys would never go hungry."

Terrence was snoring loud enough to vibrate the windows, so I just left him, and then brought plates to Sveta and Estéban. The kid eyed his platter of plain tortillas like they were poison. "Just try one. If it stays down, try another."

Sveta just sat up and tucked in, mechanically shoveling down food without tasting it. With her plate cleared in record time, she handed it back, then lay back down, turning her back to the room.

"Guess you're welcome."

And just so I wouldn't be a liar, I even went out and walked the perimeter around the property. Well, I walked part of it. It was getting dark, and I didn't have a flashlight, and after the eleventy-billionth mosquito bite, I decided it wasn't worth it.

If the Perez family wards weren't enough to protect us, then we had much bigger issues to deal with. Y'know, things like what the hell tried to crawl out of that water basin, and how did Paulito even *do* that?

Somewhere around midnight, when I dozed with my head resting on the kitchen table, Terrence staggered out into the light, making some grumbly noises that I took to be a demand for tea. I put the kettle on as he slumped on one of the benches.

"So. This might be a good time to explain a bit more to me about blood magic and what the hell happened back there." I took the seat across from the old man, giving him an expectant look.

Terrence shook his grizzled head, silent for a long time, long enough that the kettle started whistling and I had to get up to deal with that. As I poured the water, he finally cleared his throat.

"We don't know a lot about it, really."

"We meaning who?"

"Good, god-fearing decent folk." He took the cup away from me, stopping just short of making the grabby hands motion at it. "The kind of people who practice blood magic aren't generally invited over for afternoon tea."

"Yeah, I get that." I waited for him to sip at his tea for a few minutes before I pressed him again. "How does it work?"

Terrence shook his head, running a hand over his wild hair. "Normal magic… Mine, Carlotta's, the bint's, anyone's… It draws from the soul, your own soul. With blood magic, you draw power from other souls, other lives."

"But Carlotta was using your power in there, drawing from your souls."

The old man shook his head, giving me a

scathing look. "It's about the will, boy, about the intent. We gave her our power willingly. With blood magic, it's taken by force. For some things, that's more powerful, the hatred and anger that go with it. You'd never want to set defenses with blood magic, they'd be erratic, unpredictable. But attacks…or summonings…blood calls to it."

"Why don't more people use it?" Unless you counted my suspicions about the Korean sorcerous that I'd dubbed Mystic Cindy, I'd never actually seen a practitioner of blood magic.

Terrence snorted. "Because your own blood will only be sufficient for so long. Then you have to use someone else's. Then it has to be a death, just a small one, and then, finally, only a human death will keep up the power you need. Once people start dropping, the authorities tend to notice."

I got the feeling that he didn't just mean the police. "The Catholic order… St. Silvius. That's what they do, isn't it? They track down blood magic."

"Mmph. Sometimes. Tried to get Ivan in on the action about ten years ago, but he told them to get stuffed. Said it was our calling to help lost souls, not to police our own. I think he mostly didn't like that they couldn't tell him what they were *doing* with the casters once they had them."

"That's…ominous."

"Mmph." He slurped at his tea. "But still…we're going to have to tell them. Short of killing the man, I don't think we have the ability to stop whatever he's doing here. If the Order has means…"

He was right, as much as I hated to admit it. "I know a guy in the Order. I can make a phone call if we can head down into town."

Terrence shook his head. "I've got my own contacts. I'll handle it. Carlotta's not going to take kindly to giving one of her kin over to them. Best she be cross with me, not you."

"All right. When do you want to go?"

"Morning's soon enough." With a sigh, he heaved himself up off the bench again. "I'll get a bit more shut-eye, then take the truck down once the sun's up."

"You can't go alone."

He snorted, raising one hairy brow at me. "You're no one to tell me I can't, boy. I've been doing this longer than you've been alive, and you still got all those other souls to think of. You're keeping your scrawny arse right here where it's safe." He walked off into the house, muttering under his breath about youngsters and their gall.

And once again, Jesse sits on the bench. Literally, in this case. I was getting damn tired of being sidelined for my own good.

The scrying had been an unmitigated disaster, and Paulito would be on guard now, watching for us. We still had no idea why the demons were helping him, or what he intended to do with the stolen armor and weaponry. And all I could do was sit here and play nursemaid til everyone was on their feet again.

It ate at me the rest of the night, and what little sleep I got was the opposite of restful.

The next morning saw both Terrence and Estéban upright and functional, and out in the driveway working on Miguel's bike again. They'd worked for hours, only stopping briefly for lunch when I insisted. Currently, they were both covered in grease and grime, and had tools and equipment strung out for what seemed like forty yards.

"So here's the thing that bugs me." I had perched myself on an overturned bucket, handing them things as needed, and largely thinking out loud about the events of the previous day. Occasionally, one of them would make a noise in acknowledgement, proving that I wasn't actually talking completely to myself, but for the most part, the small but intricate engine was taking up their attention. Me, I just kept yapping, because it helped to sort out what was going on in my head.

"The thing is, they're not getting anything out of it. The demons, I mean." Estéban flailed a hand at me, and I slapped a crescent wrench into it, whether that was what he needed or not. "You said they're not fighting for souls, they're fighting for their freedom, which they really already have. So why would a creature like that voluntarily show up to get its ass kicked if they're not being paid? Something doesn't add up."

Terrence grunted in reply, and I handed him a rag to wipe his greasy hands. "Think that might do it, boy. Let's try to start her up."

With a pensive look on his face, the kid hit the ignition, and was rewarded with the instantaneous sound of the engine roaring to life. Well, buzzing to life. The bike wasn't really big enough to roar. Estéban looked up at the both of us, grinning like his face would split. "We did it."

I couldn't help but chuckle. "Good job, kid."

They tinkered with the thing some more, testing out the throttle, tweaking things I didn't really understand. Everything was apparently to the old man's satisfaction, because they finally powered it down and he gave a satisfied nod. "If you take good care of her, she'll run forever. Just gotta keep up on the maintenance."

"I will. I'll take good care of her." Estéban reverently ran his hands over the bike's seat. "Miguel would be happy that we got her running."

Terrence snorted, eyeing the mechanical carnage they'd left strewn all over the driveway. "You boys better get to picking this up. I'm going to head down into town, make a few phone calls." Oh sure, *we* had to pick up the mess. The kid and I rolled our eyes at each other, but started gathering up the tools and spare parts while Terrence took over my bucket throne, leaning on the cane that he had miraculously not needed until just this moment. "And as far as your demon fighting puzzle, I think you've reached the point where there's only one solution, and it may be worse than not knowing."

"Oh?"

"The only way to find out what deal that boy has made with them is to ask him. Only we can't find him, can we?" I waited patiently, hoping the old codger had a point. "So you're left with asking the one other thing that knows the answer."

Esteban and I both paused in our cleaning to look back at Terrence with raised brows. He just gave us a challenging look. "Are you really suggesting that we summon up a demon and have a chat?"

"I didn't say any such thing. Just saying that it's the only alternative you've been left with."

I knew the answer to this already. "Not only no, but hell-the-fuck no." I'd summoned one demon, ever, and I still felt pretty slimy about it. Whatever we needed to know, it wasn't worth it.

The kid, however, had a thoughtful frown on

his face. "We could. We know its name." At that simple suggestion, the demon name in question swam to the forefront of my mind. The souls in my skin twitched, and I grimaced. The look on Estéban's face said that it was doing the same to him. They wanted to be spoken, the names. Nearly living creatures in and of themselves, they wanted to be set free into open air, tainting anything that was close enough to hear it. Every single demon name I'd ever heard still lingered inside my head, like an abscess just waiting to pop. I swallowed hard, and tried not to taste the bile at the back of my throat.

"That's a dangerous road to start down, kid. It's not really something you can take back once it's done." Another name swam dangerously close to the surface, one that belonged to a creature I'd nicknamed The Yeti. That one I could still taste on my tongue, where it had passed into the world not quite a year ago. It would be easier to say it the second time. I knew that instinctively. My right shoulder flared white hot for a second, startling me into a wince, and the names retreated, bullied back by the pure life force I was carting around.

"Do we have a choice?" The question wasn't rhetorical, he truly wanted an answer.

"There's always a choice. It just may not be a good one." When demons were involved, the choice was never a good one. I'd learned that.

Terrence heaved himself off his seat, hobbling his way toward the kitchen with what I was pretty sure was grossly exaggerated stiffness. "Well, you two ladies figure it out. I'm taking the truck, I'll be back after while."

Estéban sighed and bent to finish gathering up the tools, rolling them carefully up inside their worn leather case. "Mama would murder us anyway, if we did it."

"We couldn't do it here," I conceded. "Not inside the wards. That's just…beyond wrong." I frowned, hearing the words come out of my mouth, and quickly corrected myself. "Not that we would actually do it. Just sayin'."

"Right. It'd have to be somewhere else. Away from people. Wouldn't want to put them in danger." I picked up one of the tool boxes, and he took the leather bundle, and we went to put them away. "Need to be a shadowed place too. They don't like sun, but I don't think we want to tackle this at night." I gave him a raised brow, and he shrugged. "Hypothetically."

"We couldn't hold it, you know. Circles don't really trap them. We'd have to give it a reason to stay and talk. Give it something in exchange for any information we get. It won't deal for free."

"Hypothetically."

"Right."

"It wouldn't have to be a soul we offered it. If we could figure out something else that had value for it." Souls were not the only thing demons would bargain for. I knew that. They'd take a smaller deal first if they thought it would get their mark hooked. The first one is free, the second one always costs. "A favor would be too much, but…a name, maybe. A single name, not a whole name."

Names and voices were odd things for a demon. I'd been told once that all humans, all of us apes crawling on the planet's surface, looked alike to them. It was our voices that told us apart, our names spoken in those voices that let them identify just who was who. Axel knew my name, and he borrowed my voice with impunity. Every demon I'd ever fought knew my name. That was part of the deal.

The demon from the fight club had seen me, and my souls, and he'd heard my voice, but he didn't know my name. It might be enough to trade.

I realized that I'd fallen into grim silence, and the kid was staring at me with a similar look on his face. "We're going to do this, aren't we?"

It went against everything Ivan had ever taught me. And sometimes, you just have to draw a line. " No. No, we're not."

"But Jesse—"

"I said no." That was as firm a voice as I had. "Drop it. Go check on Sveta, see if she's done terrorizing your cousins." We'd left the kid-pack in charge of Sveta's convalescence, figuring sheer irritation would get her back on her feet sooner than later. "Go check on your mom, see if she's ready to try a little more food. There's lunch leftovers warming on the stove. I'm gonna go walk the perimeter."

Was that smooth? Yeah, that was smooth. 'Cause every one of you knows what I'd decided to do.

Sure, I walked the perimeter. I walked along the mystical boundary, feeling the uneven edges where one caster had gone out to one distance, one to another. It allowed the barrier to trail off gently, rather than end in an abrupt, impenetrable wall. Parts of it felt distinctly like Carlotta, but the others were older, ghosts of people long gone.

With frequent glances over my shoulder, I made sure I was as far from the main house as possible when I slipped over the border – a little part of me expected to get shocked like one of those dogs and their invisible fencing – and headed out into the trees and mountain wilds.

It was beautiful out there, the late afternoon sun shining down through the leaves, casting fluttery shadows on the ground beneath my feet. Unseen birds chorused cheerfully overhead, seemingly unconcerned about my presence. *Better vacate, Tweetie, you're not gonna like what comes next.*

I walked for probably fifteen minutes – far enough that I was fairly certain I could still find my way back, and yet leave the Perez family at a safe distance – and finally found a small clearing that would suit my purposes. An ancient tree had fallen, probably decades ago, but there was still a gap in the canopy where the sun beamed in unhindered. Exactly what I needed. They hated the sun.

Planting myself in the center of the sun-drenched clearing, I closed my eyes and took a few deep breaths. *Listen up, you lot in there. I'm gonna do something you're really gonna hate, but I need you to just go with me on this one, okay?* There was no response from my passengers, so I had to just hope they didn't decide to rip my back apart and leave me helpless with a demon wandering around and night coming on.

I palmed the demon mace canister off my keychain, ready to fog the place with cayenne and cumin at a second's notice, set both my feet in a good solid stance, took a deep breath, and said it.
"_____!"

Oh god, that sucks... It wasn't meant for human anatomy, that word. My tongue shouldn't have been able to wrap its way around the syllables of poison, bitterness, ground glass, and sulfur stench. But there it was just the same, and I could feel a greasy, unholy joy as the name escaped into the world.

I didn't puke this time. Yay me? But the world tilted at a radically unnatural angle, and the trees swam around me like water reeds. The sensation of rancid oil coated my throat, my skin, everything that vile, degenerate word could touch. I think the sun even dimmed, a pall falling over the clearing that dropped the temperature by a good ten or fifteen degrees. I didn't have time to be cold, though, what with the skin of my back burning like fire. I could almost hear the souls hissing their displeasure aloud as they swirled in agitation. I blinked my eyes rapidly, trying to make things return to their normal, upright positions before my visitor arrived.

The first thing that settled around me was the silence. The birds had taken my advice and headed for less demon-y pastures. The pleasant breeze had stilled. Hell, maybe the rivers had stopped running and the earth ceased to turn. Hard to say. It was only my second demon summoning.

With no wind to speak of, the scent of sulfur and ozone shouldn't have been able to reach my nostrils, but there it was all the same, flirting around my head. "Come on out, ugly, I know you're here."

The only response I got back was a sibilant giggle, somewhere above my head and to my left. I should have grabbed my sword before I did this. I knew that. Belatedly. Dumbass.

"All right, I'm sorry I called you ugly. What would you prefer? Fluffy? Snookums? Cuddle-pie?" The tree branches rustled, and I tracked the motion off to my right this time. I turned to keep it in front of me. The thing giggled again, sounding like a tank with air escaping. Claws rasped on tree bark, but the thing stayed hidden. "Here kitty, kitty, kitty…"

Finally, the large moon-eyed head peered its way around a tree trunk, a good fifteen feet off the ground. Safely out of my reach, I noticed. The bat-winged ears twitched and swiveled, keeping a wary watch on all that went on around it. The actions of a prey animal, I realized. This little guy had been hunted before.

"I seeeeeee you, soul-bearer." With a blink, it ducked back into hiding again, though I could still see the tip of one ear sticking out.

"Yeah, I see you too, Bats. Why don't you come on down here so we can have a chat without me getting a crick in my neck?"

"Tsk tsk tsk…" The thing tutted at me. "No no no…won't like it, chatting with you. Won't like it at all…"

I snorted. "I like to think I'm a brilliant conversationalist, actually."

It hiss-giggled at me again. "Talk talk talk! Always talking, saying nothing. Wispy words, drift like smoke…"

"What can I say, it's a gift." I took a few steps to try and get a better look, but the thing circled the trunk, keeping itself half hidden. "Come on down, let's get to know each other."

"Down is down, up is better. Up high, safe and free. Like a birdy in the tree!"

Oh god, it was rhyming. This was going to get old, real quick. I'd talked with lots of demons over the years, all with varying degrees of coherence. This one, while coherent, was decidedly off, even for a demon. Sure, it was pretty weak. I wasn't even sure which of my personal categories it belonged to.

But I'd negotiated a detailed contract with a demonic slug with more success than this.

"If I promise not to hurt you, will you come down here?" The head reappeared, the enormous eyes blinking owlishly at me.

"Swear. Swear it by power. Play me false, and poof, all gone!"

"Uh…sure. I swear on my own power that so long as you offer me no harm, I will cause *you* no harm while you are here speaking with me, on this one and only occasion." You have to be really specific, with demons. The letter of the law is everything.

The demon obviously didn't know who I was, if he thought I had any power of my own to bargain with. Still, the oath seemed to satisfy it, and there was a scrabbling of claws on wood as the thing slid down to the forest floor.

It emerged from behind the tree, walking on feet and knuckles like a tiny ape, hunched and wary as it peered around the sunlit clearing. The hairy tip of one ear caught a stray beam of light, and the thing hissed as it drew back under some overhanging brush. "Filthy sun. Why the sun? Why not the cool dark night, sweetly black?"

"Can't give you all the advantages, right?"

It snickered, hissing through its mouthful of fangs. "What does the soul-bearer want with me, hm? No one, nothing… Plaything, puppet, slovenly worm…"

It was referring to itself, I realized. Ladies and gentlemen, what we had here was the very first demon I'd ever seen with self-esteem issues. "I wanted to talk to you about the fight club. About what you were doing at the warehouse the other night."

The demon snickered and clapped its bony hands together in glee. "Oh, the fun we have! Playing, yes, playing with the angry ones!"

I crouched down so I could be more on a level with the creature, peering under the bush that sheltered it. "Must hurt, them smacking you around like that."

The moon-eyes flared red for a heartbeat. "Don't have to let them! Could eat their faces off, if I want! Only won't let me... No, no, says no eating faces...." The red faded and the bat-like ears wilted in dejection. "No eating faces."

"Who won't let you eat their faces?" Points to me for getting through that question without so much as a flinch. I had no doubts, looking at the size of the maw on this thing, that it could eat faces if it wanted to.

The demon gave me a bit of a smirk. "Wouldn't you like to know? All puzzled up, is the soul-bearer. Needing what he does not know!"

"Wouldn't have asked if I didn't want to know." This was starting to be familiar territory. This would lead into negotiations, trading for info. This I knew. "What's it going to take to get you to tell me? And don't pretend like it's Paulito. You and I both know he doesn't have the power of a AAA battery."

That tickled the little demon, and he hissed-giggled all over the place. "No! No power there. Not enough, but just enough... Enough for what wants." It slunk out from under the leaves, cautiously looking around it. I realized that the shadows were slowly creeping my way as the sun started sinking toward the ocean in the west. "What is the soul-bearer willing to give, hm? A soul? One tasty soul? Won't miss it, has plenty."

"Not a chance. Try again." I'd already decided what I was willing to part with, and while it would be better to force the demon to ask for it, I didn't think I had the time. I didn't want to be out here with it once night fell. "How about a name?"

The demon's ears perked up, the tips quivering. "The soul-bearer's name?"

"One of them. One of my names, in exchange for you telling me who is giving you orders, and what you're gaining by letting that bunch of idiots beat you up."

The thing rocked its head back and forth, the enormous ears flapping. "Hem. Haw."

I couldn't help it, I snorted a laugh at that. "I don't think you're actually supposed to *say* 'hem' and 'haw'."

The big eyes blinked at me. "Then how does it know I am thinking? Thinking is much taxing. Hard working."

I couldn't decide if the little critter was terminally stupid, or just nutty as shit. "So what do you think?"

"I am thinking… I am thinking this is yes. One name, one name of the soul-bearer, and in return I will say who is, and what gets." The very idea seemed to delight it, and it danced a little caper in its growing pool of shadow. "A soul-bearer name will be worth muchly! No worm then!"

Y'know, against my better judgment, I actually felt kinda sorry for the little thing.

16

"All right, tiger. You go first. If you tell me true, I'll give you the name."

"Yes yes, always the true, always. No lies, never never. Doesn't like. Doesn't like at all." With its weird crouched walk, it edged out again, still hugging the very boundary between sunlight and shadow. "We play with the angry ones, so doesn't hurt. Doesn't rend and tear and slash. Says, no eating faces, no winning. Lose every game, and will be pleased with us."

"Whoever is bossing you around, they want you to lose on purpose."

It nodded, ears flopping. "Yes! Small game not important, says. Big game important, and angry ones must stay angry. Anger is stupid. Anger makes mistakes."

I was inclined to agree with that. "So…the fight club is just to get them used to being around demons. Get them thinking that they're bigger and badder than you and yours. Make them cocky, make them reckless."

"Yes yes! Big show, much fangs and claws." It hissed, demonstrating, then dissolved into giggles again.

"Why?"

"Needs them." It nodded firmly at that. "Needs the blood, needs the thump thump."

"Thump thump…" The heartbeat. The life. "Your…master, for want of a better word, is working blood magic. They need the blood and the life force of the kids at the fight club to do…something. So you little ones, you do the grunt work, get your butts kicked, and your boss gets all the benefits."

First it shook its head no, then nodded vigorously, then shrugged its spare little shoulders. "Benefit is not hurting. Don't like to be hurting."

Another inch of shadow, another smidgen closer to me. Don't think I wasn't watching the little rodent. "Who is it? Who is your master?"

The thing shook its head furiously to the negative. "No name! Soul-bearer's name is not worth *that* name."

"Well you have to give me something, or our deal is off. Is it a man?"

"Nope. No male apeling."

"A woman then."

"No!" The thing chortled gleefully. "Nope nope, no female apeling either."

I gritted my teeth and took a couple of breaths for patience. "Then what is it?"

"The first. One of the very first. Older than old, older than apes, than rats and rocks and trees…"

Lovely. "A demon, then. A very old, very powerful demon."

"Older than demons, older than oldest. The first."

The cold chill down my back had nothing to do with the fading sunlight. The souls in my skin stirred, twisting in unease. "What is it using the blood magic for?" I'd never heard of a demon using anything but souls.

"No!" The rat actually stamped his little clawed foot at me in anger. "No! Gave you the wants! Now give me the name! The soul-bearer's name!"

I sighed and stood up, stretching the aches out

of my legs. "You did. You did what I asked, so our deal is held. My name is Dawson."

The moon eyes fluttered closed with an expression of ecstasy. "Dawwwwwwson. It is a good name."

"I've always liked it." Time to go. I had no clue what to do with the information I'd received, but maybe Carlotta or Terrence would have an idea. "See ya later, scrawny. Maybe think about getting yourself a new boss. Your current one seems to be treating you shitty. Check into a union or something."

I turned to go, only to have the little critter dart around in front of me again, clawed hands held out imploringly. "No! No leaving! Stay….talk… Could say more, for another name maybe perhaps."

"Not a chance. One is all you get. See ya." I tried to walk around it again, and again he skirted the edge of the shadows to get between me and the trees.

"Something else, then? What's trade, hm? I know things. Things Dawson wants."

"I doubt that. You don't seem strong enough to have any good secrets." Oh yeah, I was playing the little guy now, and I should probably feel really bad about taking advantage of a weaker being. But hello…demon? "What could you possibly know?"

As I'd hoped, the bat ears quivered in outrage. "I know much! I am small, yes, but forgets I am there. Says things. Big game things! Things Dawson needs to know."

I crouched down again. "Dazzle me, but you've only got fifteen minutes to come up with something. Once the sun gets below the trees, we're done."

The thing hopped back and forth on its two clawed feet for a moment, thinking, then snapped its fingers. "Know where the weapons are! Armor and blade, stained with blood."

As much as I'd love to get those back for the kid, it wasn't vital enough to trade for. "We can replace those. Try again."

The little demon frowned, ears wilting in concentration. "Know...know how he did it, the angry one. Blood in the salt, monster climbs through. Rawr." It mimed gnashing jaws with its clawed hands.

"Dude, I'm so the last person who needs or wants magic lessons. No trade. And you're running out of time."

It hissed at me this time, the moon eyes flaring red. "Stay! Know more secrets! Dawson cannot leave!"

"Why are you so keen on me staying here?" The creature flinched at that, ducking its head like it was about to be hit. "Are you stalling me?"

A slow smile crossed its face, and it nodded its head, the ears flopping a little. "Yes, there's the secret. Voices heard, plans made... That's what Dawson will trade for."

"What plans? Whose voices?"

"The youngling's voice...you know the voice." The next thing that came out of its throat was not its own raspy sibilant demon speech, but a pair of voices I knew all too well.

"Where are you? Are you in a safe place?" *Estéban.*

"Yes, I'm safe, but they're coming for me." *Paulito.* "I'm almost to the ruins, but I don't think I'll make it to the house."

"No, stay there, I'll come get you." It was eerie, hearing the kid's voice come out of that fanged mouth, but demons were nothing if not perfect mimics. It was also dizzying, listening to the thing switch back and forth between the two voices with ease.

There was a tremble to the voice that belonged to Paulito. "Why would you do that? After what I've done?"

"Because you are family, that's why."

"Estéban... I... I'm scared."

"Just stay there, I'll be there as soon as I can." The thing even mimicked click of the phone hanging up, and then a dial tone.

"When did this happen?" It could be false, I knew that. Something invented, just to tempt me into giving something up. But I had to say, in all the years I'd been dealing with them, I'd never once seen a demon lie. The knot in my gut said it was all too real.

"Moments ago. Days ago. Hard to say." Once again using its own voice, the thing shrugged its shoulders with a sly grin. "Worth a trade? Another name?"

"No. But this is." I took a moment to carefully frame my words. This was gonna be a doozy. "The cousin's a douche and the kid's walking into a trap. I know that much. They're going to the ruins, where there's old magic and someone's been messing around already. I know that too. But you tell me now, and you tell me true. Is your master, the first, going to try to sacrifice Estéban for something? To get his blood to power some kind of magic?"

It made sense. The fight club, and probably Paulito's blood alone, was no longer enough to power whatever they were trying to do up at those ruins. The chicken death hadn't been big enough, either. Terrence had said that the next step was a human death.

The scrappy little demon gave me a slow grin. "Yesssss. Now a name. Pay your debt."

"It's James!" I shouted it back over my shoulder, because I was already running.

The tree branches whipped against my face as I pelted through the forest, and I had a vague thought that I sure hoped I was running in the right direction when I blasted through the Perez wards without even realizing I'd reached them.

People paused in their tasks as I raced through the compound, outright hurtling one garden fence when it sprang up in my way unexpectedly, and the kitchen door slammed open hard enough to bounce when I hit it at full speed. "Kid! You here?"

"Señor Jesse! You come!" One of the kid-pack appeared, grabbing at my wrist and yanking. "Come now, Señorita is hurt!"

I let myself get dragged down the hallway to Carlotta's room, where Sveta sat slumped at the end of the bed, a bloody towel pressed to the back of her head as Carlotta examined the wound. The boys, clustered around her attentively, all parted like the Red Sea so I could get close. "What happened?"

Sveta spat something at me in Ukrainian, then winced and wobbled where she sat.

It was Carlotta who supplied the answer. "He is gone. *Mi hijo*, he hit her, and took the truck and left." She pressed an icepack against the back of Sveta's head. "Why would he do this? What is happening?"

"Did he get a phone call, right before this happened?" Both women gave me blank looks, but one of the little ones nodded.

"*Sí!* He went in the other room, so I do not

know who it was."

"I know who it was," I muttered. "And I know where he's going."

"I will come with you." Sveta tried to stand, only to sink back down onto the bed, her face pale.

"You're gonna sit right there, and Carlotta's going to watch you for a concussion. I'll get him." I fixed my gaze sternly on the pack of boys. "You do everything your mother tells you, and if Señor Smythe gets back, you tell him to get ready to take on casualties and repel boarders. You use those exact words, *entienden*?" The kids might not understand what I was saying, but the old man would. I got a round of solemn nods in return.

"Bring him home, Jesse. *Por favor*."

"I will. I promise."

I turned to leave when Sveta's hand shot out, grabbing my arm in a grip like steel. When I looked back to her, her ice blue eyes were grim. "He took The Way."

Well shit. Nodding my thanks, I bolted out of the house again.

Terrence had one pickup truck, and Estéban had taken the other, so that left me the donkey, which was not really going to happen, or Miguel's bike. It had been probably fifteen years or more since I'd last ridden a motorcycle, but as the engine sputtered to life, I figured it was like riding a bicycle. The body doesn't forget. "Man, I hope you guys knew what you were doing with this thing."

I admit, I drove at speeds that were unsafe for road conditions, and it was only a miracle I didn't lay that thing over and get turned into street pizza. I didn't know how much of a headstart the kid had on me, but I had to make up time. The sun was setting, if nothing else. And whatever "the first" was, I did *not* want to confront it in the dark.

I would have missed the turn off toward the ruins if the grasses hadn't been mashed flat by something recently driving over them. The kid was there already. I planted my foot on the road to make the corner, the bike's back tire throwing up a spray of gravel in all directions

The overgrown trail was rough, and I nearly bounced myself over the handlebars a couple of times, trying to muscle my way through. Only when I saw the truck ahead of me did I abandon the bike, tossing it carelessly on its side in the bushes.

The hood of the pickup was warm, and the engine ticked softly as it cooled. I couldn't be too far behind him.

The path seemed even more tangled than the first time we were there, almost like the vines and bushes and closed in behind Estéban as he passed. I knew I sounded like a herd of drunk water buffalo, coming through the brush, but I didn't really have time for stealth. And with two hundred and seventy-five souls riled up and beaming, it wasn't like I could hide from anything magical anyway.

The souls were on fire. Had been since I tore out of the little clearing, leaving the sly little demon behind. Whether my passengers truly understood what was happening, or were just reacting to my emotional state, I couldn't say. Regardless, whatever cloaking powers Axel's spell had given me, they were pretty moot now. Even I could tell that much.

The foliage gave way abruptly to the wide meadow, the surface of the tall grass swaying in the twilight breeze. I stumbled to a halt, trying to quiet my breathing so that I could hear. To my left, there was a path through the grass, and on examination, the stalks had been sliced neatly through. He had seriously used my sword as a weed whacker. I was so going to kick his ass.

I heard the voices first, and once I had a direction, it was easy to see the three dark heads sticking up over the weeds, halfway across the clearing. They'd gone further in than we had before, had to be standing almost dead center in the midst of all the fallen stones.

The shortest one, the one that I hadn't expected, was Reina, standing just behind Paulito. There was a strange excitement in her dark eyes as they flicked between the two men. Just what the hell was she doing here? The tattoos on my skin writhed and burned white hot, and I had a sick feeling that I wasn't going to like that answer when I got it.

Paulito must have been standing on one of the rocks, head and shoulders taller than his younger cousin. Even at that distance, I could see the sneer on his face. They were speaking Spanish to each other, and while I couldn't follow it all, the mocking was obvious. He was taunting the kid, no doubt for falling for such an obvious trap. He gestured with one hand, and I realized he had the machete with him, flailing it around like a magic wand.

In the wide open clearing, it wasn't like I was going to approach unnoticed, so I didn't even try. I took the trail Estéban had cut, noting where he'd skirted a few of the aging stones. Wouldn't do to go tripping over one of those and splatting on my face in the midst of the fast escape I was sure we were going to have to make.

I came up behind the kid, making enough noise that he'd know I was there, but stopped about ten yards away. The kid's head twitched slightly in my direction, acknowledging me, but he kept his eyes on Paulito. Reina's gaze, though, it found me, and a pleased smile curved her very pretty lips.

"Having that blade doesn't make you a champion, Paulito."

The switch to English was for my benefit, and Paulito's eyes flicked to me and back to his cousin with a smirk. "Just because your papa was champion doesn't mean that you are one either. You're just a boy, and you have no *idea* what kind of power I have at my disposal."

"I know you're using blood magic, black magic. It will kill you, sooner rather than later, and your soul will be damned with it. I don't know what she's told you," His gaze darted to Reina and back quickly, "but she has lied to you." The kid still had my sword, I realized, pointed down but held in a position he could easily fight from if necessary. "Just come home. Mama will forgive you, we can talk. You can still walk away from all of this."

Paulito threw back his head and laughed. "Reina doesn't lie. Reina doesn't *need* to. What makes you think I want to walk away from this? This will get me everything I ever wanted."

"It won't." Estéban shook his head, and I could see his shoulders droop for just a second before he squared himself again. "I am taking you home. You get to choose what condition you're in."

"Is that a threat, *primo*?" Paulito hopped down off his perch with a dark chuckle. "You really going to use a sword on me? *Tu familia*?"

"*Si tengo que.*" Estéban brought The Way up, settling into a ready stance just like I'd taught him. "Jesse. Whatever happens, stay out of it. This is family business."

Dammit, kid. Not that I really knew what I was going to do anyway. I was unarmed, without even my boot knife, and my sword...well, it was being borrowed. Even at my very best, going up bare-handed against a crazy dude with a machete was probably not going to work out very well for me in the end. All I could do was stand back and watch. The Way wasn't Estéban's weapon, it wasn't even one he'd practiced with extensively, and I could only hope I'd taught him enough to get him by.

As Paulito advanced on his cousin, Reina moved too, so I mirrored her, circling the pair until we formed the four points of a square. There was a stone directly behind me, and two small ones the size of softballs to my right. The small ones still had enough magic in them to cause my souls to lean that direction, making me feel off balance. Across the grass, my eyes met Reina's, and she gave me a small grin.

It was Paulito who broke first, and I felt a glimmer of pride for my student as he stood his ground while his cousin charged at him, bellowing with rage. The machete came down, a clumsy overhand strike, and Estéban calmly stepped out of the way, deflecting the blow and sending Paulito stumbling off-balance into the weeds. The kid came back to center, simply waiting.

The older man whirled, charging again, and again the kid parried, using his cousin's momentum against him. With Paulito's back to him, Esteban had the perfect opportunity to strike, to end this, but again he waited, simply bring the sword back up into a ready stance.

"*Puta! Cobarde!*" Paulito spit at him. "*Pelea,*

cabrón!"

"No."

Paulito came at him again, and this time the blades clashed in earnest, the longer katana keeping the shorter machete at bay. The kid's form was shit, his balance too far forward on the balls of his feet, but he still had more training than his cousin and it showed. The pair of them trampled an ever-growing ring in the tall grass as Paulito tried frantically to get inside the kid's guard, trying anything to reach him. For his part, Estéban kept mostly to defensive maneuvers, and after his second counterstrike where Paulito came away with stinging knuckles and nothing more, I realized he was using the flat of the blade instead of the sharpened edge.

"Kid, we don't have time to play! The sun's going down!" It was something I felt more than saw, the green glow of the spellstones brightening with each passing moment. We were maybe fifteen, twenty minutes away from serious darkness. Whatever "the first" was, the middle of a dark, spell-trapped hole in the woods was not where I wanted to meet it for the first time.

"Come on, *kid*!" Paulito's chest heaved as he tried to catch his breath. "Run home to mama before dark, because the monsters will get you."

They came together again, and the sound of clashing metal and grunts of exertion filled the clearing. Paulito was pushing harder, realizing that his cousin wasn't about to hurt him, and I knew it was only a matter of time before he closed on the kid and forced some kind of end to it. I seriously feared that when it came down to it, the morals I'd instilled in the kid were going to get him killed.

Almost as soon as I'd thought it, there was a

surge in the fight, and somehow the two cousins wound up in a close clench, the two blades pinned between their wielders as they stared at each other from inches apart.

Paulito grinned, a filthy, dark expression. "You cannot defeat me, *primo*. You will *have* to kill me, or I will gut you and leave your body here for the animals. And then I will cut the head off of every brat your mother spawned, and end with her."

Wow. That was some world-class super-villain-level hatred there. I saw the moment the words registered with Estéban, saw the switch flick behind his dark eyes. *Don't kid, don't do it.* But I knew better. Of all the buttons for Paulito to push, that had been the one. Whatever training I'd managed to instill in the kid, that was about to go right out the window.

With a roar that surprised even me, Estéban gave a heave, shoving Paulito back with a force that sent the older man staggering. And instead of waiting, the kid followed with a flurry of blows that Paulito blocked only through blind luck. There was no finesse, no style, only rage behind those strikes, and if any single one of them landed, they were going to remove body parts.

Estéban backed his cousin through the grass, Paulito just this side of outright running away. They got so far away that I realized I could only see them illuminated by the green glow of all the stones around us. Night had fallen, and the pair of idiots had fought their way into the dead center of the clearing. It was only a matter of time before Paulito tripped on a rock and went down, and then the kid really was going to kill him. I was sure of that. He'd kill him, and spend the rest of his life hating himself for it.

"Kid!" There wasn't even a flinch to show he'd heard. "Estéban! Let it go! Stand down!"

Maybe it was the sound of his name. Maybe it was just that he'd been conditioned for so long to obey my voice. But for a split second, he hesitated. And in that second, I saw the machete come up, the blade ominously dark in the green light. "No!"

There was a clang as The Way met the machete, the kid's block coming up impossibly fast, and then a grunt as Estéban executed a nearly perfect spin kick and took Paulito square in the chest, launching him off his feet.

Silence fell over the clearing as all eyes watched Paulito, sprawled on his back and gasping like a landed fish. He'd dropped the machete, and it lay at Esteban's feet, though I'm not sure the kid even realized it. Reina, silent for so long I'd almost forgotten her, inched forward to see better, and but my eyes were all for Estéban. *What are you going to do now, kid?* The next few moments were going to tell me just what kind of teacher I'd been. Would he let him live?

And suddenly, Estéban's decision didn't matter anymore at all, because Paulito started screaming.

17

I thought at first he'd landed on a fire ant hill or something. Paulito flopped around in the trampled grass, tearing at his shirt with frantic fingers. His screams grew higher, breathier, cries of agonizing pain and fear. But in the dark, we couldn't see anything assaulting him.

Estéban took a step forward and I held a hand out to him. "Don't. Stay back."
Something…something was happening.

It was the smell that caught me first. It wasn't cloves. It might have been, at one time, but now it was old, mildewed, rotten. There was something sickly sweet about it, like rotting meat, and something behind even that that was…ugh. Clotted blood, my mind told me, though why I knew what that smelled like, I couldn't say.

Old magic. The moment I thought it, my vision started that dizzying flicker, showing me the real world in one breath and the magic beneath it in the next. The spellstones, even the ones that didn't glow to the naked eye, sprang up all around us, and the on-again-off-again sight gave them a strobe effect, flashing in the corners of my vision.

Paulito had fallen into a pool of leftover magic. I could see it, surrounding him like a green cloud of gas, the tendrils of it winding around his chest, his arms and legs. The ancient power, long since altered from its original intention, crept into his mouth like invading vines, and his voice choked off as his back arched painfully.

The first crack of breaking bone was like a

gunshot in the clearing. Paulito's left arm suddenly jutted at an impossible angle, a jagged spur of bone gleaming whitely in the dark. No blood though, I realized, and even worse, the bone seemed to be growing, lengthening.

"*Madre de Dios...*" The kid crossed himself.

In the dark, in the tall weeds, it was hard to see everything that happened. There were more sounds of breaking bone, of muscles and tendons tearing. Paulito occasionally let out an agonized gurgle. Something dark sprouted from his skin, looking almost like scales, only to have them slough off and fall away, leaving raw, weeping sores behind. The fingers on one hand fused together, while the ones on the other hand grew four extra knuckles, and the newly sprouted claws dug deep furrows in the soil.

His joints snapped and reformed at angles that weren't natural in human anatomy, and his spine had grown, that much I could see, adding at least another foot to his height if he were able to stand upright. He made it to his feet once, tottering on knees that bent backwards as he howled his agony to the night sky. The voice was no longer human. After that, he collapsed in a heap and was still. The wisps of magic around him died away, soaking into the ground as if they'd never been.

Estéban swallowed hard, and I had to admit I was doing my best not to vomit too. "...Paulito?" He had to be dead. No one could survive...whatever that was. "*Primo?*"

I was just about to call it, advise coming back in the daylight to tend to burial duties, when the mass on the ground twitched, stirred. *Oh shit.*

What rose to its feet wasn't Paulito anymore.

Only the T-shirt hanging in ragged tatters off its spiked shoulders revealed that this had once been a human man. The oozing skin had hardened in places, forming a shell that gleamed in the green spell light. The arms were longer, spikes of sharp bone jutting from the elbows in such a way that they'd never be able to straighten. One hand had melted into something like a pick, and the other was all spidery fingers and claws.

The legs were animal-like, bringing the thing up to stand on its toes, powerful thighs ready to propel it forward. More bone spikes had grown out of the spine, clear up the back of the neck and protruding out the top of the skull, and when it finally turned to look at us, the face was...indescribable. Suffice to say that there were fangs everywhere, and more of that dark, chitinous armor.

The monster-formerly-known-as-Paulito turned its whole body, the neck frozen in one position by the extrusions of bone and armor, and its gaze zeroed in on Estéban. Opening its gaping maw, it bellowed, and the sound shook the night.

"Run, kid!" But he had nowhere to go. We were in the middle of nowhere, with no cover, nothing to hide behind or take shelter in.

The creature sprang, its impossible limbs launching it a good ten feet in the air. Esteban waited until the very last second, then dove out of the way, rolling to his feet as the thing crashed down where he'd been just seconds before.

Whatever was left of Paulito in there, it obviously remembered the grudge against his cousin, because the monster kept focused on the kid like I wasn't even there. As stealthily as I could, I tried to circle closer, intending to reclaim the fallen machete and join in on the fight. Turns out, I wouldn't need to.

The thing swiped at Esteban with the thin, claw-tipped fingers, and screeched as they met spell-blessed metal. The Way was wickedly sharp and layered with so much magic, it sliced through shell and bone like it was butter.

The kid was fast, as fast as I was really, and that was what saved him. The creature was ungainly, unbalanced, and it cornered like a brick. Estéban darted under its reach, slicing at where hamstrings should be, and the thing bellowed in pain, dropping to its…knees? On all fours, it looked more pathetic than dangerous, but it tried to lunge at the kid again as he came around in front of it.

Estéban only stepped back a foot or so, removing him safely from the range of the thing's slavering jaws. *"Vaya con Dios, primo."* And the katana came down, a perfect strike. The gruesome head bounced once on the flattened grass, and the huge body slowly toppled over to land on its side. A pool of dark fluid slowly formed under the severed neck.

"Yessssss……!" We both whirled at the voice, turning to find Reina still standing there. I'd totally forgotten about her. "Yes! It is done!"

The ground beneath our feet gave a sudden lurch, and a crack opened up in the earth, splitting the clearing right down the center. All I could do was try to keep my feet as the quake vibrated down to the very core of the mountain we stood on. It went on forever, it seemed, and when things were finally still, Estéban and Reina stood on one side of a six-foot-wide crevasse, and I stood on the other.

Estéban, still with my sword in his hand,

turned to face the woman. "What have you done?"

The dark woman threw her head back and laughed, a joyous carefree sound. "Oh, I did nothing. You did it, little champion. It was all you. *Gracias*." And with one negligent wave of her hand, an unseen force hit Estéban hard enough to throw him a dozen yards, and when he landed, he didn't move again.

"Kid!" I started to run forward, only to find myself on the crumbling edge of the opening in the earth. In the dark, it was impossible to tell how deep it was, and even with a running start, I wasn't sure I could clear it.

"Be careful, soul-bearer." Reina sauntered forward, her hips swaying artfully as she approached. "After all of this, I would hate to have to fish you out of a hole in the ground." She peered over into the chasm, shaking her head in obvious amusement.

The souls in my back stilled, suddenly, the first time since this whole thing started that I hadn't felt them creating a riot under my skin. I felt them watching her warily, like rabbits under a hawk's shadow. "Who are you?"

She chuckled, shrugging her bare shoulders. "Reina will serve our purposes, I suppose. It means 'queen' in their language, did you know? Though how you all keep such things sorted in your tiny brains, I will never understand."

"It's you." I knew it, even as the words escaped me. "You're not working for the first...you *are* the first."

She smiled coquettishly, shrugging again. "It is one way I am known, yes. Though there are some that would argue whether or not I am *the* first, or simply *a* first." Her smile took on a dark gleam, and she tilted her head, eyeing me up and down. "Some like your dear friend, The Architect."

A chill ran down my back, and I was suddenly very aware of Axel's spell. I'd only heard him called The Architect one other time, and I still didn't know why. "I don't know what you mean."

Reina snorted her disgust. "You reek of The Architect. Do you think I cannot smell it on you, the stench? He sent you, did he not? You can return to him and tell him that you failed. I walk the earth once again, free."

The spellstones had gone dark, I realized. The moon was just barely peeping over the trees, not quite full, and the light we stood in was white, not green. "The ancient priests…they didn't defeat a great evil here."

"No. Oh, they tried, valiant little things. But all they were able to do was confine me here, temporarily."

"A thousand years or so is an odd definition of temporary." One step at a time, I started making my way along the edge of the crevasse. If I couldn't go over it, I'd have to go around it. I had to get to Estéban.

"For your short-lived kind, yes, I suppose it is." She strolled along with me, like we were taking a flirtatious jaunt through the woods on a moonlit night. "In recent decades, though, the bindings started to weaken. I was able to project my image out, a little farther every year. Trying to make contact, you see."

She paused, looking down, and I realized she'd come upon what was left of Paulito. "He was so easy to manipulate. So much hate and envy." Nonchalantly, she nudged the massive body with one foot, toppling it over into the gaping hole in the ground. "I told him what he wanted to hear, and he brought me what I needed to break the bonds."

"Blood."

"Death." Her eyes flashed red for the first time, lighting up the night for a heartbeat. "A human death, to be specific. I knew, if I could get both of them here, that one of them would die. It didn't matter which one." The glare in her eyes died down, and she smiled at me again. "I was not counting on you, though. The soul-bearer. Even here, in my prison, they whispered of you."

"Yeah, people tend to do that." I stepped on something that wasn't rock, or grass, and it moved slightly under my boot. Glancing down, I realized that I'd found Estéban's machete, forgotten in all the chaos. "So, uh, what's the plan now? You're loose. You've got a couple thousand years of movies and pop culture to catch up on. What's a single demon do for a night on the town? Disneyworld?" I ran my mouth, because it's what I do best, and slowly tried to work my toe under the hilt of the machete without her noticing.

She laughed softly, and I was glad that I could entertain the nice lady demon. "You talk a lot. I mean, you all do, but you more than most."

"It's a gift."

"And you think that if I reveal my plan to you that you will be able to stop me in some way? Or perhaps take the information to The Architect in exchange for some reward?" She shook her head, her dark hair falling around her face. "Foolish. First of all, The Architect knows very well what my plan is. My confinement merely postponed it, it did not change it. Second, I could tell you every single thing I'm planning, and it wouldn't make a bit of difference. The end result is inevitable."

"That's some major self-confidence there."

"I am eternal. You are less than half a grain of sand in an infinite hourglass."

"Nice imagery. Almost modern."

"I try." She tilted her head to the side. "And as amusing as this is – what do you really think you're going to do with that blade, anyway? – I find that I am anxious to be away from this place sooner rather than later. So we must discuss the multitude of souls that you are carrying with you."

Well crap. Since she'd seen it anyway, I did a little kick with my foot to flip the machete up into my hand. Looked pretty slick, and there wasn't a single person here to appreciate it. Story of my life.

I felt better with a blade in my hand, even if it wasn't mine. Still had no idea what I was going to do with it, though. I didn't think taking on the queen bitch over there was going to be as simple as sticking the pointy end of a sword between her ribs.

"The souls are not up for discussion. They're mine." My shoulders grew warm at that, a feeling of approval radiating out from the tattoos.

"They're a commodity. They can be bought and sold, like anything. And I am willing to buy them from you."

My skin rippled, the souls expressing their distress at that thought. "What's the going rate for a soul these days?" Not that I was actually going to take her up on it, I just had to buy some time until I figured out what my next course of action was.

"For these? Oh…I'd say a life would be sufficient. One pure, untainted life, in exchange for two hundred and seventy-five souls."

"My life?" I had to laugh at that. "Listen, lady, I don't know who told you I was pure and untainted, but they told you some vicious lies."

Reina grinned. "Who said I was speaking of you?" Her head turned, ever so slightly, and one hand stretched out toward a dark form on the ground, one I'd been trying very hard not to think about. *Estéban.* "He has a valiant heart. I can feel your touch on his soul."

No... "Leave him out of this."

She raised a brow at me. "What is it worth to you? The advantage is all yours here, you must realize. You get his life, safe and sound. You rid yourself of your cumbersome burden. You free yourself of the pursuit that you must know is coming. You can just...walk away. The alternative is that someone – myself, perhaps, or maybe your dear Architect – will rip that power out of you, and leave you a smoking husk on the ground. The souls will still be gone, and you will have gained nothing."

"When you put it like that, you make it seem like there's no choice." I couldn't see well enough to know if Estéban was still breathing. Reina could be jerking my chain all along. But if there was a chance... I couldn't let the kid die. I'm sure Reina knew that. That was the point, after all.

"No one would blame you, soul-bearer. Under the circumstances, you are taking the only option you have available."

She was right, to a point. Given the choice to let Estéban die, or give up the souls, yeah, there was only one acceptable result. However, there was a third option she hadn't even considered. Hell, I shouldn't be considering it. "You forget one thing."

"Oh? What's that?"

"I could just take these two hundred and seventy-five souls' worth of power, and I could blast

your sorry ass back to Hell where you belong." I
could do it. I'd burned up one of the souls before to
save my own neck. Surely this much mojo behind a
blow like that would be enough to give even a demon
as old as this one pause.

Her eyes narrowed, and for the first time, the
pleasant smile dropped completely. "You would dare
that? They will die, you realize. Every human who
gave their soul over to you for safe keeping will cease
to be at that moment. Two hundred and seventy-five
lives sacrificed to save one boy? Is that really what
you want?"

Of course it wasn't what I wanted. In my
perfect world, we were all going to walk out of this
alive, but I didn't always get what I wanted. It was a
bluff. I just had to hope I could be convincing
enough, for long enough.

I'd forgotten to take into account the souls
themselves. They were aware back there, after a
fashion. I could feel them perk up the moment I
suggested burning them up, using them to banish the
Reina-demon. I braced for the pain, preparing to
have my muscles knotted into uselessness, but it
never came.

Instead, the tingling sensation, the ever-
present zing that told me they were there, started to
spread. The tattoos spread up the back of my neck,
into my hair, and down my arms, until I could see
them shining white in the darkness as they coiled
around my wrists, like frost on glass as they covered
my hands. Under my jeans, it was the same, the
feeling of hot-cold threads tracing designs on my
skin, all the way down to the soles of my feet. The
dark clearing lit up like someone had turned on a
floodlight, and all of it came from me, blazing in the

night.

I might be bluffing, but the souls were not. They made it perfectly clear that they had chosen, and I could feel a deep satisfaction from them, as if deciding their own purpose had been all they wanted all along.

"I don't know that what I want is going to matter very much." They closed over my eyelids last, and I blinked out of reflex at the brightness. When I opened them again, I was again spell-sighted, the dim stars above us now excruciating in their clarity. Each and every blade of grass that swayed in that clearing drew my attention. The odors of old and new magic, of sulfur and cloves and rotting, decaying flesh threatened to choke me, and I could feel bits of it clinging to the inside of my lungs.

It was like that first night, the night the souls had blasted their way into me. I was drunk on it, and even in the face of certain doom for myself and for my multitude of passengers, I wanted to laugh with a giddy sense of joy. This was being alive.

Reina hissed in displeasure, I'm sure at the light, and my eyes landed on her next. It was…not what I'd expected.

I'd seen one once before, and the sight had nearly ripped my sanity out of my skull. To look upon it is both indescribably beautiful, and so terrifying that a person should run screaming and never stop. The last time, I'd groveled with my face on the ground, and considered myself pretty damn brave for the effort.

This time…it wasn't the same. Reina was an angel. Or maybe had been, at one time. Under the human guise she donned, her true form was wreathed in hues of gold that artists haven't even invented yet.

Gold and white and silver, just like the old crazy homeless guy in L.A., Felix. But where his had been a pure light, agonizing in its perfection, hers bled into browns, reds, blacks at the very edges. Where his had seemed to rise right into the sky, hers was grounded firmly to earth, leeching into the soil below our feet, tainting all that she touched. Her, I could look upon without pain, without feeling like my brain was about to go trickling out my ears.

And I realized, juiced up like I was, that I wasn't the least bit afraid of her. "You should go now. They really want to fry your sorry ass, and I don't know that I can stop them."

The area that should be her face colored in mottled shades of blood red and sickening orange. "Do you think you can do me harm, worm?"

"I'm willing to give it a shot. And even if I'm wrong, that'll be two hundred and seventy-five souls that you'll never see. Pretty sure sacrificing themselves will put them back on the big G's good list. They won't be headed down."

She wavered, weighing the odds, and in the end I was pretty sure it was greed, not fear, that won out. "This is not over, soul-bearer. We will see each other again." In less than an eyeblink, she vanished, leaving behind the stench of sulfur.

I took a deep breath, closing my eyes, but it didn't help. I could still see the blood pulsing in my eyelids, taste the salt on the air from the ocean so far out of sight. "When you're ready, guys. I think we made our point."

The souls receded slowly, but finally every iridescent tattoo was back under my shirt where it belonged, and I could open my eyes to find only the darkness of a moonlit forest night. "Estéban…"

It took me a bit to find a place where the chasm narrowed so that I could cross it, and then longer to make my way back to my protégé, still just a dark heap in the grass where he'd landed.

His skin was warm when I touched him, which was my first relief, and then I found a pulse, slow but steady in his neck. "Thank you," I whispered, and I couldn't even say for sure who I was grateful to.

I know you're not supposed to move people, in case of more injuries, but I had to roll him over onto his back to try and get a better look. He had an egg-sized lump on his skull, and there was dried blood on a small stone next to him. Just bad luck in the landing. "Kid. C'mon, kid, you gotta open those eyes." I patted his cheek gently, all the while the words 'traumatic brain injury' running through my head.

Finally, his eyelids twitched, then fluttered open, though he was having a hard time focusing on me. "Jesse?"

"Yeah, kid." I couldn't help it, a small laugh escaped, probably not appropriate to the situation at all. "Christ, kid. Helluva time you picked for a nap."

"I'll do better next time." His eyes darted this way and that, trying to see past me. "Where is she? Reina, where....?"

"She's gone. Gone back to wherever bad things go when they're not out being evil."

"Did you kill her?"

"No. Missed my chance."

"We have to tell Mamá, we have to…" He made the mistake of trying to sit up before I could stop him, and almost passed out again.

"Easy there, you're in no shape yet to go

traipsing around."

His face was pale, I could see that even in the darkness. "How do we get home?"

"Well, kid, it's like this." Settling into a more comfortable position, I very carefully shifted him so that his head was pillowed on my thigh. "I'm gonna sit here and keep you awake all night, because of the concussion I know you have. And when the sun comes up in the morning, all bright and shiny, your mom is going to send out the cavalry to come find us. And then we'll go home."

"Can't do that," he mumbled, his words slurring just slightly. "Not safe here, the old magic."

"You let me worry about that. Just stay with me, okay kid? Why don't you recite your multiplication tables, to start. And then maybe we'll talk about baseball stats or something."

He blinked at me, uncomprehending, so I prompted him with the first one. "One times one is…?"

"One. *Uno*."

"Ooh, tricky hm? Gonna go for both languages? Okay, smart ass, two times two."

"Four. *Cuatro*."

"Three times three."

"Nine. *Nueve*."

18

Dawn came with Estéban's head still resting in my lap. He'd drifted into a normal sleep at some point, and so long as he still protested when I pinched his arm, I let him have it. If nothing else, it gave me time to think. There was a lot I had to sort out, after all of this.

Our clothes were damp with dew by the time I heard an engine in the distance, and fifteen minutes later, Sveta came bursting through the trees at the edge of the clearing, gun in one hand, and her bared shaska blade in the other.

"Time to wake up kid, the cavalry's here."

"Mmph." Still, Estéban blinked his eyes open slowly, and they looked a little better than they had last night.

"Sveta! We're here!" I waved my hand until she located us. "Watch out for the big hole in the ground!"

Between the two of us, we managed to get Estéban back to the vehicles, Terrence waiting in the second pickup truck. I loaded Miguel's bike up into the back of the other, and we caravanned back up to the Perez compound.

As far as injuries went, we were all going to be okay. The kid was going to be on light duty for a week or so until his brain unscrambled, but I think that was the only thing that kept Sveta from kicking his ass. She was a little pissed about getting clocked in the dome.

Carlotta was back on her feet, though she'd declared herself merely a supervisor as the kid-pack assembled breakfast with their usual chaotic efficiency. She grabbed my hand as I walked past, pressing a kiss to my knuckles before releasing me. Her way of saying thanks. I gave her a small smile, then went to collapse. I was too old for all-nighters.

In the boys' room, I carefully placed The Way back in the case where it belonged, and laid the machete on Estéban's bunk. They'd ensconced him in his mother's bed, being the biggest and most comfy, with Rosaline keeping careful watch on him for the concussion. Sinking onto my own low cot, I rested my head in my hands for a long time, only now allowing the shakes to come.

Eventually, I laid down and slept, the rest of the truly exhausted. No dreams came, no visions of Gretchen Keene toppling to her death, or of a large arena with a mysterious figure at the other end. Just darkness, quiet and peaceful. When I woke, I started packing up my gear.

"You cannot leave yet! We have not yet figured out how to remove the souls!" Carlotta was understandably against the plan.

"I didn't intend to live here forever, Carlotta. You've seen enough of it now, you have a good place to keep working from. I'm going home to my wife and my children." That was one thing I'd decided during my long vigil. The world was going to Hell, in a fairly literal sense. I couldn't stop that, but I *could* go be with my wife while she gave birth to my second child. I could play with my daughter, and teach her katas and how to make the world's best PB&J sandwich. I was pretty sure I didn't have a lot of time left, but I could choose how I would spend it.

Now that I'd declared what I was thinking of as "the nuclear option", I didn't think the demons would be coming after me so overtly. They wanted the souls intact more than they wanted me dead. It would buy me some time, buy Carlotta and Terrence more time to figure out a solution.

Because of course, Terrence was staying in Mexico. No one was surprised when he made his gruff declaration, but Estéban and I hid our grins. Seriously, old people in love are adorable.

Carlotta made a few token protests. "Who is going to protect Jesse, then? Sveta cannot do it alone."

"I am." Every person in the room turned and blinked at Estéban, but he held his chin up and didn't flinch at all. "I've thought about this a lot. Mamá..." He leaned over to take her hands. "I'm not sure that I can be a champion, not like Papa and Joaquin and Miguel. I'm not sure... I'm not sure that I believe what they believed, about all of this."

Carlotta nodded slowly, simply waiting for him to go on.

"But what I do believe is that Jesse is a good man, and that he fights for the right things. I think I can better serve at his right hand, than by risking my life for people who may or may not deserve it."

I raised a brow at him. "Practiced that in the mirror, did you?"

The kid blushed, but chuckled. "Like twenty times."

His mother just looked at him, reaching out to smooth a stray lock of hair off his forehead. Her fingers traced his jaw, rough from not shaving for a few days, like the rest of us, and then she straightened the collar of his T-shirt even though he didn't need it. "Oh, *mi hijo*." She turned to look at me. "Do you agree? Do you think that my son can protect you?"

I didn't hesitate. "Absolutely. There's no one else I'd trust as much." The kid flashed me a beaming grin that made him look every bit as young as he was, and I just gave him a nod. I meant every word. If it was all going to come to an end, there were very few people in the world I'd rather have with me.

"Señor Zelenko will not like this…" Carlotta tried again, and I just shook my head.

"I'll handle Ivan. Don't you worry about him." Sveta snorted at my statement, but when I gave her a challenging look, she just raised her hands in acquiescence. "All right, you two. Pack it up. We're heading home as soon as we can get a plane."

As soon as we could get a plane turned out to be two days later. Despite the lack of body, the Perez clan gave Paulito a suitable funeral, and neither Estéban nor myself felt like telling them exactly how he died.

I cornered the kid a couple times, just to see how he was handling it. I mean, he *had* killed his own cousin, even if that thing hadn't really been Paulito anymore.

Estéban paused in making repairs to the goat fence, eyeing his hands for a moment. "That monster was not my cousin. The transformations are irreversible, he could not have been saved. It was a mercy killing."

"You sure you're okay?"

"Do I have a choice?"

Our exit from the Perez home was like our departure from my house, only magnified by like a thousand. Every member of the clan had to come say farewell to their departing hero, and that process in and of itself took nearly an hour. Paulito's mother pressed tearful kisses to his cheeks, and blessed him in the name of every saint I'd ever heard of, and he promised to pray for Paulito's soul which made her weep harder. All through it, the kid's eyes stayed dry, his stance firm. Even when Carlotta held him close and whispered quietly to him, he only hugged her in return then waved a smiling goodbye to his family.

Homecoming was sweet, but I think my family was happier to see Estéban than they were to see me. Mira fussed over the still-visible lump on his head, and Anna latched onto her adopted big brother and refused to let go for at least the first hour I was home. I could see that Estéban was just as happy to be back home, and despite all he'd been through, there was something lighter about him than when we'd left.

The first thing I asked of him and Sveta, though, got some pushback.

"Did *you* get hit in the head?" Sveta glared at me suspiciously.

Esteban nodded his agreement. "This is a bad idea. Those wards are strong, there's no reason to dismantle them."

"I have my reasons. Just do it. And then I'm going to introduce you to someone we're going to be seeing a lot of, I think."

Reluctance in every gesture, the pair of them set about taking apart Terrence's carefully constructed wards around my back yard. Standing out by my water garden, I felt when the last of them snapped, the ever-present tingle under my skin fading away into nothing. I took a deep breath and rolled my shoulders, and even the souls in my back felt a bit more relieved to not have that constant pressure on them.

"All right. I want the two of you to stand back on the patio, and for the love of everything, do *not* say anything. Especially not your names, understand?" Their expressions said they didn't, but they obeyed, watching me warily.

I waited until they were standing back by the sliding glass door, then turned to face out into the yard. "Axel." I got no response, at first, at least none that was visible. But my eyes weren't my only sense, and the hint of sulfur teased my nose. "I know you're here. Come out. I want to introduce you to some folks."

A few more moments passed before the tall figure emerged from behind a sapling tree that shouldn't have been big enough to hide a pencil. I heard Sveta's breath catch behind me, and held up a hand. "It's all right. He's fine."

Axel raised a pierced brow at me, glancing over my shoulder to look at the pair on the patio. He hooked his thumbs in his belt loops, looking for all the world like a slouching, petulant teenager. "Didn't know you were going to out me like this."

Estéban immediately disobeyed my prohibition against speaking. "I know you. I've seen you here before."

The demon tilted his head and smirked faintly. "Ah yes, the student. Now I remember."

"It was time for them to truly meet you." At the sound of my voice, Axel's attention swiveled back to me. "Their lives are on the line, right next to mine now. They needed to know what we were dealing with."

"And are we? Dealing, I mean?" Axel's eyes flashed red, finally betraying his irritation. "Do you have any idea what you have *done*, Jesse?"

"Which part? The part where we broke a really pissed off fallen angel out of her prison, or the part where I threatened to detonate the little tac nuke you've got riding around in my skin?"

He threw up his hands. "You have no idea the ramifications of these events. The power balances that have been tipped, the moves that have to be scrapped now and rethought…"

"Of course I don't." That made him pause, and he tilted his head at me. "You've been very careful to keep your little intrigues to yourself. Well, this is me, telling you that it ends now."

The man-demon narrowed his eyes at me. "What do you mean?"

"I mean that you're gonna pull up a chair, right here on this patio, and you're gonna lay it all out for me. No deals, no bargains, just information. You're going to tell me what this little war is about that you've got brewing. You're going to tell me who Reina is and why she's so pissed at you. And you're going to tell me how the hell you intend to get me out of this shit that I never signed up for."

Axel blinked at me like I'd slapped him in the face. "I can't just…"

"You can. And you will. I'm done playing."

His eyes darted to our audience and back to me again, looking uncertain for the first time since I'd known him. "And you want them to hear all of this."

I nodded. "They need the chance to walk away. The one I didn't get."

"We're not—"

"I would never—"

Of course that set both Sveta and Estéban to talking over each other, despite the fact that they'd been told not to speak. "Quiet, both of you. Grab some chairs. I think we're going to be here a while."

The kid obediently grabbed a few plastic chairs, dragging them around our patio table, and I went and took a seat, kicking one out in invitation to Axel. After a moment of eyeing it like it was a striking snake, he came and sat as well, stretching his long legs out. "It will have to be the Cliff's Notes version, or we'll be here all night."

"Hey, we got nowhere to go. Start at the beginning."

He was right. Even with the abridged version, we were out on the patio most of the night. Mira brought us drinks and sandwiches at one point, frowning intently at the demon on her deck even as she slid a glass of lemonade in front of him. Axel managed to smile politely and thank her, even if he didn't touch the beverage at all.

Hours of chatting boiled down to a few basic facts. There were two factions in Hell, which was something I pretty much knew already. To say they didn't get along was putting it mildly. You had the one side, represented (or lead? Axel managed to avoid that question) by Axel and those allied with him. And then we had the other side, who until a few days ago had been without their leader. Of course, it was Reina, whatever her real name was. Their war had been put on hold a thousand years ago when she got put on ice, but as the spells around her weakened, the demons had started to rebuild their ranks, once again choosing sides.

The good demons – and wasn't that an oxymoron? – believed that it was their duty to test the souls of the world, to make deals, to follow the rules as laid out. It was a job, a purpose, and they took it very seriously.

"But why? I mean, what are you supposed to get out of it?"

Axel shrugged, looking at his hands as they were clasped in his lap. He'd spent a lot of the night like that, eyes downturned, lacking all of the bravado and charm I was used to from him. "Maybe...maybe they think that if they do their jobs well enough that they'll be allowed into heaven someday." He didn't even choke on the word. I was a bit proud of him.

"Demons want to go to heaven? Even the angels that fell?"

His chuckle was bitter. "You will never find so devout a creature as a fallen angel, Jesse. They're the ones who know what they're missing."

The other group, what I mentally tagged as the rebels, didn't give two figs about the rules, or about what duty they may have been assigned, once upon a time. They were tired of being stuck in Hell and they didn't see why they couldn't just come up and take the world for their own. They viewed themselves as superior to the human race, short-lived, weak things that we were. We were a fuel source to them, nothing more.

"But, if there are angels, why are they not fighting the demons?" Estéban had given up remaining silent hours ago, but at least he hadn't said his name. Even as cooperative as the demon was being, I knew Axel was mentally cataloging everything he could, and if I could keep their names from him, it would be a start.

I raised my hand before Axel could respond. "I actually know the answer to this one. I talked to one, once." That got all their attention. "He said that it was not their war, that Hell would have to take care of their own."

"That's it?" Estéban blinked at me in disbelief.

I shook my head. "I asked him why God hadn't sent help, because there were humans down here dying over this mess. He just said 'what makes you think He didn't?'"

Axel snorted softly. "Not surprising. It's always someone else's problem, where most of them are concerned."

"So what happens next? Now that the queen bitch is loose?"

Axel sighed, and I realized that he looked weary. I didn't even know he could. "I honestly don't know. I was arrogant enough to think I had a few years at least before I would have to deal with her. Now... Well, I know a few strikes she'll make first, to weaken me and to strengthen herself." He chuckled, suddenly. "Do you know how odd is it so think of her as 'her'? It's not like we actually have gender, not like your kind."

I couldn't help it, I had to smirk a little. "You telling me that's not how little demons come into being? When a mommy demon and a daddy demon like each other very much..."

"Ew." He actually kicked my shin, half-heartedly. "You say such disgusting things sometimes. Why do I talk to you?"

"Because I'm just so damned awesome." I stretched my arms and laced my fingers behind my head with a smug grin.

We parted ways soon after that, the human factor needing to make up on their sleep, and the demon participant needing to...well, go be demon-y.

I lay in bed that night, my very pregnant wife

curled up against my chest, and I dreamed of the tunnel and the figure at the far end of the arena. This time, every time he was there, I felt an immense sense of relief. The times the hard packed field remained empty, dread seeped into my very core, and Mira finally woke me to tell me I was mumbling in my sleep. That was new.

Axel showed himself more often after that. Sometimes, it was just to walk past the window of It as I worked, catching my eye to let me know that he was in the area. Sometimes, he showed up just to play a game of chess with me in the back yard. My two shadows would always be nearby, keeping an eye on the demon, but we'd agreed to let him come and go as he pleased for now. If Reina made an appearance, Axel was the only one likely to be strong enough to put her in her place.

In the meantime, the world was going to shit. Just watching the news told me that much. It had been going on for a couple years now, but with Reina on the loose, things got worse. There were earthquakes where there'd never been any before. Typhoons and hurricanes. There were random shootings in pretty much every city you could name, even riots on a few occasions. Dictatorships were under siege in unstable countries, and to hear the talking heads tell it, everybody's finger was on the button. I hated to say it, but I kinda knew how they felt.

I was a tiny little country in the big demon world, but I'd gotten my hands on a nuke, and I was fully capable of using it. They wouldn't come for me, because they couldn't be sure I wouldn't do it, and I couldn't actually use it without ending two hundred and seventy-five people who had absolutely no idea what was going on with their souls. We were at the ultimate stalemate.

I got way less flak from Ivan than I'd expected. I could tell, when we talked on the phone, that he wasn't happy with my decision to replace Terrence with a half-trained kid, but in keeping with Ivan's plan to have me as his replacement, he didn't contradict me.

"You are to be having good judgement, Dawson. I must be believing this is a good thing." Ivan sounded tired, more often than not, lately. It was starting to worry me. I'd never heard him be anything but larger than life, as equally passionate in his laughter as he was in his anger. Now, he sounded…old.

Carlotta and Terrence kept in regular touch, but even I could tell that they weren't getting anywhere. What we needed was some kind of vessel to house the souls. They could go to a demon, which wasn't going to happen, or a human – and I wouldn't have done that to my worst enemy – which left us right where we were, sitting on our hands doing nothing. It was slowly driving me nuts.

I channeled that energy as best I could into work, and into training Estéban. Even Sveta got in on the action, showing off her own unique fighting style and settling in as part of a team rather than a lone wolf type. Somewhere along the way, she and Estéban had reached some accord about him thumping her in the head, but he still tended to flinch a little when one of her strikes would come his way during sparring. She'd just grin slyly, and I knew one day she wasn't going to pull her punch, and it'd be on him if he couldn't block it.

We'd been home for nearly a month when I

got an unexpected visitor. I was in the yard, tending to my bonsai trees (the poor things had been sorely neglected), when the souls on my back gave a warning ripple that usually heralded Axel's arrival. But, when I looked up, there was no sign of the punk-haired demon.

The birds had gone silent, however, and inside the house, I heard my daughter's Mastiff start raising all kinds of hell. Chunk could sense it, too. "Hello...?" My mind raced, weighing the idea of using a garden rake as a weapon versus the odds that I could actually move fast enough to reach the house and my sword.

Just when I was about to bolt for the door, the leaves rustled in the tree above me, and a little moon-eyed face poked out. "Hello, James Dawson!" The scrappy little demon gave me a fanged grin, hairy ears quivering with excitement.

"Well, hey there. Didn't think I'd be seeing you again." I leaned on the rake, craning my neck to look up at it. "You coming to spy on me for your master?"

The thing sneered. "Forgets about me. Bigger game now, doesn't need me. And I have two names! Better than worm, so I left."

"Oh! Well...good for you." I know it was a bad idea to engage, but the little guy amused me, okay? "What are you doing here?"

"Come to see about more names! Things to trade, secrets to know." It nodded its head hard enough that it almost overbalanced and pitched off the branch. Only its vicious looking claws saved it.

"I don't really think I need to trade for anything today, but...thanks for thinking of me?" What do you say to that?

The demon's ears wilted, and he sighed. "Even James Dawson does not need me."

Cripes, it just looked so dejected. "Well, no, I just don't need you right *now*. I might need you later. Maybe."

"Say true?" It perked up a little, eyes round with hope. It'd be almost cute if it wasn't so into eating faces.

"Well, sure, maybe." I had an idea. A no good, very bad, possibly dangerous idea. "How would you like to just work for me?"

The demon gave me a suspicious look. "Doing whats?"

"Just what you always do. Sneak around, be forgotten, see what you can hear that others miss. Just…let me know what the other demons are talking about."

The thing wrinkled up its nose as it tried to parse that. "And James Dawson would pay? With names or other niceness?"

"We'll figure it out on a case by case basis. I wouldn't want you to short change yourself if you got something truly big in the future, right? Big secrets get bigger niceness." God, I couldn't believe what was coming out of my mouth. "But we'll start with a retainer. Do you know what a retainer is?"

It shook its head. "No. Whats?"

"It's like a very small payment, in advance. Just so that you know you work for me."

"And no secrets? Just…niceness?"

"Yup. Just so we both know I'm your boss."

The thing slid down the tree trunk to a lower branch, crouching just above my head. "What gives?"

"I'll give *you* a name. I'll give you a name

that can be yours, for your very own. And it's a name you don't *have* to answer to. I can say it, and if you don't want to come, you're not forced to. You can make your own decisions."

The huge eyes blinked at me once, twice, three times. "A name...for me? A choice for me?"

"Sure, why not?"

The demon settled on the tree branch, kicking its clawed feet in the air as it pondered that. Finally, it nodded. "James Dawson will give me a name. On retainer."

I bit back a chuckle, and did my best to nod solemnly. "All right then. I think you'll be...Henry. You like that?"

The thing's face split into a wide, toothy grin. "Yes! I am Henry, for James Dawson. We have a deal."

"All right, Henry, go on now. I'll see you soon, okay? After you've had a chance to listen and learn more secrets."

It didn't even wave at me, it just poofed into a cloud of black mist that dissipated on the breeze.

This may or may not work, but maybe now I could get some info that wasn't filtered through Axel. Maybe now, I could start to plan my own moves.

ALSO FROM K.A. STEWART:

Peacemaker

AN ARCANE WEST NOVEL

AVAILABLE NOW FROM INTERMIX!

Chapter 1

The bead of sweat rolled down Caleb's nose to hang there, quivering, before it fell to join its brothers in the fabric of his denim shirt. It was a testament to the length of his journey that he hadn't even bothered to mop his face in the last hour. Beneath the low brim of his hat, he squinted toward the horizon, his gaze following the seemingly endless chain of telegraph poles as they disappeared against the haze of the distant mountains .

"Are we lost?"

Caleb sighed, leaning on the pommel of his saddle. "They said follow the telegraph wires. So we are."

"This isn't a road, you know. This is barely a path. Maybe the poles are a mirage, leading us to our doom."

Caleb turned to look at his companion, pillowed on Caleb's own coat on the rear of the transport. "We're optimistic today, aren't we?"

The odd creature sniffed, its quivering nose a clear expression of irritation. "You try riding back here while this thing goes to pieces. See how optimistic you are." The rabbit-like animal gave a toss of its head, nearly gouging the man with its spiny antlers.

"Hey, watch where you swing those things." The jackalope just rolled its deep brown eyes and sulked. "And it's not really a comfortable ride up here either."

Somewhere in the last fifty miles, the

transport had developed some kind of hitch in its hindquarters, resulting in a nasty grinding noise and lurching stride. Caleb wasn't an arcanosmith, but if he had to guess, he'd say the bearings had frozen up. No surprise, with the constant dust and heat they'd been suffering for the last two months.

"Hopefully, they'll have a smith at the next stop, and we'll get it repaired." If the next town didn't have an arcanosmith, they'd be stuck for at least a month until one could be sent on the stage from Kansas City. That was going to put Caleb seriously behind on his circuit.

The jackalope grumbled under its breath as Caleb kicked the transport back into a trot. The normal wheeze and sigh of the mechanical construct was marred ruined by the grinding in the back end, and every other step was enough to painfully jar his teeth together. If they couldn't get it fixed, he was going to shoot it himself.

They'd ridden for another twenty minutes before the furry passenger remarked casually, "I think I see a crack in the casing."

"What?!" Caleb nearly knocked the jackalope off its perch, turning in the saddle to examine the glowing blue casing at the transport's flank.

The animal scrabbled frantically with its claws to remain aboard. "Damn, Caleb!"

The casing was pristine, not a single flaw marring the transparent surface. Beneath it, the blue arcane energy whirled serenely with no sign of having found an escape route. Caleb's heart pounded in his ears as he fought to calm himself. "That wasn't funny, Ernst!"

"Well, it was before you tried to knock me off the transport." Ernst smoothed his brown fur, twitching his long ears to express his displeasure.

"You do that again, and I'll skin you for a hat."

"You have no sense of humor, you know that?"

"So I've been told." The man turned to face forward again. The dusty track stretched out before them, barely visible in the tall prairie grass. Only the never-ending line of telegraph poles marked where the road might be. "It can't be much farther. We ride any more west, we'll wind up in Indian territory." The Rocky Mountain range had been claimed as the land of final retreat by many tribes in recent years, leaving a nearly impassable wall across the budding U.S. frontier. Only the desperate and the foolhardy ventured close to that wilderness these days. *Which one are you, Caleb?*

"You know, it's possible that they gave you bad directions." Ernst settled himself in his little coat nest again. "They didn't seem to warm up to you."

Caleb didn't respond, only kicking the transport into motion yet again. The last town had seemed rather cold, welcome-wise. As had the one before it. If this was how the entire circuit was going to be . . . He was sorely tempted to turn and ride back east, if it wouldn't mean career suicide. *What little career I have left.*

His "career" currently consisted of a lonely, miserable circuit in the wilds of the frontier. Over the course of the next year, he'd range from the southern-most reach of the U.S., skirting the still-contested Texas-Mexico border, all the way to the north and Canada. He would mark a trail straight down the eastern slope of the Rocky Mountains, the very edges of what was considered the borderlands, and cover everything between there and Kansas City. Such was the life of an itinerate lawman.

The mountains to the west never seemed to get any closer no matter how long they rode. The behemoths merely sat there, watching over the grassland from a bank of purple mist. Small clouds played ring-the-rosie around the peaks, teasing with a promise of rain that never came. The lack of moisture showed in the prairie grass, which had long ago gone brown and brittle in the summer heat.

Caleb finally broke down and wiped at his face and neck with a bandana, fanning himself with the wide brim of his hat. It brought middling relief at best.

"Can't you just put the heat elsewhere? I'm turning into stew back here."

The man eyed the dry prairie and shuddered. Yes, he could have taken the heat around them, shifted it elsewhere. But anywhere he put it would spark a fire, and in a dry environment like this… "Better stew than turned to charcoal."

"Says you. You're not wearing fur." The antlers jabbed Caleb in the back again, and he grimaced.

"Enough! I've got four days of stubble on my face, five gallons of sweat in my shirt and not an ounce of water in my body, and my ass feels like someone's been at it with a carpet rod. If you don't like fur, shift form. Not another word out of you until we hit town." Immediately, Caleb felt bad for snapping, and his shoulders sagged. They were both hot and increasingly miserable, but that was no reason to bite the poor creature's head off. "Sorry, Ernst."

The jackalope gave a peculiar little purr,

indicating that there were no hard feelings. "Wake me when we get there."

About an hour later, "there" appeared suddenly out of the tall grass like a jack-in-the-box. It was a decent- sized town, bigger than the last two they'd visited, and Caleb stopped the transport long enough to evict Ernst and inspect the transport one last time.

Built to resemble the horses they had replaced, they had four metal legs that moved with arcane-powered gears and pistons. Though some inventors back east were experimenting with arcane powered wagons, on four wheels, the transport design made them better at irregular terrain and simply had more power. Transports were capable of great speed and, strength, and only rarely had to be recharged with arcane energy, as opposed to a horse, which had a limited range it could travel in a day, and had to be fed and watered often.

This particular model had been one of the newest available when he'd left St. Louis, a gift from his director. *A banishment present.* It was fast, to be sure, but it had been designed for paved city streets and short country strolls. The extreme conditions of the west were taking their toll on it, and quickly. The ball joints in the knees were still moving freely, but the gears in the rear workings were grinding audibly, and it was only a matter of time before it wheezed its last. Caleb simply didn't have the knowledge to repair it himself, and once it quit, they'd be on foot. In this heat, it'd be a death sentence.

Mindful of protocol, Caleb shrugged into his heavy duster and adjusted the star badge pinned over his heart with a sigh. *Wonder if they wouldn't be happier to see me without it.*

As if his familiar knew his thoughts, the jackalope mused, "We could just say no one was home and go on to the next one." The plucky creature hopped around the dusty trail a few times, stretching his furry legs.

"You know as well as I do, this thing won't make it to the next town." In spite of his misgivings, Caleb squared his shoulders and tugged his hat down over his eyes. "Come on, one last short ride, and then we can turn this heap of scrap over to someone else." He scooped Ernst up, depositing him on top of the battered trunk attached to the back of the transport, and swung himself into the saddle.

As they rattled and clanked their way into the town, Ernst peered at the high sign spanning the width of the road. "And what's the name of this place? Dusty Hollow? Dry Gulch? The Backside of Hell?"

Caleb smiled a bit to himself as they rode under the sign. "Hope."

The townsfolk stopped to watch the stranger ride into their town midst, as Caleb had known they would. He tipped his hat to those who would make eye contact, but most kept their gazes down, only daring to stare only once he'd passed them.

They rode past a small barber shop, what appeared to be a dressmaker's shop, and several nondescript structures that might have been personal dwellings. A church with a modest steeple dominated the north side of town, and a half-constructed something sat just beyond that. There was no sign of a hotel or boarding house until Caleb spied a card in the window of the tavern that said "ROOMS TO LET".

"Looks like this is our best bet, Ernst." He dismounted, stretching muscles that were cramped and complaining from the long hours in the saddle. Even after three months, he was still green enough that the long rides hurt. "Watch the transport., I'll be right back." If the jackalope grumbled about being reduced to guard duty, Caleb missed it as he stepped up on the wooden walk.

The inside of the tavern was just as hot as the outside, but the dimness was a startling change after hours under the ruthless sun. Caleb pulled his hat off, surveying the room to allow his eyes time to adjust. The tables were empty but clean, and a piano stood in one corner, carefully covered with a linen cloth against the predations of dust . On the far side, the staircase would presumably lead to the promised rooms for rent, and the bar stood to the right of the swinging doors, backed by mirrors and a wall of glass bottles of varying alcoholic content. There was even a cold box, hissing softly as the arcane power in its tubes cooled the air within. All in all, it was one of the nicer places they'd been, lately.

"Hello? Anyone here?"

An answering yell came from a doorway on the right, and it the door soon swung outward to admit one slender fellow with dark black hair and shockingly blue eyes. He grinned through his beard, drying his hands on a towel. "How kin I help ye?" The brogue was unmistakably Scottish.

"Looking about a room to rent. I saw the sign in the window."

"Oh, yessir! Rate's two dollars a week, meals not included." The dark-haired Scot came out from behind the bar, offering his hand, but his smile slipped a bit when he saw the star pinned to Caleb's coat, the six-gun on his belt. "The last Peacemaker used ta take rooms out at the Warner ranch, about ten miles south of here."

Caleb took the offered hand for a firm shake, feeling a faint tingle against his skin. If he had to guess, he'd rate the barkeep on the low end of the power scale. Nothing someone like Caleb couldn't handle. "My transport's not going to make it another ten miles, so I think I'll just stay here if that's all right. Name is Caleb Marcus." Digging his wallet out of his coat, he presented five dollars to the tavern owner. "For meals, too."

The Scott's eyes lit up at the sight of the money in advance, but there was still a caution there, a wariness that Caleb had seen in the other towns he'd visited. "Teddy MacGregor. Owner of this establishment."

"Well, tell me, Mr. MacGregor. Do you happen to have an arcanosmith in this lovely town?"

The man snorted, retreating behind the bar to put the money safely away in his cash box. "That'll be just Teddy, thank ye. And we got a smith on the west end of town that can do for most things. Otherwise, you'd have to ride out to the Warner place. Abel keeps his own arcanosmith out there."

"I'd rather shoot the thing myself than ride another mile." Caleb grinned and was relieved to see the tavern keeper return the expression, though the man's gaze kept drifting to the right side of Caleb's face. Inwardly, the Peacemaker sighed, but if the Scot wasn't going to ask, he wasn't going to bring it up.

Finally, Teddy shook himself and tossed Caleb a key attached to a large chunk of wood. "Up the stairs, last door on the left. We serve food from five to nine, and whatever you'd like to drink until midnight."

"Thank you, sir." Tipping his hat as he put it back on, Caleb stepped back out into the searing summer sun. He glanced to the west and paused to look at the mountains, suddenly looming large over the plain. When did they get so close, and why did it feel like they were watching him just as much as he watched them?

A clamor of childish voices drew his attention, and he smirked when he saw Ernst atop a convenient barrel, surrounded by curious youngsters. He could hear the jackalope purring over the din, and the children oohed and aahed obligingly.

"Enjoying yourself?" Caleb leaned against a pole, grinning at his companion. Any time he lost Ernst, he could be certain to find him in the arms of the nearest child. The furry creature just rolled his eyes in absolute ecstasy, carefully holding still to avoid jabbing anyone with his antlers, which, Caleb noted, he had blunted for safety's sake.

"Is he yours, mister?" One of the older boys, all of seven maybe, looked over at Caleb. "Is he yours, mister?"

"Well, we travel together. So, in a way, yes."

"He's so cute!" The children seemed to understand not to pick the small animal up, contenting themselves to with stroking his downy-soft fur, exclaiming over his long, supple ears.

"That's a helluva scar, mister," said another boy, sandy-haired and freckled, and he got swatted by what had to be his sister for his language.

Caleb idly fingered the smooth scar that cut down his right cheek idly. "It looks worse than it is."

One of the girls, braver than the others, went on tiptoe to examine the man's face. "Can you see out of that eye?"

Caleb chuckled and nodded. "Perfectly." Children were so innocent in their curiosity. Very few adults would have asked him about the scar, which began at his jawline and extended upward right into the iris of his eye, leaving a stark white line across the hazel.

"Abigail!" The alarm in the woman's voice was enough to make Caleb alert, scanning for any danger as the woman hurried across the street to snatch one of the little girls from the throng. "Don't you be bothering the Peacemaker now, you hear? None of you all! Git home!" The youngsters scattered like a flock of startled crows.

"They weren't bothering me, ma'am, really…" She didn't seem to hear him as she shooed the children quickly away, darting worried glances back over her shoulder. She and her daughter disappeared into the dress shop.

"Well, you're a sure conversation stopper, aren't you?" Ernst leapt to the transport's saddle in one graceful bound, his ears drooping in disappointment.

"Seems like it." The curtains twitched on the dress shop when his gaze passed over them. They were watching. "There's a smith just down the street. Let's see if we can get this contraption fixed."

Tripping the appropriate lever, he urged the transport into motion, cringing at the grind and clank in the hindquarters. It was a wonder it had made it this far.

The smithy, once discovered, was labeled simply "SMITHY", and the heat rolling off the forge made the oppressive summer day seem positively spring-like. The smith himself seemed oblivious to it, wearing a thick leather apron over his shirt as he labored over the glowing coals. Orange coals, Caleb noted, not blue. Unusual.

"Hello there!" The smith kept working with no response to Caleb's hail. "I was told you might be able to repair a transport.?"

That at least earned a grunt in answer, and after a few more moments, the smith laidy his long tongs aside and stepped away from the forge. He was older than Caleb expected, his hair already gone white, and there was no warmth in his pale eyes. "Ja. I can do, yes."

Ah, not white hair, but very pale blond then. The Swedish accent gave everything away. Caleb nodded him toward his malfunctioning machinery. "It's got some kind of hitch in the back end."

Wiping his sooty hands on a rag, the smith came out to inspect the transport, paying no mind whatsoever to Ernst perched on its back whatsoever. He made thoughtful noises as he circled the construct, bending to look along the belly workings, poking at the transparent casings in a few places.

Caleb finally broke the silence. "Can you fix it?"

"Hmm. Ja. Maybe. Bearings seized up here." He poked with a grimy finger. "Gear stripped here. No parts. Need to make new."

"And how long will that take?"

The Swede pursed his lips thoughtfully. "Week? You come back, one week."

Caleb's heart sank. That was going to put him behind schedule. "You don't happen to have another transport I could rent in the meantime, do you?"

"Ja, maybe. Dollar. Tally up price for repairs when done." There was humor glinting in the smith's eyes, but Caleb was too tired to even guess at the joke. He forked over the dollar, eyeing the few remaining bills in his wallet dubiously. If the repairs took the last of his cash, he was out of luck until he reached a town with an actual bank.

"I'm Caleb, by the way. Caleb Marcus." He stuck his hand out to shake, and for a moment, the smith eyed it like a striking snake. Finally, the Swede gripped his hand, pumping it once.

"Sven Isby."

The Peacemaker fought to keep the surprise off his face. There was no tingle in Sven's skin, not even the faint hum of a low-level power. There was only the warm calloused hand, and the sense of…nothing. The man had been scoured. The smith raised his chin in challenge, almost daring Caleb to say something. Caleb forced a smile. "I'll check back with you in a couple days to see how it's going."

"Ja. Do that. Rented transport stored around back." That seemed to end their dealings, as Sven went back to his forge and began working the huge bellows.

Caleb retrieved his saddlebags, throwing them over one shoulder, and his trunk, which he propped on the other. Ernst hopped up, his slight weight barely noticeable, and Caleb took his staff out of the scabbard on his saddle. He waited until they were around the back of the building before he asked, "Ernst, did you notice—"

"Yes." Caleb could feel the creature shudder, even though he was perched on the trunk.

"Could you tell—"

"Looks accidental. Trauma as a child."

Some of the tension in Caleb's chest eased. Accidental scourings were tragic but did happen, most often before a child learned true control of their his own power. But better that than someone who had been scoured deliberately. That was reserved only for the most dangerous of criminals.

The fact that the town had accepted the blacksmith as a contributing member and business owner, despite his disability, only served to highlight the differences between the borderlands and the urban sprawl back east. In the city—any city, really—it was nothing to see packs of scoured or barren men, living rough in alleys or slums, making do with society's scraps, the occasional odd job, and the few charities that catered to such. No one wanted them. No one wanted to see them. They were a reminder of what could so easily go wrong.

For all that he didn't have a lick of power about him, Sven Isby was a lucky man.

The humor in the smith's eyes made sense as Caleb surveyed the "transport" he'd been rented. Ernst snickered from his place atop the trunk. "You paid a dollar for this?"

Well, it was at least a construct. It was also tall enough that Caleb couldn't see over its withers. With the broad back and extra pinion hooks, it had obviously been designed for hauling, not riding. It was also at least four generations out of date—it had actual reins instead of levers—and some of the metal pieces gleamed brightly where they'd been replaced with newer parts over the years. Still, the soothing blue glow of the arcane power swirled within the casing as Caleb inspected it. "Better than nothing, I guess. It could have been a horse."

Ernst traded his trunk seat for the back of the hauler. "Comfy up here! Lots of room to spread out." And he proceeded to do just that.

Muttering to himself, Caleb took the reins and led the lumbering monstrosity back toward the tavern. Each steel hoof was as large as a dinner plate, and Caleb grimaced, just thinking about getting a foot caught under one.

The streets were largely deserted, an oddity for this late in the afternoon, but Caleb could feel the eyes on him as he walked the length of the town. And not all of the gazes were friendly. He fought the urge to funnel a trickle of power into his staff. Lighting the runes was impressive- looking, but showing off would be beneath him. "What the hell is wrong with this place, Ernst?"

"Must be your innate charm."

Somehow, Caleb didn't think so.

With the rented transport left at the tavern and his things stored safely in his room—he kept his staff, out of sheer paranoia—Caleb went in search of the one thing he'd been missing for the last month, without much hope of locating it. Through some miracle, he found it at the general store.

"Ernst, I may have died and gone to heaven." He could see at least two tins of his favorite cigarillos on the shelf, and if there were more in the back, he might be tempted to buy those, too, before he left town. He hadn't had a decent smoke in longer than he liked to contemplate.

The jackalope, now without a convenient place to roost, hopped his way around the store, idly sniffing at things on the lower shelves. "And how much are the repairs going to cost you?"

Caleb sighed, examining his wallet again. No, no more bills had materialized into it. Reluctantly, he only plucked only one tin from the shelf.

The storekeeper had eyed them from the moment they walked in. His eyes looked like two black beetles under his bushy, salt-and-pepper brows and, following followed them as they perused his wares. Ernst got barely a glance, unusual in most places, but the Peacemaker badge had earned a wary scowl. The general feeling of hostility was starting to weigh on Caleb, and he scowled right back as he seat the tin on the counter. "Just this, please."

There was no mistaking the surprise on the storekeeper's face, his prominent eyebrows rising almost to his hairline. He stood up from his stool, revealing that he towered a good four inches over Caleb and weighed a good deal less. Good Lord, the man was gangly. "Um . . . er . . . six bits." Caleb counted out the seventy-five cents from his wallet, pushing them across the countertop. The storekeeper bit one, then dropped them into his till and took his seat again.

Caleb leaned his elbows on the counter. "Can I ask you something, sir?"

"You can always ask." There was caution in his voice, but Caleb read curiosity in the set of his lanky shoulders.

"Why is everyone in this town treating me like I'm about to eat their children?"

At least the tall man had the good grace to blush. "Well, sir . . . To be perfectly frank, you're new, and no one really knows you yet. But the last Peacemaker . . . he made it real clear that he wasn't required to pay for anything. Which was fine, really! 'Cause this close to Indian territory, we surely appreciate all you do for us. But . . . sometimes maybe he took a bit more than folks was really comfortable with, you understand?"

"Yeah, I understand." Caleb gritted his teeth. It explained a lot about the reception he'd received, all over the circuit. "Maybe you could do me a favor and let folks know that I'm the new Peacemaker, and I pay my own way."

The old storekeeper's face broke into a slow smile, like he could scarcely believe his good fortune. Good gossip was better than a bag of gold dust, if everyone came to see what the storekeeper knew. "Yessir. I could do that." He offered his hand. "Hector Pratt."

"Caleb Marcus." There it was, the tingle of faint power just beneath the skin. More than Teddy at the tavern, but still relatively average. Caleb often wondered what people felt when they shook his hand.

"Well, Agent Marcus." The storekeeper offered him a jar of lemon drops. "Welcome to Hope."

About the Author

K.A. Stewart has a BA in English with an emphasis in Literature from William Jewell College. She lives in Missouri with her husband, daughter, two cats, and one small furry demon that thinks it's a cat.

K - 5 - 9 / 20 11/21 11/22

MAR 1 4 2017

CPSIA information can be obtained
at www.ICGtesting.com
Printed in the USA
FSOW04n2043020317
31486FS